AF269014

THE PLOT PACT

THE BAR DOWN SERIES #1

CALI MELLE

Edited by Amy Pritt
Proofread by Emma Cook | Booktastic Blonde LLC
Cover Art by Essasketch
Cover Design by Cali Melle

PLAYLIST

Softcore - The Neighbourhood
Dancing With Our Hands Tied - Taylor Swift
Supercut - Lorde
uh oh - Tate McRae
Man I Need - Olivia Dean
One Way - 6BLACK, T-Pain
Down Bad - Taylor Swift
So Easy (To Fall In Love) - Olivia Dean
Stay With Me - Sam Smith
About You - The 1975
Chains of Love - Charli xcx

For the ones who kept going, even when life continued to knock them down. Even when no one could see you were quietly drowning.
You're stronger than you'll ever realize.
Give them hell, babe.

CHAPTER ONE
JADE

My soft pink, manicured nails tap rhythmically against the mahogany top of my desk. My heart thrums against my ribcage, a bit erratic and uneven as I stare back at my agent, Meredith, through the screen. Her lips are moving, but I am no longer focused on anything she is saying.

One sentence hangs heavily in the air, settling around me, the weight astronomical.

"They're going to drop you if we can't come up with something else fast."

The worst words any author wants to hear in regards to a publishing contract. At the ripe age of twenty-nine, I have managed to stay on a steady schedule, pumping out four books a year for one of the biggest publishing houses in the country.

My first deal with them fell into my lap by the grace of God. I met my agent through a mutual friend and she was immediately interested in my debut romance novel. It was something I worked on while in the trenches of college, mainly because I loved to write and was dragging my feet on what I wanted to major in.

I ended up majoring in English Lit and had my first book deal secured before graduation.

"Jade."

The stern sound of her voice snaps me out of it, forcing me back into the moment.

"Sorry." I let out a deep, ragged breath, shaking my head. I twist my lips to the left, biting down on the inside of my cheek. While my brain went on a side quest, it had to have miraculously retained at least one word Meredith said.

She arches a perfectly sculpted brow. "So, what do you think?"

Heat spreads across my cheeks and I nervously tuck my hair behind my ears. "I—uh—I didn't catch everything you said. You kept freezing."

The lie tastes bitter on my tongue, but desperate times call for desperate measures. Inspiration has been fleeting lately, and so is my attention span. This is an extremely important conversation with Meredith that deserves my undivided attention.

But all I can think about is how the hell did I end up here?

"No worries," she says, offering me a polite smile, although her tone has an iciness to it. "I was saying, instead of circling around the same projects that are giving you trouble, put them aside. Take the next week or two off and find your muse. Find it, wrap your fingers around it, and hold onto that motherfucker."

I chuckle softly, my shoulders relaxing, just in the slightest, as Meredith's expression warms. "Say I find my muse and choke it—I mean hold onto it, very tightly." I smirk. "Then what?"

"You know your editor, Nina, trusts you to put out a quality book that will have readers flocking to their nearest bookstore as soon as it drops. The publisher knows you'll make them money, we just need a concrete idea. One you can follow through with, preferably."

They want a new romance from me and every idea I have been trying to write isn't working. It all feels like the same recycled bullshit. Rinse and repeat. Boy meets girl, they get close, they fall in love, the end. Unproblematic and sweet.

About as boring as my current life.

Even the break-up I went through a few years earlier didn't affect my writing mojo like this.

"Just unplug. Go to a yoga class or meditate or some shit. Anything to get your mind off of this spiral you're trapped in." She stares at me through the computer screen. I love Meredith, she is a shark of an agent, but sometimes she scares me. "You can do this, Jade. You are capable and your success can attest to it."

Emotion lodges in my throat. I swallow hard, pushing it deep down inside, tucking it back into Pandora's box. I am not going to risk having another breakdown on camera with my agent. She didn't take me on as a therapy client. We both have jobs to do and I am the one not holding up my end.

If only I could go back in time and tell bright-eyed,

bushy-tailed Jade that the pressure of producing and being creative could be crippling.

"I have to head off for another meeting, but we'll chat toward the end of next week, okay?"

"I don't know what to write," I blurt out, the words tumbling from my lips. It's not news.

Meredith is silent for a moment. "Let me think of some ideas and you do the same, then we'll see what we can come up with on our next call." She rolls her wrist, her eyes flicking down to her watch. "Gotta run. Bye, Jade!"

Meredith's face disappears and relief immediately floods me. I lean back in my seat, my body relaxing against the back of the chair. I push my fingers through my long hair, my nails running along my scalp. Tilting my head back, I gaze up at the white ceiling and push my feet against the floor to slowly spin in circles.

What a trend that has become recently.

Meredith is right. I can do this. This isn't my first time writing a book. I've done it time and time again. I've experienced writer's block before, it just never felt quite this bad. Like I am stuck in quicksand, every movement sucking me deeper into the suffocating depths.

Taking time off wasn't unheard of. Authors did it all the time. However, my situation is a bit different. After having a few successful series with the same publisher, they asked me for something new, something fresh. I didn't have to go through the pits of writing a pitch and having Meredith take it onto submission with other publishers, hoping one would want to buy it.

They wanted me.

They wanted anything written by me.

Too bad I can't fucking write anymore.

With a huff, I sit upright in my chair.

You're a bad bitch, Jade Wilson. Get your head out of your ass.

Enough of wallowing in my self pity and despair. Meredith telling me to trash the ideas I'd been struggling to write is a welcomed relief. I can't write something I'm not feeling. Perhaps, I need something fresh. Something new.

Something exciting.

I put my feet flat on the floor, abruptly standing up from my desk. I'm not going to find the idea sitting here inside my apartment. Sometimes the muse will drift in through an open window and wrap itself around me like a cloak of the finest silks. Other times, I have to go out and find it.

And this particular time, I just might find it where I least expect to.

———

"Don't hate me, but I can't stay long." Nicole glances at me, tossing an apologetic smile in my direction. "Like I have to grab my drink and go."

Nicole and I met our freshman year of college and have been best friends ever since. We shared a dorm throughout our undergrad years and had an apartment together for two years after we graduated. When her longterm boyfriend Ben proposed to her, we both moved into different places. Now, she and her husband live a few blocks away.

Although, not for long. Ben got a promotion, which has them moving to New York in two months.

"Where are you running off to?"

"I have an unexpected meeting with the superintendent." She sighs and rolls her eyes. Nicole works for the local school district as a school counselor.

"Are we still going out next Friday night?" I ask, stepping to the side and pulling open the door for a couple walking out of the coffee shop.

Nicole glances at me and walks inside as I motion for her to go ahead. "Yeah. Eight o'clock, right?"

We are meeting some friends from college to go out for the night. Ben is our designated driver, although in the city, most places are walkable.

"Yeah," I nod as the door closes behind us and we head over to the counter. Usually I come here during off times, when there aren't as many people. Today, it's pretty busy. Nicole walks over to one of the tablets to put in her order. "Do you know what you want?"

I shake my head, grabbing a menu from the basket on the counter. "Go ahead and order, since you need to run. I might try something new."

"Ooo, who are you today, Miss Wilson?" She winks with mischief dancing in her eyes. "Or should I say Candy Stone?"

I scrunch up my face, blowing out a breath before laughing. Nicole and I had the worst fake IDs in college. Her name was a little more believable. Mine sounded more like a stripper name than a legal one.

Those names became our alter-egos when we needed to be bad bitches. It's like a false sense of confidence comes out when I pretend to embody her persona.

"I wish I were her right now," I say with a sigh, my chest deflating as I glance down at the menu. Nicole knows I've been struggling creatively, although she doesn't know how bad it's gotten.

Hell, I didn't fully realize how bad it was until thirty minutes ago during my call with Meredith.

"What's goin' on, babe?" Nicole says softly as she finishes her drink order and pays. She turns back to me. "Is work stuff still stressing you out?"

I purse my lips, slowly nodding. "Yeah. It's uh—not good. I need a story or something that my agent can bring to my editor."

Nicole frowns. "You need something to inspire you. I feel like you've just been running yourself ragged trying to pull some kind of inspiration from within."

"Excuse me."

A deep voice from behind us cuts in. I glance over my shoulder, the same time Nicole does. A man—late twenties I'd say—looks at both of us with a soft smile pulling across his lips. "Hi, sorry for interrupting."

I glance at Nicole and her eyebrows are already cinching closer together. Not a good sign. Nicole can be a bit confrontational from time to time. She's not really a fan of men who are strangers.

I quickly fix a smile on my face. "Do you need something?"

"I was just wondering if you guys were done with the tablet," he says, smiling sheepishly. His gray eyes glance at the counter, then back at Nicole and me.

"Oh, yes." I grab Nicole's wrist, pulling her away from the counter. She's still assessing him like she can't decide if she wants to tell him off for speaking to us or if she's curious. Ben passed her test during our first year of college, although she did put him through the wringer.

"Sorry about that," I offer, the two of us stepping out of his way.

"No worries." He smiles, dipping his chin before walking past us.

I turn my back to him, paying him no more attention as I look at Nicole. "We'll talk more about it tomorrow or something."

Nicole looks back at me. "Can I help in any way? There has to be something I or someone can do to help you."

"I don't know, girl," I say with a shrug just as one of the baristas calls Nicole's name. "I'm on a mission to find my muse, I think."

"It's out there, we just need to find it for you," she offers with a smirk, pulling me in for a hug. "I gotta run, but text me later, okay?"

"Yeah, of course." I take a step back from her. "Good luck at your meeting."

She rolls her eyes. "They are the bane of my existence." She takes a few steps past me, past the now empty ordering station, and grabs her drink. "Love you!"

"Bye! Love you!" I call back to her, watching her for a moment as she jogs out of the coffee shop. I turn back to the counter, tucking my menu back into its basket.

I tap on the screen, following the prompts to place my drink order as a heavy sigh escapes me. Instead of being adventurous and trying something new, I get the same thing I always do.

I'm not feeling like Candy Stone—*not today*.

CHAPTER TWO
MATTEO

"THE FIRST TIME I SAW HER, THE WORLD AROUND ME WENT QUIET. I DIDN'T RECOGNIZE HER AT FIRST, ALTHOUGH MY SOUL KNEW. IT KNEW SHE WAS THE ONE IT HAD BEEN LOOKING FOR." - JULIAN HART, PAINTED INFERNO

"Matty, throw me that roll of tape."

I tug once more on my laces, loosening them before grabbing the roll of white tape to my left and tossing it around Cam Shaw and over to Theo. I've known Theodore Simmons most of my life. Our families have always been close since our dads played for the Aston Archers together.

He's one of the younger kids on the team, but I promised his dad and mine that I'd take him under my wing when he came into the league at nineteen.

"Boys, we need to get our shit together."

The voice of our captain, Warren Cross, echoes through the locker room as he drops down onto the bench. He tosses his helmet onto the floor in anger, his damp hair shifting as he shakes his head.

He's not wrong. The first half of the season wasn't bad,

but it's like after the beginning of January, we've been on a downhill slope. We've been on a losing streak for three weeks, which is borderline embarrassing.

Practice this morning was absolutely grueling with no pucks and just skating. A few of the guys were running for the nearest trashcan after we got off the ice.

"We need to figure out what the problem is and fix it."

Something has been off and the synergy just isn't there. Whatever we had going at the beginning of the season vanished. Now, we're drifting lower in the standings with every game. We had a shot at play-offs and if we don't turn things around, there's a chance we might not even be in the race for a wildcard spot.

Dropping my gaze to the floor to avoid Cross's gaze as he looks around the locker room, I slide my feet from my skates and wipe the blades down with a towel. I know I'm partially to blame for the downfall of the Hillford Ice Hawks.

Since the new year, I haven't scored a single fucking goal.

And as a power forward, that's completely unacceptable.

"I mean, it could be a multitude of things," Theo offers. I look at him and he shrugs his shoulders as he continues to wrap the tape around his stick's blade.

Cross clicks his tongue and shakes his head. "I don't know. No one's been injured for long enough to make a real difference. We're not scoring goals like we should be. If we can't produce, what the fuck are we doing here?"

Guilt immediately strikes my chest and I feel his eyes on me. I'm bent forward again, pulling the clear tape from my socks. I'm not the only one who hasn't been putting up points, but as someone who averages one point per game, I know I'm one of the main culprits.

"Who's been changing shit up?" Shaw chimes in as he rises to his feet. My eyebrows tug together and Theo mumbles something to himself. "Should we all shave our heads or some shit?"

Theo huffs. "Here we go again."

Hockey players are known for their superstitions and quirky habits. I toss the tape into the trash can and slip off my socks and then my shinguards. The smell of sweat, melted ice, and musk fills the room as everyone strips out of their gear. No one's bothered by the scent. It comes with the territory.

"No, for real," Shaw insists, his eyes trailing around the locker room, scanning each and every one of us with scrutiny. "Someone must have changed something up and whatever it is, it's not working."

Murmurs and mumbles break out throughout the room as the guys all start to disagree with him. Cross tilts his head to the side, his gaze locking with mine. The way he studies me is a tad unnerving, although it's not unusual from him. He's highly calculated, but quick to confront.

"Matty."

I inhale deeply. "What?"

"You're the only one who hasn't said anything."

I purse my lips and shrug my shoulders. "I don't think I've been doing anything different or out of the ordinary."

"That's not true," Gray, our goalie, cuts in. I whip my head to the side, my eyes narrowing on him. "Your New Year's resolution, remember?"

No way...

We ended up playing on New Year's Eve and afterwards, we all drank champagne and made resolutions.

Realization dawns over me. My eyes widen as I stare back at him. That game was the last one we won.

"Oh shit." Shaw, Cross, and I all say at the exact same time.

"That's gotta be it," Tyson, one of our wingers says, nodding eagerly. "That last girl you were seeing around Thanksgiving. What was her name?"

I swallow roughly. "Robin."

She knew the deal when we first started talking. I told her from the gate that I don't date for love. I don't do attachments, commitments, or strings. It's mostly just something to occupy my free time. Who doesn't enjoy a little companionship every now and then?

She swore she was cool with it, but things ended up changing, as they always do. She wanted more and I didn't. We ended things right before the holiday.

"Right, right." Tyson's head bobs again. "You haven't talked to anyone since your resolution, have you?"

On New Year's Eve, my resolution was to eliminate distractions, which meant swearing off dating. All the women I spoke to only saw one thing: a successful, professional athlete. Of course they always wanted more.

More is something I will never want from anyone.

"Holy shit," Shaw says slowly, turning to face me. "That's gotta be the reason why."

"Shouldn't it be the opposite?" I retort. "Getting rid of outside distractions should have me more focused on the game."

Shaw smirks. "Theoretically, but I think you might be the exception."

"It can't be," I argue, shaking my head at him, refusing to accept it as a possibility. "There's no way."

"But what if there is?" Theo says, a smirk tugging on

his lips. "Dude, what if you need the distractions? What if you're playing like shit because you're overthinking it or something?"

"Hey, I'm not playing like shit."

A few of the guys snort.

"You haven't scored since the New Year's Eve game," Gray reminds me.

"On and off the ice," Shaw chimes in, laughter chasing his words.

I rise to my feet, shaking my head at all of them. "Okay, fuck you all. It's not my fault the entire team is playing like shit and on a losing streak. There's no fucking chance that's the reason behind it."

"I mean, who's to say it isn't?"

All eyes are on me and judging by the looks on every single face, they might all be buying this.

"Think about it," Theo says, rising to his feet as he walks over to me. "You're one of our high energy guys. We all feed off of it. If you're down, whether we realize it or not, we match that."

My jaw drops. "You're not seriously blaming me."

"Not directly," he explains, frustration washing over his expression before it fades. "At the end of the day, we're each responsible for the way we play. There's a synergy, a cohesiveness to our team. If one of us is off, it has a ripple effect."

I chew on his words, letting them sink in. Again, there's some truth behind them. Normally, when someone's having a bad day, the rest of the team can pick up the slack. But after getting our asses handed to us time and time again, it wears you down.

"Am I supposed to just throw my resolution out the window?"

"Maybe," Cross says, shrugging his shoulders. "It wouldn't hurt to try, right? You just need a distraction off the ice. Someone to feed that boisterous ego of yours."

"You do have a tendency of being a little more showy when you have someone to impress."

What the fuck is this? An intervention? I didn't sign up to have the entire locker room tell me about myself. I already know I'm a bit overly confident, if you will.

"It's a theory to test."

"A theory," I snort, rolling my eyes dramatically. I grab my clothes to head to the wash room. "Yeah, whatever, I'll think about it."

There's no way I can't not think about it now that they planted the little superstitious seed in my mind. I love my teammates. We truly are like family and they're great guys, but fuck them all right now.

―――

My hair is still damp from the shower, making it difficult to ignore the chill in the air as I climb out of my car. As much as I don't want to believe it, there could be some truth to what the guys were saying. I'm just as superstitious as the next guy on the bench. What if they're right? What if I'm the reason behind our losing streak?

Self doubt isn't something that melds well with my confidence. My ego doesn't like it.

My footsteps are heavy and I pull the hood of my sweatshirt over my head to block the snow flurries dancing in the air. January in Massachusetts tends to be pretty brutal, especially where Hillford is, not far from the coast.

I tuck my hands into the pockets of my winter coat and

put my head down as I walk down the sidewalk. There's a coffee shop on my way home that is part of my routine. On days I have to be at the rink, whether it's for practice or a game, I always stop here on my way home. And I always order the same exact thing: an extra sweet caramel macchiato.

At least there's one thing I haven't done wrong to mess up the way I've been playing.

The coffee shop is busy when I step inside, seeking reprieve from the falling snow. Baristas behind the counter move about in a flurry, taking orders, making drinks, and calling out the names of customers.

Along the left side of the counter are two self-service tablets to place your order. I typically just order from there and now is not going to be the time I do anything differently. The one on the left is my preferred tablet. The one on the right is already occupied and there are two women standing in front of the one I like on the left, although neither of them are paying any mind to the screen.

I pull my hood down, brushing my hair from my forehead as I slowly approach. Their backs are to me and as I step up behind them, I can see the screen clearly.

"Thanks for your order," it says in bold black letters.

"Excuse me."

They both glance over their shoulders to look at me. The woman on the right immediately narrows her eyes, spinning her body to face me head on. Her friend stares back at me for a moment, her auburn hair shifting along her back as her soft blue eyes do a quick scan of my face.

A smile spreads across my lips as my gaze trails across her delicate features. She's gorgeous, but not in a loud obnoxious way. It's more so the quiet, tender kind of beauty. The kind that demands your attention and slides under your skin like a sharp needle.

Who are you?

"Hi." I offer an apologetic smile, noticing the faint freckles peppered over the bridge of her nose before bouncing back to her eyes. "Sorry for interrupting."

They both look to be in their twenties, although it's hard to tell which end. They're both facing me now. Blondie on the right has her eyebrows pinched together like she wants to cinch my throat closed. I look back at the softer blue eyes.

"Do you need something?" She smiles, but it's tense.

I clear my throat, running my hand through my hair. Charming women is my strong suit, but she has me feeling off my game. That makes two games now—fuck. "I was wondering if you guys were done with the tablet." I glance behind them at the counter before meeting their eyes once more.

"Oh, yes," the one with freckles says, grabbing her friend's wrist as she tugs her away from the counter. Her friend is still looking at me like she doesn't know what to do with me. "Sorry about that," she says, as they step out of my way.

"No worries." I nod, keeping my distance as I walk around them and step up to the counter. A hint of vanilla and raspberries dances in the air as I pass them. Soft and subtle, like she only pressed down for half a spray when she put the perfume on. It has to be hers.

Shaking my head to myself, I punch my order in, knowing the placement of every button by heart. I press the one to send it to the baristas before walking across the shop to the bathroom. Pausing just outside the door, I can't help myself as I turn my head to the side, looking for her.

My heart thumps a little harder and my eyebrows tug downward when I don't see where she was last.

"You goin' in?"

A gruff voice behind me breaks through my thoughts. I look at him, giving him a curt nod as I pull open the door and slip inside. I know her blue eyes and those freckles scattered like constellations are going to haunt me. A smile tugs on my lips.

This is just the kind of distraction I've been trying to avoid.

And maybe it's the exact thing I've been missing.

CHAPTER THREE
JADE

"I couldn't look away as he manipulated the clay with his fingertips, sculpting perfection. Julian Hart has the hands of a God." - Clara Foss, Painted Inferno

My face scrunches as I pull my drink away from my mouth. I don't know what they put in it, but it tastes like shit. Maybe they changed their syrups because I order the same thing every time and it has never tasted this bad.

Setting it down on the table, I prop my elbow, dropping my chin down onto it as I flip open the notebook with my other hand. A blank page stares back at me. A shiver of intimidation rolls down my spine. This is the worst part of the process for me lately. Coming up with an idea that is going to stick. I click my pen.

A blank page is a new beginning.

I hate new beginnings.

My hand falls away from my chin and I sit there, one hand wrapped around my coffee and the other clutching my pen like it's the only thing keeping me afloat. I have to come up with something. I need the story of a lifetime to save my career at this point.

If I can't follow through, I'm screwed. Maybe it's time to hang up my writer hat and find a different job. Thankfully, if there's one good thing my parents taught me, it was to be smart with my money. I don't live beyond my means and after receiving the seven-figure advances I have in the past, I made sure to invest a large portion of it.

My degree in English Lit might not get me far, but at this point, anything sounds better than writing. I'm not too young to go back to grad school. I could become a teacher or a professor.

I need to stop stalling. I need to get some ideas down on paper. If there's one thing everyone should know about me, it's that Jade Wilson is not a quitter. The publisher asked for my agent and me to come up with an idea. I've stretched my time as thin as I possibly could.

Get your head out of your ass, Jade. All you have to do is write.

The tip of my pen scratches across the paper. Short and sweet. I smile as I read the two little words: *Fuck this.*

"Jade."

A deep voice calls out my name, immediately pulling my attention away from my notepad. Confusion floods me, my face scrunching as I glance in the direction it came from.

"Jade?"

This time it's a bit louder, sounding more like a question. My stomach flips and my heart races. The coffee shop is still filled with customers and I have no idea who's calling my name.

I slowly rise to my feet. "Yeah?" I look in the direction of the voice and that's when I see him. His gray blue eyes meet mine from across the room and a slow grin lifts the corners of his lips. My heart skips a beat, but I ignore the fluttering sensation. It's just a byproduct from the anxiety of hearing my name being called out.

His stride is long as he closes the distance between us. Confidence radiates from him, rolling off him in waves as he walks through the shop. I swear to God, not only do the women glance in his direction, but so do the men.

Who the hell is this guy?

He stops on the other side of my table, his right hand wrapped around a coffee cup and the left grabbing onto the back of the wooden chair. "Jade?"

My name sounds like it's exactly where it belongs, rolling off his tongue like he's tasting it.

Jesus Christ, what is my problem?

It has to be the fact that I've been abstinent for the last year.

"Hi," I say softly, my brain momentarily short circuiting so the sound comes out more like a whisper. I tilt my head to the side, my eyes bouncing between his. "You know my name?"

A soft chuckle rumbles in his throat. He leans forward, the tendons in his hands flexing as he sets down the cup and spins it to face me. His eyes flick to mine and back to the coffee as he taps the tag on the side. "I think you have my drink."

Heat immediately spreads across my face. My mouth falls open and I quickly spin the other cup to check its tag. "Matty?"

"That would be me." He smiles, his expression warm as his eyes meet mine once more.

"Oh my gosh, I'm so sorry," I say in a rush, shaking my head as I silently beg for the floor to open beneath me. I would accidentally grab the wrong cup. And not just the wrong cup, but the one that was supposed to go to the hottest guy in this coffee shop. "I don't know how I managed to get my name and yours confused."

A smirk tugs on his lips. "Guess you were just thinking of me before I gave you a reason to."

My stomach flutters while it simultaneously sinks. I'm not immune to banter, but at the same time—ugh. There's nothing more unattractive to me than a man who confuses his cockiness with confidence.

"Yeah, I don't think that was it." I shake my head at him, my expression flat. "I have a lot on my mind. I wasn't paying attention."

"No worries," he says, shrugging with indifference as he takes his cup. My eyes are trained on him, slowly widening as he doesn't stop lifting the cup until it's to his lips. He tilts it back, taking a sip of the sickeningly sweet, piping hot liquid.

"What are you doing?" I'm momentarily horrified and equally intrigued by whatever might be wrong with this guy. "Why are you drinking that?"

His movements are slow, his throat bobbing as he swallows. His brow furrows. "What do you mean? Why wouldn't I?"

"Um, because I already drank out of it?"

His eyes slowly search mine. "Still not understanding the problem, Sunny."

Sunny?

"I'm a complete stranger who drank out of your drink." I stare back at him in disbelief. How is he still not getting it? Ugh, he's attractive and ignorant. The worst combination. "How do you know I don't have some kind of sickness or disease?"

He tilts his head to the side. "Well, do you?"

"No." My face contorts and I shake my head, huffing out a frustrated breath. "That's besides the point."

He stares at me, his expression giving nothing away before his face cracks. His head tilts back, and his chest shakes with laughter. And fuck me for loving the way it sounds. Completely and utterly free. "Shit." He runs his hand through his hair. "I like you," he chuckles as he looks back at me. "Can I sit?"

"Uh—" *What the hell is happening?* "Sure?"

Matty drags the chair back, the feet groaning across the floor. He's unfazed by the sound and takes a seat across from me. "Getting your cooties is the least of my worries right now," he chuckles, leaning against the back of the chair as he takes another sip of his drink.

I reach forward, grabbing mine before I bring it up to my lips. I pause, my eyes still on him. "Did you drink out of mine?"

"No, *Sunny*," he says, rolling his eyes, exaggerating his new name for me. His dark hair's a bit longer on the top, falling just above his eyebrows in tousled waves. It shifts as he shakes his head. I wonder if it's as soft as it looks. "Even if I did, I don't have cooties either."

"Good to know," I mumble, tearing my gaze from his as I take a slow sip. The bitter liquid hits my tongue and I immediately thank the coffee gods. This is exactly what I was searching for, not an abomination of sugar and caramel like whatever it is he's drinking.

He's silent across from me, but I feel the heat of his gaze as he scans my face, studying and assessing like he'll be taking an exam on me tomorrow. "You come here often?"

I can't help myself as I let out a laugh. "Please tell me that line doesn't actually work for you."

He doesn't laugh. My breath catches in my throat as I meet his stare once more. "No, I mean I've never seen you here before. I come here almost every single day after I leave the rink and not once have we run into each other."

The rink. He's a hockey player. That explains the whole athletic look he's got going on. I shrug. "I do come here often, just not normally this time of day."

"Hmm," he muses, lifting his cup to take another sip. "I guess we both have luck on our sides today." He falls silent for a moment, his head nodding at my notepad. "What are you working on?"

I slide the notepad from the table, carefully closing it before I set it back down. "Are you always this... invasive?"

Matty smirks. "You have no idea how invasive I can be."

Jesus Christ. I need to excuse myself from this table before I either clock him in the jaw or go home with him. Either feels like an acceptable response at this point.

"Look, Matty," I start, my voice dropping lower. "I don't know who you are or who you might think you are, but you're more attractive with your mouth closed. You should learn to think before you speak."

His eyes are on mine. A string of laughter escapes him, his eyes bright and cheeks flushed. "Don't stop there, Sunny. Keep judging me when you don't know a single thing about me."

"What is actually wrong with you?"

"Probably a lot." He shrugs, still chuckling. "I've taken quite a few hard hits during games."

When he first said rink, that sent off a tiny alarm inside my head, but there's the confirmation I needed.

"Hockey player is an immediate red flag."

"Why?" He leans forward, folding his arms on top of one another, focusing on me. "You get hurt by one before?"

I narrow my eyes on him. "Something like that. It was a few years ago."

"Would I know him?"

"Aiden Scott."

A muscle in his jaw tightens. He takes a long, slow sip of his drink.

"Wait, you actually know him?"

"I do," he says, dipping his chin and sucking in a deep breath. "He plays dirty, but acts like a baby whenever he gets a taste of his own medicine. Don't care for the guy, honestly."

"Yeah, me neither," I laugh quietly. Aiden and I dated during his first two years in the league. We met through a mutual friend while I was still in college. I broke things off with him after pictures surfaced of him out with another girl in a different city. "You play for the Ice Hawks?"

Matty bites back a grin. "You really don't like hockey, do you?" A soft laugh falls from his lips, sliding against my eardrums like silk. "I do. My real name's Matteo Ford, but everyone calls me Matty."

His name is familiar, even though his face isn't. And trust me, he has a face that would be hard to forget. Aiden complained about him before, although I didn't pay much attention to the things he said. Like Matty, there wasn't enough space in the room for his ego.

"I've heard of you before."

His face lights up. "Careful, Sunny. You're gonna have me talking without thinking again."

"Learn some self control," I quip, rolling my eyes.

Amusement fills his eyes, his gaze scanning my face

once more before he pushes his seat back and rises to his feet. "I enjoyed this. We should do it again. Same time and place next week?"

I tilt my head back, staring up at him as I narrow my eyes and purse my lips. "You wish."

"Can I at least get your number?"

"Nope." I lean back in my seat, looking up at him with the sweetest smile. "Maybe you'll get lucky and see me here again."

"Damn," he breathes, the word barely audible. He lets out another soft chuckle, shaking his head. His expression is unreadable, but the curiosity in his eyes is impossible to ignore. "Okay. I *will* see you again. One way or another."

"Are you always this arrogant?" I huff, arching an eyebrow.

"Not arrogant, just confident," he says with a wink before leaving me alone at the table. I can't help myself as my eyes follow after him as he heads out of the coffee shop. He pauses just outside the door, his gaze colliding with mine through the glass. A slow, sure smirk lifts his lips before he walks away.

What the hell just happened?

CHAPTER FOUR
MATTEO

"I SHOULDN'T HAVE BEEN STARING AT HER, BUT I WAS MERELY STUDYING THE COMPETITION. WE WERE BROUGHT TOGETHER FOR A COLLABORATIVE EXHIBITION WITH THE BEST ARTISTS IN THE WORLD... AND I HAD EVERY INTENTION OF BEATING HER." - JULIAN HART, PAINTED INFERNO

"Matty, crash the net!" Shaw yells at me as he takes the lead, skating into our offensive zone. He passes over the blue line and I'm right after him. One of the D-men for the other team blocks him, forcing more space between Shaw and the net as he pushes him closer to the boards.

There's less than a minute left and we're tied with the other team, 1-1. Theo managed to sneak a goal past their brick-wall of a goalie early in the second period. We knew this one was going to be a tough game, but we have a chance.

Shaw's up near the red line, waiting in the corner. The muscles in my legs fire as I push my way toward the crease, turning with the play as I knock my shoulder against one of their defensemen.

"Asshole," he snaps, bumping into me harder.

The puck moves across the ice, leaving Shaw's stick. Theo receives the pass, his head on a swivel as he looks for an opportunity for a shot. I'm shoulder to shoulder with the defensemen and he's trying to tangle up my stick.

I skate half a stride in front of him, the puck sliding back to the point. Cross slaps his stick, calling for the pass. The goalie's moving along the crease, trying to see past me as I use my body as a screen.

"Get the fuck off," I bark at the defenseman who's still fucking with my stick. My eyes are glued to the puck as the guys try to get a scoring chance. "Net, net!"

Shaw fakes their players out, his body shifting as if he's going to pass the puck, but instead he shoots it at the net. I'm too far to the right of the goalie and somehow, he sees it coming. He slides to the right, catching a piece of the puck with his blocker as he stops it from soaring past him.

It all happens so quickly, although for a moment, it feels like time is suspended. The puck deflects off his pad, coming right at me. I don't waste the chance to take a shot as it connects with my stick's blade. My body shifts, the muscles in my arm firing. A quick flick of my wrist as I spin in front of the net sends the puck right past the left side of his torso.

He slides across the ice, but he's just a fraction of a second too slow.

The horn sounds through the arena. My heart pumps harder, faster at lightning speed. Holy fuck, it finally happened.

"Fuck yes!"

The four other guys on my line skate over, gathering around me as we take a second to celebrate. "It's about damn time, Ford," Cross says, laughter wrapping around us as he taps the backs of my legs with his stick.

I lead the way, skating past the bench, giving all my teammates fist bumps before heading back to center ice for the faceoff. Whenever a line scores, Coach has been keeping those players on the ice to keep the momentum going.

Theo skates to the dot, checking on me, Shaw and the defensive pair on our line, Cross and Vasily Volkov before he gets into position. My knees bend slightly, my hands gripping my stick as I place it on the ice.

"Finally broke your streak, huh, Ford?"

I glance at the winger from the other team who's lined up with me. A smirk tugs on my lips as I see who it is. "Yeah," I nod my head, shifting my gaze back to the ice, waiting for the puck to drop. "Thanks to your ex-girlfriend."

"What the—"

The puck drops before he gets the last word out. Theo tangles up his stick with their center, pushing his body into him, creating space between them and the puck.

My feet move quickly from muscle memory and I take possession of the puck, dipping past Aiden Scott with a smirk on my face as I head down the ice. We enter their defensive zone and get another shot on goal before the final buzzer sounds.

Scott gives me a smug look, although there's a hint of curiosity in his expression. I'd be willing to bet he doesn't even know which ex-girlfriend I'm talking about. Rolling my eyes to myself, I ignore him. I don't need to instigate anything, not after the game is already over.

I skate over to the net, falling in line behind Theo as we

all skate past Gray, tapping the top of his goalie helmet. "Great game, Gray. You played your ass off."

"So did you, Ford." He gives me a toothy grin. "We're fucking back, baby."

Theo wraps his arm around the top of my shoulders. "Matty! You were unstoppable tonight."

"That's a little generous. I scored one goal."

"After not scoring any in the last few weeks, I'd say you were on fire."

Theo laughs, releasing me and bumps his shoulder into mine. We all file off the ice and down the tunnel to the dressing room at the end of the hall. The energy in there tonight is vastly different than it has been the past few weeks.

"Matty fuckin' Ford!" our assistant coach, Coach Frost, calls out as I walk in. The guys break out into hoots and hollers. "Goddamn, we missed you."

"Asshole," I mutter under my breath, laughing as I pull off my helmet and walk over to my spot. Physically, I've been here, but recently, I disappeared on the ice. Until tonight.

Everyone starts stripping out of their gear and Cross rises to his feet. "Alright, boys. I think we know who the player of the game is tonight without even saying it." He holds up the hawk mask, his gaze pinning on mine. "We're a family. We all feed off each other's energy, and tonight, someone truly brought what we needed. He stepped up and pushed himself, which made all of us push even harder."

Our head coach stands off to the edge of the room, a hint of a smile on his lips, but he doesn't dare to fully let it show. He looks over at me, his dark gray eyes meeting mine.

Coach Ford is ruthless. He has high expectations of all of us and me being his nephew doesn't grant me any free passes. If anything, he pushes me harder than anyone else.

Cross strides over to me, holding out the hawk mask. "You earned this tonight, fair and square."

I take it from him, pulling it over my face as the guys break out, chanting my name. "Matty! Matty! Matty!"

Adrenaline courses through me and I climb up onto my seat, curling my fists as I start to hold my arms out to the side, elbows bent. I tip my head back, letting out the most obnoxious, high pitched hawk call that sounds like a war cry.

The room breaks out in similar variations of the sound and honestly, we all just sound like a bunch of psychotic men mimicking raptors from a dinosaur movie. Shaw was the one who informed us that they actually use hawk calls when they make those movies.

A pointless piece of information, but oh well.

I jump down, my bare feet hitting the floor as I pull the mask off and toss it down. "We're gonna do exactly what we did tonight, every night. We're so fucking back. No one is going to be able to stop us."

Theo whistles and the other guy's clap. The energy in the room is insane, you'd think we just won the biggest game of the season. I sit back down on the bench, busying myself with my gear as I put everything where it goes.

"What's your secret, Matty?" Anderson, one of the other centers, calls over to me.

"Yeah, did you break your resolution?" Tyson chimes in.

I shrug, glancing at the two of them. "I don't know. Not really."

"Not really?" Theo questions me, casually slipping into the conversation.

I grab my clean clothes to head to the showers. There's no one I'm talking to, although, there's someone I can't stop thinking about. "I met a girl at the coffee shop the other day, but that was it."

"What's her name?"

Her name rolls off my tongue. "Jade."

"No last name?"

I laugh, shaking my head. "I didn't get it."

"You get her number?"

A chuckle rumbles in my chest as my mind drifts back to Jade. She had such an attitude, I liked it. "She wouldn't give it to me."

The thought of chasing her has me by the balls. That's got to be where the excitement and the distraction truly comes from. The chase before getting what I want.

"You gotta see her again. That will be the real test of the theory."

"I will."

"You didn't get her last name or her number, but you guys made plans to see each other?"

"No," I say, confidence welling inside my chest. "But I'll see her again, I know it."

Cross stares at me as Theo snorts. "You're crazy."

"He is, but somehow it always ends up working out. Just watch, he'll end up running into her or something."

My chest shakes with laughter. "I refuse to believe that what I want won't be mine. It's worked out so far in life."

"It's worked out pretty damn well, I'd say," Tyson chimes in.

Without another word, I dip my chin and excuse

myself from the locker room. "Matteo," Coach's voice follows after me as I stop into the hallway. "Good game tonight."

I turn back to my uncle, meeting his gaze. "Thanks. I know I've been off lately, but I swear it's gonna change."

"I hope so," he says, nodding at me. "I know your dad's been worried about you. You should give him a call."

The mention of my father feels like a thorn in my side. The last time we spoke, we ended up in a heated argument about my supposed lack of effort on the ice. My father didn't raise his prodigy to not be producing during games.

"Uncle Cale, remember, here I'm not your nephew."

The muscle in his jaw tightens. "At the end of the day, you are, regardless of where we are. You will not get special treatment from me or game time without earning it. Get over your pride and whatever your little temper tantrum was and call your father."

"Coach…"

He gives me that look. The same one he used to give me and my cousins when we were about to get a stern talking to. "Get a shower and go home, Matteo."

"Okay. Goodnight."

"Goodnight," he says, nodding once more as he pulls his keys from his front pocket. "Keep playing like you did tonight. It helped the team."

"Yes sir."

My uncle gives me one last look before spinning on his heel and heading toward the hall that leads to the exit. I run a hand through my damp hair, grabbing the back of my neck as I slip into the washroom.

The pressure settles on my chest. I scored tonight and

we won, but that was just tonight. I need to do it the next game and every one that comes after.

And if the guys are right, if it's because of Jade, I need to find her.

CHAPTER FIVE
JADE

"Julian Hart was good at what he did, maybe even better than me. I'd never be the one to tell him that. We were partners, but also competitors. And Clara Foss did not go down without a fight." - Clara Foss, Painted Inferno

Throwing back my third shot, I hold my breath, swallowing quickly as the vodka burns my throat on its way down. Ellie, my and Nicole's other best friend, just finished her last semester of her doctorate program, so it was only right that we come out to celebrate.

All my friends have things worth celebrating in their lives. New jobs, new career path…and then there's me.

I'm now at the end of my deadline. Monday morning my agent is expecting to have something in her inbox.

And you know what I've got to send to her?

Nothing.

I let out a breath, propping my elbow on the bar as I push my forehead against my hand. The bass from the music pounds against my eardrums, a steady, yet fierce rhythm. My legs are sore from dancing, although the alcohol has me feeling relatively numb right now.

When Nicole and I graduated from college and moved into our first apartment, we met Ellie. She lived in the apartment next to us and we ran into her the second night we were there. She came over with her eyes puffy after a breakup and a bottle of wine. She was new in town, only moved there because of her ex and work.

Three glasses later, she asked us if we wanted to go egg her ex's car and the rest was history after that.

Nicole's on the dance floor with her husband Ben, Ellie's out there with them and some other friends, and I'm stuck at the bar with Ben's friend, Eric, whispering in my ear.

"What do you say?" Eric says, his fingertips trailing along the side of my forearm. "You ready to get back out there?"

Eric's attractive, but finance guys are not my thing. He's had his eye on me for a few months now, according to Ben, although I've never fed in to any of his advances.

"I dunno," I say, half slurring my words together as I roll my head to the side to look at him. His fingers linger, slowly curling around my forearm and sliding down along my wrist. "I'm pretty drunk."

"So am I," he laughs, his face flush as he leans closer. His hand encapsulates mine, his fingers pushing between mine. "What do you say we get out of here instead?"

My breath catches in my throat. Panic immediately swirls in the pit of my stomach, regardless of how tipsy I am. Is he hot? Yes. Is he a guy I'd consider going home with? Absolutely.

But not when I'm drunk and not when I'm not sober

enough to know if it's something I might regret in the morning.

It's been a year since I've slept with anyone and I'm not sure this is the guy I want to break my streak with.

"Not tonight," I say softly, shaking my head as I turn back to the bar, grabbing my water instead. I need to sober up and get the hell out of here. Alone. "I'm not going to leave my friends."

"Why not? They're not even with you right now." He runs his fingers along mine, turning in his seat to look out at the dance floor. "I'm sure they won't care."

He wraps his hand around mine, pulling it away from the bar. My eyes flash to his and he's inching my fingertips closer to his lap. "Feel what you're doing to me, babe. You got me all fired up after you were rubbing against me while we were dancing."

Oh my god, no.

I immediately jerk my hand free from his grip. "What the fuck is wrong with you? I didn't say you could do that." I hop down from my seat, grabbing my purse and my coat. "I said no. What about that word made you think I want to touch you in any way?"

His eyes narrow on mine as he spins around in his seat to face me. He lowers his feet to the ground, straightening his legs as he stands up. He sways, ever so slightly. "You were all over me while we were dancing."

"We were dancing, that was it." He takes a step toward me and I practically jump backwards away from him. I collide with a warm, solid body behind me. "I'm so sorry," I say in a rush, my words slurring as I turn to face the person.

I stumble as I turn, the room half spinning with me. Large, warm hands dart out, wrapping around my biceps to steady me. I stare at the chest in front of me, my eyes slowly trailing upwards until I meet his gray eyes.

"Matteo?"

The corners of his mouth twitch. "Hey, Sunny." His expression hardens, his eyebrows drawing close as he scans my face. My chest heaves, my heart beating harder. His eyes flick behind me. "This guy bothering you?"

My breathing hitches. "Oh—um, no. Everything's okay."

"You can go, man," Eric says, stepping up beside us, puffing his chest.

My body falls rigid. Matteo's hands are still holding me upright. His eyes shift to mine. "Do you want me to leave?"

I swallow roughly, my nostrils widening. My hair dances along my back as I move my head back and forth. "No. Eric was just leaving." I look over at him. "Weren't you?"

He scoffs, rolling his eyes. "Don't get your hopes up with her," he says to Matteo, giving me a dirty look. "She's just a tease."

Matteo's fingers tighten around my biceps, not hard enough to squeeze, but almost as if holding onto me is the only thing stopping his hands from curling into fists.

Eric turns and walks away, Matteo's eyes following him. His expression is unreadable, but his eyes are dark. Distant and cold.

"Matteo."

His eyes slice back to mine.

"You can let go of me now."

He blinks. Once. Twice. Warmth chases away the cold. His throat bobs as he swallows hard then clears his throat. I notice his absence as soon as his hands fall away from my arms. "Sorry." He lifts his hand, running it through his tousled hair. "Who was that guy?"

I shake my head. "A friend of a friend. I just met him tonight and don't plan on ever talking to him again."

Matteo tilts his head to the side, his eyes doing a slow scan of my face. They don't stop as they run down my bare neck, along the scooping neckline of my dress. "Did he hurt you?"

"No, no." I swallow roughly, meeting his gaze as his eyes bounce back to mine. "He just misread the situation and thought I was interested, which I am not."

I don't know why I added that last little piece. It doesn't matter to Matteo. He doesn't need to know whether or not I'm interested in some guy he doesn't even know.

The room shifts. I feel like I'm going to overheat. Warmth surges through my veins. I only had a few shots and one mixed drink, but I don't have much of a tolerance.

"I'm gonna head out."

Matteo's brows furrow. "Are you here alone?"

"No, my friends are somewhere," I explain, waving my hand dismissively, not bothering to look for them. I'll text them; they'll understand. "I'm only a ten minute walk from here, it's fine."

I pull open my purse, finding my phone and a hair clip. I gather my hair, pulling it away from my neck to secure it with the clip.

"I'll walk you."

My heart skips a beat, my eyes widening slightly. "What?"

"It's dark outside. I'm not letting you walk alone."

"I—uh." I pause, looking around the room. The music is still pounding, people are still dancing, and the lights above are still flashing. "What about whoever you're here with?"

Matteo smirks, cocking his head to the side. "Are you worried I might be here with another woman?"

The air grows thick around us.

"I'm not worried about anything that concerns you, Matteo Ford." I pause, lifting my brows. "Besides, if you were here with another woman, why would you be leaving with me?"

His lips part, his tongue darting out to wet them, and my traitorous heart stumbles again. His eyes are hooded, slowly searching mine, like he's taking a moment to choose his words carefully.

"I'm not here with anyone else," he says, his voice low and hoarse. "I've been hoping I'd run into you again." His fingers brush against mine as he takes my coat, opens it up, and waits for me to slide my arms in. I do, turning around as he slides it up over my shoulders.

He leans in. "Come on, Sunny." The side of his face brushes against mine. He moves beside me, his hand brushing against mine, but he doesn't slip his fingers through mine.

The back of his hand rests against mine, as if he's testing the waters. It's like he's silently telling me it's okay, he's not going to push me. He wants me to be the one to make a move. He doesn't pull away. He stays there, the heat radiating from him. A hint of a woodsy yet bold scent infiltrates my senses.

My heart beats harder, skipping a beat every three beats. It's because of my heart issues, not because of him. My heart would *never* betray me like that.

I straighten my fingers, the backs of my fingertips

grazing his. The music is so loud, but I swear I hear the sharp intake of his breath. "I don't want to go home."

He arches a brow. "No?"

I chew on the inside of my cheek, shaking my head. "I just want to get out of here. It's too loud, too crowded." I pause, the corner of my mouth lifting. "And there's no food."

A ghost of a smile drifts across his lips. "I know just the place."

CHAPTER SIX
MATTEO

Jade bumps her shoulder against mine, stumbling to the right, in my direction. "Sorry," she mumbles, hiccuping and then letting out a soft laugh. "I don't normally drink."

I glance down at her, my expression softening as she accidentally bumps into me again. "It's okay," I say, bending my arm to offer her my elbow. "Here, hold onto me."

Jade's steps stutter and her gaze flicks up to mine. She hesitates, a wave of distrust passing through her eyes. I don't know how much she's had to drink but judging by her inability to filter her expressions, I'm sure it was more than the legal limit.

"It's just my arm, Sunny. You're going to end up eating concrete if you keep stumbling the way you are."

43

A lopsided grin pulls on her face. "Then I'll look how you probably do without your fake teeth in."

My eyebrows tug together. "What?"

"You're a hockey player." She narrows her eyes. "You mean to tell me all those perfect teeth are real?"

I snort, shaking my head. "Sorry to disappoint, but I've managed to keep all mine so far."

Jade laughs and my heart jumps. It's a soft melody, sliding against my eardrums, seeping into my veins. She surprises me as she slips her arm through mine, the inside of her elbow hooking around mine.

We're both silent, except for the sound of her occasional hiccups as we walk farther down the street, toward the intersection. On the left corner, there's a small diner and we stop out front when we reach it.

Jade tilts her head back, her auburn hair falling down her back. Her lips move as she reads out the name of the place, but the words are barely audible.

It wouldn't matter if they were anyway. The only thing I can hear is the sound of my blood whooshing past my ears as my heart pumps harder with every beat.

She's fucking breathtaking.

She straightens her head, turning to look at me with a sheepish grin. "Would you judge me if I said I've never been here before?"

My mouth falls open, my eyes widening. "You've never been to Diane's before?!" I stare back at her, mocking surprise, although she's too drunk to tell the difference. I bite back a grin, swallowing my laugh. "Not having their waffles is the highest crime one can commit in Hillford."

"Well, I suppose you'd better turn me in then."

I shake my head, winking at her as I pull open the door. "I would never." I tug on her arm, guiding her into the diner. "We still have time to change that before someone else does, though."

Jade smirks. "Well, you're the only one who knows my secret."

"It's safe with me."

The diner's relatively empty, since most people who come at night are probably still at the bar. One of the servers from behind the counter waves at the two of us.

"Pick whichever table you'd like!"

Jade is the one who leads, pulling me to an empty booth in the back corner. She unthreads her arm from mine and slides into one of the bench seats. I slide into the one across from her.

"I already know what I want," she announces, a smile pulling across her lips as she shrugs off her coat.

I arch a brow as I slip off my own jacket. "Is that so?"

"Yes." My eyes are drawn to her lips and the way they roll as she releases the syllable. My throat bobs as I swallow hard, forcing my gaze away from her mouth.

I don't know what the hell my problem is.

"Hi!" The server from behind the counter steps up next to our table, almost as if she was summoned by Jade's words. "I brought you both menus, if you want to look over them."

"I think we both know what we want, don't we, Sunny?" My voice is low and thick with tension as my eyes bounce to Jade's.

Her nostrils widen, her pupils dilating as she stares back at me for a beat. Her tongue darts out to wet her perfect plump lips and I wish my tongue was hers. I close my eyes, the muscle in my jaw tightening.

"I'll take a water, a black coffee, and whatever he's having for food."

I open my eyes, arching a brow at her before looking at our server. "I'll have the same to drink, but my coffee with cream and sugar. We'll both have the stuffed Nutella waffles with strawberries and bananas."

She jots it down on her notepad, smiling at the two of us before she excuses herself from the table.

"Those waffles sound like a sugar overload."

"It is, but you won't regret it, I promise," I say, smiling at her. "Plus, you need something to counteract all the alcohol you drank."

She blows out a breath, pushing her hair from her face as she quickly shakes her head. "I swear I didn't drink that much." She purses her lips. "I have a low tolerance and needed something to take the edge off."

The edge from what?

The words die on her lips as our server comes back with our waters and pours us each a mug of piping hot coffee. She leaves some cream and sugar in the center of the table for me.

Jade slowly lifts the hot liquid to her lips, not even flinching as she takes a sip of it. I overload mine with cream and sugar, slowly stirring it as I meet her gaze once more.

"Is everything okay?"

Her chest rises as she sucks in a deep breath. She swaps her coffee for her water, taking a long sip before setting it back down on the table. "I don't know. I'm just stressed and out of time and probably fucked."

My eyebrows cinch together. I have no idea what she's talking about as she speaks the words in a rushed exhale. "What's going on? Is there anything I can do to help you?"

She lets out a harsh laugh. "Unless you can come up with the best story idea ever, then no." She opens her mouth, then closes it, her face scrunching up before she sighs. "I'm an author and the publisher I've been working with asked for a new idea and I'm supposed to have something by Monday but I have nothing."

My curiosity is piqued and I tilt my head to the side. "You're an author? What do you write?"

"Romance," she admits after a beat, almost as if she wasn't sure she wanted to say it aloud.

"No shit," I breathe, a soft laugh following. A grin tugs on my lips. "That's really cool. I've never met a real-life author before."

Jade arches a brow. "Do you even read?"

"Not often, but it is a skill I have."

Her shoulders shake with laughter. A pink tint creeps across her cheeks and her lips lift into a slow smile. "Seems like you have a lot of those, but none that benefit me."

I stare at her for a moment, the last three words hanging in the air around us. She doesn't seem to notice, probably because she's still sobering up. She takes another sip of her coffee and then her water.

She has no idea how we could benefit from one another again. I don't know the first thing about her job or what she does, but I know how to tell a story.

Which could also be the perfect distraction for me.

"Let me help you with your book."

She sits back in her seat, crossing her arms over her chest. "What?"

"You need inspiration for your story. Let me help you."

She's silent for a moment, her arms falling away from her chest as she reaches for her mug. Her eyes don't leave mine as she assesses me. Her gaze is piercing, intrusive, and fuck me, I like the way she's looking at me right now.

Like she doesn't know if she should leave my ass sitting in this booth alone or if she should indulge in the crazy idea I presented.

"What do you know about love, Matteo Ford?"

"You can call me Matty," I offer, shrugging. "Everyone else does."

Her eyes burn brighter. "I'm not everyone else."

Holy fuck.

"No," I rasp. "You're not, are you?"

"You didn't answer my question."

Lifting a hand, I rake my fingers through my hair. "It's not really my thing."

"And you think that qualifies you to help me write a romance story? About the one thing you don't believe in?"

"I didn't say that," I correct her, bringing my own mug to my lips to take a sip now that it's cooled down some. "I don't date for love or romance. It's just something to occupy my time. Something to keep me busy. It's not that I don't believe in love, I just know it's not for me."

She nods her head, the movement slow and exaggerated. "Let me change your mind."

My body freezes. "What?"

She chuckles, leaning forward as she folds her arms on the table. I don't miss the swell of her breasts, the way they lift as they press against her forearms. I tear my gaze from them.

"Oh god," she breathes, her eyebrows lifting. "No, not me, not like that. I have no interest in athletes." I can't read the emotion on her face. "I don't actually know what I meant by that. I'm drunk."

I lift a questioning brow. She's not as drunk as she was.

"What I meant was, I don't believe that. I think there's

love out there for someone, if you open yourself up to the idea."

"Yeah, well, I'm not," I say, forcing out a laugh and shaking my head. "I'm not big on commitments."

"Yet you want to help me come up with a story line."

Jesus, she's relentless. I let out a frustrated breath and the moment is severed as our server reappears with our food. She sets a plate in front of me and one in front of Jade. Each one has two huge waffles with Nutella seeping from them. They're piled high with strawberries, bananas, and whipped cream.

"Can I get you anything else?"

Jade shakes her head, looking to me for confirmation then back to the woman. "We're great. Thank you."

"Enjoy!"

The silence stretches between us as Jade stabs her waffles with her fork and slides her knife through them. She lets out a soft moan as she takes a bite.

"You were right. These are delicious."

Satisfaction washes over me and I take a bite of mine. "Told you."

We're quiet as we both dig back in, but my mind is fixated on both of our problems. There's a simple solution, she just doesn't know it yet.

I need to keep her around, at least until the end of the season.

"Helping you helps me."

Jade swallows a mouthful of food and chases it with a gulp of water. "What?"

"I play better when I have a distraction that's off the ice. It's like reverse psychology. If I think I have something to prove or someone to impress, I'm more focused. If I don't, I overanalyze every move, and it fucks me up."

"Okay…" She stares at me, locked in, but doesn't fully understand what I'm getting at.

"I swore off dating as my New Year's resolution and everything's gone downhill since. We were on a losing streak and I didn't score the last few weeks, until I ran into you."

Her face slowly breaks into a smile. "Are you saying you've been thinking about me, Matty?"

The nickname sounds weird coming from her. "Matteo."

Her smile stretches, her eyes burning brighter. "You didn't answer my question, *Matteo*."

Electricity rolls down my spine. Fuck. "Yes."

She pushes another forkful of food past her lips, slowly chewing as she studies me for a beat. "How can we help each other?"

"You can be my distraction, and I'll help you with your book. It sounds like you need someone to help you brainstorm and I need something to help me keep my head out of my ass."

"Hmm," she murmurs, her eyes glued to mine as she lifts her mug to her lips and takes another sip. "A deal we can both benefit from." She pauses, tilting her head to the side. "What kind of a distraction do you need me to be?"

"Anything, honestly." I shrug my shoulders. "Obviously, the other day was all it took for me to have something else to think about."

She levels her gaze on mine. "Are you—" She purses her lips. "I'm not exchanging sexual favors for your help."

My eyes widen, and I shake my head immediately. "No, no, that's not what this is. I just like the chase. I perform better under the pressure of impressing someone."

"Sounds like you just like to show off."

"Well..." I smirk. "I'd hate to waste those many skills I have that you referred to earlier."

She snorts, rolling her eyes. "So, you'll be my muse? Let me draw inspiration from you and your cocky attitude and I just have to talk to you, hang out with you?"

"Basically." I shrug again, laughing at how ridiculous it sounds. "We're both in a bind and desperate times call for desperate measures, don't they?"

"You do have a lot of qualities I look for in a character..." She cocks her head. "Why don't you just find someone else to distract yourself with?"

My eyes roam across her face, over her freckles and back to her blue eyes. "I'm not interested in anyone else being my distraction."

She's quiet again. Assessing, studying. "Okay," she says after a moment. "Fuck it. I'm out of options, so why not?" She runs her tongue over her top row of teeth. "Just until we don't need each other anymore?"

A smile tugs on my lips. "Exactly."

Her expression is unreadable. "I have one rule."

I tilt my head to the side, my eyes scanning her face. "What's that?"

"No catching feelings."

A chuckle rumbles in my chest. "I don't catch feelings, Sunny. That won't be a problem." I extend my arm, holding out my hand to her. "So, do we have a deal?"

Her eyes don't leave mine as she slides her palm against my waiting hand, giving me a swift shake.

"Deal."

CHAPTER SEVEN
JADE

Why do I feel like I made a deal with the devil?

I stare down at the entire thread Nicole sent to me with people talking about Matteo and the women he's dated. It doesn't look like he's ever been in a confirmed relationship, although it's not unusual for him to be seen in public with different women.

Maybe he's just the devil disguised as a hot hockey player with a known playboy reputation. The one who has enough confidence for his entire team.

Regardless of who he is, I woke up yesterday morning with a massive hangover and a brain brimming with inspiration. I filled a few pages of my notebook with random thoughts and ideas.

"So, let me get this straight," Ellie starts after she finishes chewing a piece of her sushi roll. I lock my screen, not needing to see anymore. I've already done enough of my own research too. "You left us Friday to go to a diner with Matteo fucking Ford and ended the night by making a deal with him?"

Chewing my own food, I slowly nod my head. "Yeah. Pretty much."

"I don't understand his side of the deal," Nicole chimes in from across the table. "There has to be something more than just talking and hanging out with him, right?"

"I don't know," I shrug, shaking my head as I set my chopsticks down on my now empty plate. "I told him I won't be exchanging any sexual favors."

Ellie claps her hands. "Yes, girl, establish those boundaries."

"Hockey players are known for their superstitions. If you think about it, it makes sense."

Aiden had some weird ones when we were dating, although I didn't pay much attention to them. He kind of kept me separate from the hockey world, which at the time, felt weird, but I didn't question him on it.

Looking back now, I couldn't have been any stupider.

"He said he scored a goal, and they broke their losing streak after we met."

Nicole's eyes widen. "You're his new good luck charm."

"Like those rabbit foot keychains."

Nicole and I both look at Ellie. Nicole's face contorts. "Um, maybe not exactly like that." We share a quiet laugh before she looks at me. "What about you? Any progress with your book?"

"The spark I needed—it's come back to me," I admit, a smile creeping across my lips as my stomach does a somersault. "I've been jotting down notes and have a few ideas that feel promising. I'm just not sure what I want to do yet. But to answer your question, yes."

I need to have something for my agent tomorrow, but I feel a hell of a lot more hopeful than I did before. I have twenty-four hours to get something ready for her.

"You found your new muse."

The smile spreads across my face. "I think I did. Although, this whole situation is a first for me."

Ellie waves her hand dismissively. "It's fine. You're just doing it for the plot."

That's exactly what this is. Something about him leaves me feeling inspired and he's already agreed to help me figure out this story. It's like our very own pact, in a way. I help him, he helps me.

A laugh bubbles in my throat. "Oh my god, it's a plot pact."

"Literally," Nicole laughs, her head tipping back as the three of us cackle. She straightens and gives me a pointed look.

I look back and forth at both my best friends. "I'm going to miss you guys."

Nicole looks sad and Ellie's face contorts. "I'm not going anywhere," she says. "We'll still see each other when I'm home."

I'm immediately embarrassed by the amount of sensitivity I'm showing. Ellie's new degree earned her a promotion... one that requires a great deal of traveling.

"You're right," I admit, nodding my head. "Sorry, my mind is just all over the place."

Nicole smiles. "I'm just a few hours away." Her eyes squint with a hint of mischief. "Just so you know, we're going to need all the details with your new little friend."

Details? Matteo and I are not dating. We have a mutual agreement—an understanding. We're both using each other and no one is going to be benefitting in a way that will be anything worth sharing.

"I told you, it's not like that."

"For now," Ellie says with a wink. "Nicole's married and all the men I've met suck. I'd rather just hear your stories instead."

"I have nothing to tell other than fictional ones."

Ellie sighs. "Why are all the good men fictional?"

"Because they're written by women," Nicole chuckles. "Well, except for my husband. It's like he crawled right off the pages of a romance novel."

I lift a brow. "You practically trained him."

Nicole smiles, lifting her finger as she presses it to her lips. "Shh. That secret is only for the girls." She glances around like she's checking to make sure no one is listening. "We can't let the men know."

"My lips are sealed."

Ellie nods in agreement. "I'll never tell."

The conversation shifts away from men and we finish up our meal before the three of us go our separate ways. My footsteps are light as I head down the street, making my way back to my apartment. I've spent so much time writing myself in circles or just avoiding the creative process in general. I've been afraid of the future, because I wasn't certain I'd have one in this career.

And for the first time in a long time, I'm ready for whatever comes next.

———

I stare down at my notes. Ripped pages from my notebook are askew across the floor. Some with the words scratched out and others are rolled up into tight balls of frustration.

Not a single idea feels like *the one*. I need a story unlike anything I've ever written before.

I need a story that everyone is going to stop their lives for and rush to the nearest bookstore to purchase.

I pinch the bridge of my nose. Maybe I'm not good enough anymore. Maybe I need to just call it quits and find another job. I feel the inspiration, but I'm too indecisive. Too afraid. What if the idea I go with isn't enough to salvage my career?

My phone vibrates, and I sigh, picking it up. My heart skips a beat when I see his name.

MATTEO

You alive?

It's been two days since we shook hands and made a deal. I gave him my number after he walked me home in the wee hours of the morning. It was a stipulation to our agreement. How else would we use each other if we didn't have a way of getting a hold of one another?

JADE

Barely. This book is going to be the end of me.

MATTEO

What's going on? Maybe I can help.

I don't know if he can help, but at this point, I will take anything I can get. I have so many ideas, I just need to figure out which one sounds the best.

JADE

Can I call you? I think it would be easier.

MATTEO

Yes.

Ignoring the nervous ball twisting in my stomach, I tap on his name to call him before I get the chance to second guess myself. I'm not sure Matteo is the person I should be bouncing ideas off of, but his part of our pact is to help me, so…

"Hey," he says, answering on the second ring. He sounds a bit breathless. "Shit, hold on."

There's a rustling sound in the background, maybe a door slamming and then he's back on the phone. "Sorry about that."

"Everything okay? I didn't mean to bother you."

"You're never a bother, Sunny. I just got home from dinner at my friend's." He pauses for a second. "Theo."

"Why do you call me that?"

He's quiet for a moment, then asks, "Call you what?"

"Sunny," I say, my voice barely above a whisper.

"Because you're like the sun. You shine brighter than everyone else around you. I know if I get too close, I'm bound to be burned."

My heart stumbles over itself before breaking out into an unsteady rhythm of erratic beats.

"So, how can I help?"

Right. The reason why I called him.

"I have too many ideas and I need help picking the perfect one."

"Let's hear them."

Putting him on speakerphone, I open my notes app on my phone and begin to list them off. The first few are similar to books I've written before. Friends to lovers, enemies to lovers, two single parents falling in love.

"I personally like to write the forbidden stories. The ones where they shouldn't or can't be together but find a way to end up together."

"Oh, I like that," Matteo says slowly, his words penetrating my ears. "What if you work off the forbidden aspect? Like rivals, maybe?"

The idea swirls in my brain, slowly sinking its tentacles into the crevices of my mind. "This is something I can work with."

"It's a romance, right?"

"Well, yeah. I don't write anything that isn't." My fingers move quickly across the screen, my mind bubbling with ideas as I jot it all down. "They could be opposites. Bad boy, good girl. Maybe he's from the wrong side of the tracks and thinks he's not worthy of love."

"He could have trust issues and that makes him hesitant to fall in love. He doesn't think it's something he'd ever want, but she ends up changing it for him."

"This is brilliant. I think I have what I need to get started." A smile pulls across my lips as I finish typing the note out on my phone. "This little plot pact is really going to come in handy."

"Plot pact?"

I stifle a laugh, rolling back onto my side. "My friends and I came up with a name for what this is. You know like the saying do it for the plot? Except mine is kind of literal because I'm writing a book."

"Hm." Matteo lets out a soft chuckle. "The plot pact. I like that."

"Me too," I say, unable to fight the yawn that forces itself upon me. "I should probably get some sleep. I need to get up early and dive into this story tomorrow."

"Yeah, I should go too."

"Thanks for your help, Matteo. I've seriously been struggling to pinpoint an idea and you really helped."

"It's my pleasure," he says quietly, his voice tender yet thick with something undetectable. "Goodnight, Sunny. Sweet dreams."

"Goodnight."

We both linger a second longer than we should and I'm the one who severs the connection, ending the call. My chest feels lighter and as I close my eyes, the darkness pulls me under with his dark gray eyes following after me.

CHAPTER EIGHT
MATTEO

I stare out the window, my eyes drifting out into the distance that is nothing but onyx night sky. The clouds beneath us are hard to see with the lack of moon or sunlight. While the days are growing longer now that it's February, it's still getting dark earlier than I prefer.

I adjust in my seat, glancing at Cam sitting beside me. His head's tilted back, mouth wide open, and if I didn't have my headphones on, I'd be blessed with the obnoxious sounds of his snores.

The cabin of the plane is quiet, and the lights are set low. We were supposed to leave earlier today, but there were some mechanical problems, so we're getting to Colorado a bit later than originally planned.

I check the time on my phone. We still have about two hours of flying time. We'll land close to midnight, which isn't ideal. Once everyone gets settled in their rooms, it will be super late and we need to get up early for our morning skate.

Normally when we travel farther distances, we fly in the day before the game. It helps to get acclimated to the area and the time change, if there is one. We won't have much time for that on this trip. We're just going to have to push through the exhaustion. It's nothing we haven't done before.

My phone vibrates in my hand, and I can't help the smile that lifts the corners of my lips when I see her name on the screen. I unlock my phone, tapping on my messages and immediately opening our thread of texts.

SUNNY

The best thing happened yesterday, and I think it's all because of you.

My heart flutters inside my chest.

MATTEO

Oh yeah? What happened?

SUNNY

I had a meeting with my agent, which ended up also being a meeting with my editor at the publishing house. They loved the idea. She took it to her team immediately.

I just got off a call with them.

They want the book. I got the deal.

I slowly lean back in my seat, crossing my ankles as I stretch out my legs. This is great news. This is everything she was hoping for.

MATTEO

That's amazing. Congratulations!

Did you go with the idea we came up with?

SUNNY

It's similar.

I tilt my head to the side, chewing on her words.

I wonder which idea from our Sunday night brainstorming session she ended up going with, if the idea is only a similar one.

MATTEO

When I'm back in town, I want to take you out to celebrate.

SUNNY

You don't have to do that.

We have a deal. A pact. It's nothing more than that. I can take her out to celebrate without it meaning something different.

MATTEO

What if I told you I want to?

We agreed until the end of the season, right?

SUNNY

Yes.

MATTEO

Then let me take you out to celebrate.

You can use the night for inspiration.

SUNNY

Are you sure? It's not that big of a deal.

This is something that deserves to be celebrated. I don't know who made her feel insignificant in the past, but that will be changing.

MATTEO

You're right. It's not a big deal.

It's a huge deal.

SUNNY

Isn't this weird, though? This deal we made. We don't even know each other.

MATTEO

How do you think people get to know one another, Sunny? How am I supposed to know you if I don't get to see you.

When she doesn't reply right away, my finger twitches. I can unsend it, and pretend I didn't say it that way. Those words, they feel like there's too much emotion tethered to them.

This is an emotionless transaction.

I'm allowed to want to get to know her with no other intention than that. There would never be a future for us in the cards, especially when that's the one thing I will never want. She's my good luck charm for the rest of this season. If she's mine until then, we're going to get to know one another.

There's no way around it.

SUNNY

I don't think you truly want to know me,
Matteo. I'm here to serve a purpose for
you, as a distraction. Someone to pump
your ego.

You don't want to know the real me.

I stare back at my phone, words failing me for a moment. She has no idea what I want.

MATTEO

Why don't you let me be the one who
decides that?

Time is momentarily suspended as I'm trapped in a tin can flying through the sky. Damn, what did Aiden do for her to be this jaded?

But then again, I don't know anything about her and there's a burning curiosity inside of me. Most of the women I meet only ever want to talk about themselves.

Not Jade. She keeps her cards close to her chest with her poker face perfectly in place.

That alone has me wanting to dive into the archives of Jade Wilson.

SUNNY

Okay.

My eyebrows tug together, conflict washing over me. She seemed ready to extend her claws and now she's retreating. It's hard to read tone in text messages, so maybe I had it wrong.

MATTEO

Can I take you out when I get home?

SUNNY

Just as friends.

MATTEO

Are we friends now?

SUNNY

That's the only word that fits whatever
this is.

Whatever this is. *I don't even know.* We're not dating. We're not fucking. We're really not anything.
Friends it is.

MATTEO

Then yes, as friends.

SUNNY

And just for inspiration.

I can't tell if she's trying to make those lines even clearer than they already were.

MATTEO

Yes, Jade.

I have no intention of this being anything
more.

SUNNY

Good, neither do I.

I'd eat you alive, anyways.

I'm no match against the laughter that rumbles in my chest. Cam stirs beside me, his head rolling to the other side as I smile down at my phone in the dark cabin.

She's fiery, smart mouthed, and might actually have full immunity to my charm.

I think I'm fucking hooked.

CHAPTER NINE
JADE

The muscles in my hand ache from the last few hours of figuring out the ins and outs of this book. I set my pen down on the counter beside my notebook. This is the first time I've come up for air or have taken a break from it.

I slowly rise from my seat at the island in my kitchen, and scan over the scattered post-it notes with different pieces of information scratched on them.

I never said my process was neat.

My ears need a break from my headphones, so I slip them off and set them on the counter. I could use a lap around the kitchen too, but the stiffness in my knees and hips cause me to slowly unfold to stand. I have to pause to stretch my muscles. I hadn't realized how locked in I'd been, I guess I hadn't changed positions in a while.

Then again, I was curled over the counter in the same posture as a hunchback goblin.

I pick up my phone while I down a gulp of water, switching it back on for notifications to come through. There's one from Nicole, two in the group chat with the girls, and one other that causes my stomach to do a little flip.

Matteo Ford.

Communication with him has been interesting to say the least. I've found myself looking forward to his texts while he's been on the road. They left last Monday and have been gone for over a week now.

He said he'd be gone for almost two weeks while they're playing on the west coast, but to plan on going out with him to celebrate when he gets home.

Not for a date. Oh god, no, never a date.

I take another sip of my water, ignoring the pitter patter of my heart as I unlock my phone and open the message from him. A slow smile pulls on my lips as I read his words.

MATTEO

Sunny, you're on my mind again.

JADE

Sounds like a personal problem.

MATTEO

Not so sure it's a bad one, honestly.

I scored a nasty goal at the end of the third tonight.

My eyes flick to the time in the upper right corner of my phone. He's on the west coast, three hours behind me right now. I hadn't even realized it was already after two o'clock in the morning.

JADE

You're welcome for that.

MATTEO

Probably would have had a hat trick if you
watched the game.

I chuckle to myself, shaking my head. I don't get
involved with athletes, and watching a game for the sole
purpose of watching one player feels pretty involved.

JADE

That wasn't part of the agreement,
remember?

MATTEO

I think I need an addendum.

What are you doing awake? It's late.

I take a picture of the mess on the counter, and send it
to him.

JADE

Sometimes I work better at night when the
rest of the world is quiet.

MATTEO

I get that.

Do you have a title yet?

JADE

Painted Inferno.

MATTEO

I like that. When can I read it?

> After I convince myself it's not complete trash.

He doesn't respond at first and I set my phone back down, planting my hands on the counter as I stare down at the mess I still need to organize. My phone vibrates again after a moment, except this time it's not the normal short pattern from a text message.

My eyes widen as I glance at the screen. He's calling me. We only spoke on the phone one time when I was rambling to him about this book last Sunday. Other than that, all communication has been through text.

My palms are instantly clammy. I swallow roughly, feeling the vibrations of the second ring. I could let it go to voicemail. I suck in a breath, holding it for a second before answering the call on an exhale.

"Hello?"

"I hope it's okay I called," he says in a rush. My breathing quickens at the sound of his voice, low and gravely.

"No, it's okay. I just—I wasn't expecting it."

He's silent for a moment and I quickly shuffle some of my things around on the counter. My eyes are beginning to feel like they're permanently crossed. This mess will be here for me to sift through in the morning.

"You're not busy, are you?"

"No." My footsteps are light as I exit the kitchen, heading down the hall to my bedroom. "What are you doing?"

"I just got out of the shower, getting ready for bed. We have an early flight in the morning."

"Are you guys flying back to Hillford?"

"Yeah," he says. "Usually at the end of a roadtrip we fly home the same night, but since it's so late, we were able to just stay tonight."

"That makes sense. With the time difference, you guys wouldn't be back until early morning anyways."

"I sleep like shit on planes," he admits as I put him on speakerphone and set my phone on the counter. I grab my toothbrush, sliding some paste across the bristles. "What are you doing?"

"Getting ready for bed, too."

"Perfect timing," he says softly.

"I'm going to brush my teeth. Tell me about your game or something so we're not just sitting in awkward silence."

Matteo laughs softly as I wet the toothbrush and put it in my mouth. He starts to tell me how their team is turning things around. They've won every game on their road trip and his points are up. I scrub my teeth as I listen to him intently, smiling at how his voice fluctuates with emotion.

Something about him demands my attention. I know better than to get involved with him, but that doesn't mean I won't let myself feel the way his presence draws me in.

I don't bother to tell him I'm finished as I pull my hair back into a braid and walk into my bedroom. The words finally fall from his lips, the silence stretching as I'm sliding in between the covers on my bed.

"Sunny?"

"Yeah?"

"I didn't know if you were still there."

"Yeah," I breathe, ignoring the smile creeping onto my face. "I was just listening."

"I didn't call to tell you all about my night."

I lie down on my side, tucking my other hand beneath my head. "What did you call for then?"

"I was hoping you'd tell me a story." He pauses, his voice low. "The one you were working on all night."

I don't know what my hesitation is. Sharing my story ideas and brainstorming with him is what our pact is all about. "It's not about you, if that's what you were thinking." I inhale deeply, holding the air in my lungs a moment before resigning myself to the fact that I should just tell him. "It's about two people who end up falling for each other, even when they know they shouldn't."

"When they swear they wouldn't?"

I squeeze my eyes shut. "Yeah."

"Can you tell me more?"

"I told you, I don't share my work until I can convince myself that it's not trash."

"I refuse to believe anything you write is trash." Matteo is quiet for a beat. "I looked you up. Everyone loves you and your work. You didn't tell me you're famous like that."

I blow out a breath. "I feel more like a has-been lately."

"You're not," he declares. "I refuse to believe that. You're working on your next bestseller and it's going to go crazy. Don't worry, I will be telling anyone who'll listen to go read it."

"Oh god," I groan, dragging my hand down my face. I didn't consider him and his overly confident self. I didn't once think that maybe he'll go telling everyone that he helped me with inspiration and research.

I do not want to be labeled as another one of Matteo Ford's conquests.

"I should have made you sign an NDA or something."

Matteo clicks his tongue with amusement. "Am I your dirty little secret, Sunny?"

"No." The word comes out without hesitation. "I just— you have quite the reputation and ego."

"Hm," he murmurs, the sound almost detached. "Wouldn't want to tarnish yourself and your work with someone like me, is that it?" He sighs, long and exasperated. "For the record, you shouldn't believe everything you read on the internet or hear from unreliable sources."

"Are you saying that none of it is true? That you don't just jump from one woman to the next?"

"It's not like that." I detect a hint of defensiveness in his tone, then he continues a little softer, "I don't sleep with everyone I date."

My stomach sinks, although there's a bit of relief I shouldn't be feeling. His dating life isn't my concern, I should just leave it alone. "Then tell me what it's like."

The silence stretches. I shouldn't have even asked. Matteo and I have a deal—an agreement—and this is not part of it. We can be friendly, friends even, without knowing each other's secrets.

"It doesn't matter," he finally says. "I should get some sleep."

The abrupt ending to our conversation has me reeling, panic rolling in the pit of my stomach. That wasn't the turn it was supposed to take. The words I spoke, I couldn't stop them from coming out. I don't know why I said any of it.

None of it should matter to me anyways.

"Matteo, I'm sorry," I say in a rush, wishing I could take back all the words I spoke. "That was rude of me and I didn't mean to upset you."

"You didn't do anything wrong. Nothing you said was

untrue." He sighs, sounding more tired now than he did when he first called. "I'll text you when I'm back in Hillford. I still want to take you out to celebrate."

My throat tightens, hope bubbling in my chest. "You do?"

"Of course, I do."

"Okay," I say softly, swallowing hard. The fluttering in my stomach is an annoyance that needs to be extinguished. There's no reason to entertain it. Every interaction, every conversation, every second spent together—it's all for the plot.

"Goodnight, Matteo."

He lets out another deep breath. "Night, Sunny."

Again, we both linger on the phone a moment longer than we need to, like neither of us wants to hang up just yet. A smile tugs on my lips and I hear a quiet laughter from him. It's as if both of our fingers are hovering over the end call button, waiting to see who does it first.

"Goodnight," I whisper.

"Goodnight," he murmurs back, just before I press the button and end the call. I slide my phone onto my nightstand, roll onto my back, and stare up at the ceiling, my heart thumping against my ribcage.

We're both knowingly using one another, but this feels like a dangerous game we're playing. It's like we're on a slippery slope, on the precipice of falling. One wrong step and we're both going down.

CHAPTER TEN
MATTEO

FORD FAM CHAT

ELENA

Good morning, big brother.

It's Dad's birthday Friday. You're coming to dinner, right?

BELLA

Yeah, right. They haven't talked since their fight last month.

Mom's pissed, by the way.

She said you've been dodging her calls, Matteo.

ELENA

She's going to be more pissed if he doesn't show up for dinner.

BELLA

You and dad need to get over your shit already.

ELENA

Do you know who you're talking to? Matteo's allergic to apologizing.

BELLA

I feel like I'm in high school again.

MATTEO

You're not that far removed from it.

ELENA

You're the oldest, you should be the most mature.

MATTEO

I'm not wrong in the argument. Dad knows it and doesn't want to admit it.

BELLA

Oh jeez, here we go again.

ELENA

Friday night, Mom's making dinner and everyone will be there. Including you.

MATTEO

We'll see.

BELLA

You're both annoying.

MATTEO

You're the ones who started it today.

ELENA

For god's sake, Matteo. Shelf your ego for once.

BELLA

Yeah, what she said.

I stare down at my phone and sigh, my shoulders sagging as I narrow my eyes at the text thread with my two sisters. You would have thought the age gap between the three of us would have made us not as close, but it's had the opposite effect.

Our parents met, had a one night stand, and then I was born nine months later. The first five years were just Mom and me. Although I was young, I still remember what it was like without Dad around. The instability. The confusion of why the other kids at school had a father and I didn't.

Regardless of what my mother says about how she couldn't get in contact with him, I can't help but wonder if she could have tried harder. What held her back for those five years? If we wouldn't have gone to Aston, would I have even known my father?

I didn't have a bad life with them. Honestly, I had an amazing childhood. Two years after they found each other again, Elena was born and three years later came our youngest sister, Isabella. Everyone calls her Bella, for short.

They're both little thorns in my side and I wouldn't trade them for anything in the world. Although, in moments like this, when they're crawling up my ass about something—yeah, the temptation to trade them in is very strong.

ELENA

Call mom back. She's been worried
about you.

MATTEO

We've talked through text.

BELLA

She hates texting.

ELENA

Can you stop being so damn
hardheaded?

BELLA

He's a Ford, so no.

MATTEO

The two of you are Fords. You're the same
damn way.

I'm muting the chat. I have shit to do.

BELLA

Call mom!

ELENA

Or else…

I snort, rolling my eyes. Please. They both inherited our
mother's fierceness. Although, I'm not afraid of either of
them. What the hell could they possibly do? Nothing.
They're all bark, no bite.

Reminds me of someone else…another certain some-
body I know who's quick to show her claws. Someone I
can't seem to get out of my damn mind. It's what I
wanted, it's what I made the deal with her for.

Although, it's a bit unnerving.

She's supposed to be a calculated, controlled distraction. My self-control has been a bit unhinged. I'm not normally bothered by women's perceptions of me or my reputation. It's common knowledge that I don't do relationships. I'm known as the resident playboy for the Hillford Ice Hawks.

And for whatever reason, it fucking bugs me to think of her having that idea of me.

I run my fingers through my hair, then set my phone down on the counter as I prop my forehead on my hands. She's driving me insane. I can't stop thinking about her. I can't stop finding bullshit reasons to text her. She's been busy writing and I've been on the road for the last two weeks, so seeing her hasn't even been feasible.

I just got back to Hillford earlier today, and Jade and I have plans to go out in three days to celebrate her publishing deal. But I don't know if I can wait that long to see her, not now that we're back in the same city.

An exasperated sigh escapes me as I stand upright and shake my head. *What the hell is happening to me?*

My sister's voice rings in the back of my mind and reluctance weighs me down as I find my mother's name in my phone and press the call button. She answers just after the first ring.

"Hello?"

"Hi, Mom."

"Matteo." She lets out a frustrated breath. "I'm so glad you finally called, but what the hell? You're mad at your father, not me."

"I know. I'm sorry."

"I'm not going to give you the speech about making up with him again, but please tell me you're coming on Friday?"

Do I want to go celebrate his birthday on Friday? Not

really. Not after the fight we got into. Am I going to let my mother and the rest of the family down? No. I can't do that to them, regardless of my damn pride.

"Yes, I'll be there."

"Oh, thank God," she lets out a breath. "I know you and your father don't see eye to eye on everything, but he'll be so glad you're there."

I snort, shaking my head. "Doubtful."

"Matteo, I know you might not understand, but he's coming from a good place. He only wants the best for you and your sisters."

Of course he does. Carson Ford loves the three of us almost as much as he loves our mother. He wants the best for us all, but he doesn't want us to piss away an opportunity… which is exactly what he said I'm doing with my career.

"He has a weird way of showing it sometimes."

"I know, I know," she says softly, her voice trailing off for a second. "I'm glad you called. Don't do that again, do you understand?"

"Yes, Mom," I sigh. "I promise I won't."

"Good. You're my little buddy. You may be bigger than me now, but that's still what you'll always be to me."

A smile tugs on my lips. If you look up the definition of momma's boy, you'll see a lovely photo of me. I may have questions on whether or not she truly sought out my father after she got pregnant, but that doesn't change the bond she and I have. Nothing ever will, not even a fight with my dad.

Even if I do act a bit childish here and there.

"I gotta go, but I'll see you on Friday, okay?"

"Okay, I love you, Matteo."

"Love you too, Mom."

We end the call and my stomach growls in protest, reminding me that I haven't eaten since this morning. I set my phone down for a moment, abandoning it to dig through the fridge for something to eat. As I pull open the doors, I deflate a bit when I realize I have no food.

I don't go to the grocery store when I know we're going to be on the road for several games. Rather than wasting food, I prefer to eat everything I have and clean out my kitchen before leaving.

Normally I remember to get food after coming home, yet instead, I'm sitting here at dinner time with not a damned thing to make.

I glance at the clock on the stove. It's already after six. I wonder if Jade's eaten yet. Not that it's any of my concern…

Although, this would give me an excuse to see her. If she didn't eat and I didn't eat, you know, we could just eat together.

I grab my phone and don't hesitate to open our texting thread. A smirk tugs on my lips as I read over our texts from earlier when I was waiting for the plane to take off.

SUNNY

I had a dream about you last night.

MATTEO

Bet it was the best dream of your life.

SUNNY

Wrong. You took me fishing and ditched me.

MATTEO

I don't even like fishing.

SUNNY

Well, we went, and you left me.

MATTEO

Why'd I leave you?

SUNNY

I kept catching bigger fish than you.

MATTEO

That's fair. I don't like to lose.

SUNNY

I don't think I like dream-you.

MATTEO

What about real-life me?

SUNNY

Jury's still out.

MATTEO

What if I apologize for dream-me? Will that earn me any points?"

SUNNY

It might help.

MATTEO

I'm sorry and I promise to never leave you while we're fishing, which we will never do.

SUNNY

Thank you for that. I feel much better now.

MATTEO

Glad I could be of service.

SUNNY

Have a safe flight.

> **MATTEO**
> See you this weekend.

SUNNY
If you're lucky ;)

She's not like anyone I've ever met before. She's not afraid to give me shit and dare I say, I like it. That has to be the reason why I'm so goddamn hooked.

Hook, line and sinker.

> **MATTEO**
> Did you eat dinner yet?

SUNNY
Do pickles and a bag of chips count?

> **MATTEO**
> Absolutely not.

SUNNY
Then no.

> **MATTEO**
> Let me feed you.

SUNNY
Is that a kink of yours?

> **MATTEO**
> You curious about my kinks, Sunny?

SUNNY
Never.

I can't fight the smile pulling on my lips. She's a goddamn liar and she knows it.

MATTEO

I wanna see you. Let me bring you dinner.

SUNNY

Fine. If you show up with baked ziti, I'll
consider letting you in.

MATTEO

I need your address.

SUNNY

You didn't memorize it when you walked
me home? I overestimated you, Ford.

MATTEO

It was nearly four o'clock in the morning.
Give me your address.

Those three dots bounce on the screen for longer than I
would expect for her to type in her address. For a second
I'm worried she might actually not send it, right before it
finally pops up.

SUNNY

Text me when you're close, I'll meet you
downstairs.

MATTEO

See you soon.

Shaking my head to myself, a soft laugh escapes me as
I open up the web browser on my phone to find the perfect
restaurant to order take-out from.

At this point, she could ask me to fly to a different
country to fetch her food and I'd probably hop on a plane
without thinking twice.

All for the sake of our deal, of course.

CHAPTER ELEVEN
JADE

hit, shit, shit.

I don't know why I agreed to Matteo coming over. My entire apartment looks like a tornado ripped through it.

My trash isn't overflowing, but the sink is full of dishes. I quickly walk over, grabbing the different plates and dishes and arrange them all in the dishwasher. Being on a deadline has a way of making me hunker down in my apartment like a hobbit. The only thing I've been keeping up on is showering—thank God—and making sure my clothes are washed.

I do a quick walkthrough, straightening everything up, yet leaving all my work materials strewn across the dining room table. Since I've been fully immersed in the book I'm writing, I moved all my materials to the dining room table to free up the island counter in the kitchen.

It's a disaster, but it's an organized one. I know exactly

where everything I need is. It's fine, Matteo will get over it. Or maybe he won't even notice.

I catch sight of myself in the mirror along the wall near the dining room table.

Never mind the disaster on the table. I'm the real disaster here.

My footsteps are rushed as I head down the hallway, slipping into my bedroom to change into something a bit more acceptable. I switch out my wrinkled sweatsuit for a pair of leggings and a sweater.

I walk into the bathroom, brushing my hair and pulling it back into a messy bun on top of my head. I opt for a quick layer of light makeup, just to cover the dark circles under my eyes and to bring a bit of color back into my cheeks.

I'm not on a tight deadline, so there's really no excuse for my appearance other than not wanting to lose the momentum I have.

The inspiration lately has been like an overflowing well. It's all thanks to Matteo really. He's providing the muse; I'm just chasing after it.

The flirty banter between us keeps my mind stimulated. The conversation never feels flat or dry. Every time my phone goes off and I see his name, my heart does this stupid little stumble.

I'm supposed to see my cardiologist next week. Perhaps it's an electrical issue and not related to Matteo Ford at all.

I finish wiping down the counters after sweeping the floors. I drag a match along the side of the box, watching the flame come to life before I hold it to the wick of my candle.

And then my phone vibrates. Crap, how did thirty minutes go by so fast?

MATTEO

Honey, I'm home.

JADE

Coming.

MATTEO

Damn, Sunny. You couldn't even wait for me?

I choke on air. My eyes widen, water welling along my bottom eyelids as I cough loudly, struggling to catch my breath.

MATTEO

Just kidding. Hurry up, though. Food's gonna get cold.

Heat spreads across my face and I ignore the tingling sensation between my legs. I need to get laid or something by someone who isn't Matteo Ford.

Slipping my feet from my slippers and into a pair of sneakers, I briskly walk out of my apartment, hopping on the elevator to the lobby on the first floor. It's empty downstairs as I step out of the car and head to the front door.

Matteo stands on the other side of the glass, not noticing me at first. My eyes roam over his tousled hair, dropping down to his chest, then his torso before bouncing back to his face.

He's wearing a pair of loose-fitting jeans, a white shirt, and a dark bomber jacket. I can't tell if it's navy blue or black in the lighting outside. He turns his head, a plastic take-out bag in his hand and his gaze collides with mine.

Steel gray eyes stare back at me, trailing along my neck, deliberately slow before flickering back to my face. The corners of his mouth twitch.

I push the door, holding it open for him. "Hey." The word slips out on an exhale, sounding breathy. My throat tightens.

Matteo passes by me, that familiar bold, woodsy scent wafting toward me, and his lips lift into a smirk. "Hey, Sunny."

The door shuts behind him, but he stops right in front of me. The space between us is almost nonexistent. I'm acutely aware of how tall he is, standing this close. I tip my head back, my neck extending as I look up at him.

"Hey."

You already said that, Jade.

Channel your inner Candy Stone energy.

He chuckles softly, a small flicker of heat in his eyes as he tilts his head to the side. "Are you hungry?"

My stomach growls at the mention. "Starving."

"Good." His voice is low and hoarse. "I hope you like baked ziti," he winks.

"Look at you. You listen so well."

His eyebrows lift, just a fraction of an inch. The movement is so subtle, if I weren't hyperaware of him, I wouldn't have noticed. "You have no idea just how good of a listener I can be."

Heat creeps up my neck again while simultaneously spreading across the pit of my stomach. I need to get him up to my apartment... to eat, and then send him on his way before I end up doing something I'll likely regret.

"Come on." My voice catches in my throat and I clear

it, stepping around him as I turn away and head toward the elevator. "I'm on the seventh floor."

Matteo steps into the car, both of us occupying opposite corners of the elevator as the doors slide shut. Tension follows us into the space, heavy and thick. I shift my weight on my feet, tucking hair behind my ears to keep my hands busy.

I chance a glance at Matteo and his eyes are already on me, body turning to face me as he leans against the wall. My mouth is immediately dry. I lick my lips to try to bring some moisture back.

"You're staring."

His gaze draws down to my lips. "You're standing awfully close."

I swallow hard, warmth trailing down my spine. "The elevator's small."

"It is, isn't it?" His voice drops lower, the sound sultry as his eyes slowly search mine.

My body hums as electricity dances in the air. He's close enough I could touch him without even straightening my arm. He's in my space, he's in my head, and fuck me, I think I like it.

My lips part, a shallow breath escaping me. The muscles in my legs contract as I start to shift my weight in his direction. The elevator dings, knocking me back to my senses as it comes to a stop at my floor. My eyes widen, his darken, and the doors slide open.

I need to get my shit together. We agreed that nothing like this would happen.

"This is my floor," I half whisper, as if he doesn't already know.

"After you," he chuckles, sweeping his arm toward the hall. Without another word, I exit the cab and he follows, walking to my door adjacent from the elevator shaft.

Matteo stops just behind me, his body close enough that I can feel his warmth, but not close enough to touch me. I quickly unlock my door, pushing it open with haste and head inside.

He follows after, kicking his shoes off at the door as I let it fall shut behind us.

"Two rules."

His eyes flicker to mine.

"No touching me, and no reading any of my notes."

He rolls his lips between his teeth, biting down on his smirk as his head bobs. "Yes, ma'am." He swipes his tongue along his bottom lip, his eyes still on mine.

I force myself to turn away from him as I slip my feet from my shoes and back into my slippers, and head into the apartment.

Matteo meets me at the island in the center of the kitchen. He looks over at the dining room table, curiously eyeing my notebooks and post-it's from where he's standing. He doesn't move any closer to try and read them.

Relief washes over me as he sets the bag on the counter and starts pulling containers out.

"Baked ziti for you," he says softly, setting it down in front of me. I grab two glasses of water and slide onto one of the barstools.

"Thank you." I lift my chin as he pulls out another container. "What'd you get?"

"Chicken masala," he says, grabbing the stool next to me and sliding it to the side of the island so we're sitting adjacent instead of side by side. "Do you want some?"

"Oh, no, that's yours. Thank you, though."

Matteo shrugs. "If you change your mind, you can have some."

"You have siblings, don't you?" A smile pulls on my lips as he nods his head. "Sharing comes with the territory."

He lets out a breath, shaking his head. "I have two younger sisters, Elena and Bella. I swear, nothing belonged to me during my teenage years."

"How old are they?"

"Elena's 21 and Bella's 19." He takes a bite of his food, chewing and swallowing before offering any more information. "I was seven when Elena was born, but thankfully the age gap made us closer. I always felt like I needed to look out for the two of them."

My eyes widen. "Oh, wow. That is a pretty significant gap. I'm glad it made you closer, rather than the opposite."

Matteo bobs his head. "Yeah. Thankfully the two of them didn't have to go the first five years of their life with their parents not together, so their childhood was a bit different." He pauses, his face draining of color and he abruptly switches gears. "What about you? Any brothers or sisters?"

I want to press rewind and ask him what he means by that. His parents had him and then weren't together?

"No," I say after a second. "I'm an only child." I pause, piercing some of the noodles with my fork. "My parents live in England, so they're not really around."

Matteo's eyebrows tug downward. "I'm sorry. It must be hard not seeing them often."

I shrug my shoulders dismissively, ignoring the tightening in my chest. "It's fine. They moved six years ago, so it's not anything new. They moved for my father's job. We're not close... never really were"

He's quiet, his eyes roaming over my face like he's trying to get a read on me. My face remains stoic, giving nothing away. Not that there's really much to give away. I'm indifferent about them at this point in my life. I've always felt like a bit of an outsider with my family.

My parents had different expectations that I never met. The two of them were married to their careers. Their relationship was second. And I always came in third place to them. My mother wanted me to get a degree in medicine like her and my father, so I'm sure you can imagine their shock when I went on to be an author instead.

"Do you ever see them?"

"Usually once or twice a year," I say after swallowing another mouthful of food. "Mainly on holidays." Matteo's eyes are still on me as he chews his food.

"You're close with your family?"

"Oh, yeah." He nods his head, pausing to take a sip of his water. "Almost too close sometimes. My father likes to try and tell me how to live my life. Doesn't help that his brother's the head coach for the Hawks."

I can't even imagine that added layer of pressure. "That sounds rough."

Now Matteo shrugs with an air of indifference. "It's annoying, more than anything. The two of them feel like co-conspirators at times."

"I'm sure," I laugh softly, taking a sip of my water. "Do you ever feel like you're under a microscope?"

Matteo looks up at me again. He's silent for a beat. "All the time." He drags a hand through his hair. His eyebrows twitch. "Sometimes I just want to disappear, you know?"

I purse my lips, familiarity washing over me as I bob my head. "Yeah, I know."

"Wouldn't it be nice if we could?" He muses, the tension dissipating. "Not forever, but just for a little bit."

"That sounds like a dream. I'd kill for a break from reality. From the stress and the deadlines and feeling like I'm always falling behind."

Mischief dances in Matteo's eyes. "Want to disappear with me, Sunny?"

"We can't do that."

"Yeah," he sighs. The mischief vanishes and a sad smile lifts his lips. "It's a nice thought, though, isn't it?"

"It is," I agree, slowly nodding. I tilt my head to the side, lifting my eyebrows at him in warning, and say in the best impression of a stern tone I can muster, "You'd better not disappear on me, Ford."

A ghost of a smile dances across his mouth. "You can't get rid of me that easily."

Sheepishly, I duck my head and pierce a few noodles again. I can practically feel the heat of Matteo's gaze lingering on the side of my face before he digs into his own food. After a moment in silence, both of us mulling over the fantasy, we switch back to safer topics, hockey and writing.

It feels like he's only been here for a half an hour, but before we know it, two hours have come and gone, and it's time for me to kick him out before he gets any other ideas. Matteo doesn't argue. Instead, he helps me clean up and then we're on the elevator together again.

He stands beside me, arm to arm, not bothering to move away as our limbs press against each other. He stares at me through our distorted reflections in the doors. "When do I get to know what you're writing about?"

"Why do you want to know so badly?"

"I am your muse, no?" He glances at me from the corner of his eye. "It only feels fair."

My throat bobs as I swallow hard. "I don't normally talk about books before they're done." It's different from anything else I've ever written. It still feels so new, I'm afraid if I say it out loud, the entire story will blow up in my face.

"Can I read it when it's done? Before anyone else does?"

My heart beats a bit harder. "You actually want to read it?"

The corners of his mouth twitch. "Of course, I do. I'm fully invested in this now."

The elevator dings as we reach the first floor. The doors slide open and Matteo motions for me to go ahead of him. "After it's edited, I'll make sure you get a copy before publication."

"You'll sign it, right?"

A soft laugh escapes me. "Yes. I'll even personalize it for you."

A slow and steady smile creeps across his lips. "Goodnight, Sunny. I'll see you Saturday?"

My chin dips as I nod. "I'll see you then. Goodnight."

Matteo lingers for a moment longer before he slips through the door, stepping out into the night. I stare after him as he walks down the street, heading toward his car. A part of me wants to go after him, to take him up on that offer to disappear together.

Away from the monotony of daily life. Away from the stressors and the constant decisions.

It's such a tempting, yet conflicting offer. Maybe in a different life Matteo and I could have been more than just a physical attraction.

He reaches the side of his car and glances back at me with that same sultry smile forming on his mouth. The physical attraction is undeniable… and I'm beginning to wonder if I'm not the only one feeling it.

Heat spreads through my body and I lift my hand to wave at him before he drops down into the front seat of his car. Turning from the door, I let it fall shut as I step away. My mind replays the entire night, every word that was said, over and over as I ride the elevator back to my floor..

As soon as my apartment door is shut, I press my back against it, tipping my head up and letting my eyelids fall shut. My chest expands as I inhale deeply. His woodsy scent lingers in the air around me. A stupid grin tugs on the corners of my lips.

Matteo Ford is under my skin and I think that's exactly where I want him to be.

CHAPTER TWELVE
MATTEO

Coming here was a bad idea.

I should have just lied and told my sisters and mother I couldn't make it. There must have been some kind of bullshit excuse I could have fed them instead.

Shifting my weight, I roll my shoulders back, mentally preparing myself before reaching for the doorknob and giving it a turn. It opens effortlessly, and I let myself into the home I spent most of my teenage years in.

The first half of my life was spent in Aston, a little under two hours north of Hillford. When my father retired from playing for the Aston Archers, he and my mother decided they wanted a change of scenery.

My Uncle Caleb and Aunt Mia were the first to make the move to Hillford. Caleb's two years older than my father and he accepted a position as an assistant coach for the Hillford Ice Hawks after retiring. A few years ago, he was promoted to head coach.

After my father retired, he became really involved in youth coaching. He was hired as a head coach for a tier one youth program.

The house is buzzing with energy and voices, and I pause just inside the door, my eyes dropping to the mess of shoes in the foyer. There are a hell of a lot more shoes here than just my family's.

I kick my own sneakers off and shrug out of my jacket to hang on the wall by the door. My father's laughter carries through the house, and I hear the voices of two of his best friends and old teammates, Lincoln Matthews and Rowan Taylor.

That explains the mess of shoes.

I'm not surprised they're here. The two of them are more like uncles than anything else. Hockey families have a habit of sticking together after the hours and years spent in the same space.

"Matteo!"

Posey's voice comes from the top of the stairs. A smile spreads across my face as my oldest friend comes down the steps. Her curly blonde hair is pulled back in a braid resting over her left shoulder.

Posey's two years younger than me. The two of us grew up together since our fathers played for the Archers together and her mom and mine are very close. She now works for the Hillford Ice Hawks as one of our skating coaches.

"Hey, Poe," I say, pulling her in for a hug as she reaches the bottom of the stairs. "How are you? It's been a while."

"I'm good, how are you? I saw you seem to have your groove back."

"Yeah, it seems like I do." I pause, glancing at the stairs as my sister Elena and Rowan's daughter, Lucy, come down. "Hey, El. Hey, Luce." I hug the two of them. Lucy's five years younger than me, so she and Elena have always been closer.

"Where's your brother?" I ask Posey.

There are ten kids in total between the five different families that form our one Archers family. Half are out of college and the younger ones are still in school, or at least college-aged.

"Chase couldn't get away for the weekend. They had a big game in Michigan."

I nod my head in understanding. "I get it."

"Figured you would," Posey chuckles, linking her arm through mine. "Come on, your mom said the food will be ready soon."

Posey leads me into the kitchen to find everyone else. My dad, Rowan, Lincoln, and Uncle Caleb are all sitting at the table in the connected dining room. Posey's mom, Nova, my Aunt Mia, and Rowan's wife, Hadley, are all gathered around the island counter, talking about something.

My spine immediately straightens, a smile falling from my lips as I meet my father's gaze from across the room.

Carson Ford isn't an angry man, but when he thinks he's right about something, he stands his ground. At some point, one of us is going to have to apologize first. My pride says it won't be me.

"Matteo!" My mother comes rushing over to me. "*Caro.*" She kisses my cheek. "I'm so glad you're here."

"And you swear he's not your favorite," Elena murmurs under her breath.

I shoot a glare at her, and she gives me the middle finger.

"Where's Pip and Tella?" I ask my aunt.

"They're at a concert."

"Oh, yeah, that's right." I nod. I remember Tella saying she bought tickets for Pippa's birthday two months ago. I look back at my mom. "Do you need help with anything?"

"No, no, we got it." My mother smiles, wiping her hands on her apron. "Dinner's almost ready."

I make my way around the counter, hugging and greeting Nova, Hadley, and Aunt Mia. I suck in a deep breath, knowing I need to face my father. Pushing my shoulders back again, I turn to the table and head over to where all the men are seated.

Uncle Caleb nods his head in greeting, Lincoln and Rowan both shake my hand, and my father's gaze locks on mine again. The muscle in his jaw tightens and his expression is unreadable. For a second, it looks like guilt washes over his eyes before it vanishes. He rises to his feet, surprising me as he walks over and pulls me in for a hug.

"Hey, bud. Glad you could make it."

"Yeah," I say quietly. My stomach rolls with uncertainty. "Happy birthday."

My father releases me. "Can we talk?"

There's no hint of anger in his voice, yet I'm confused. I thought he was still mad at me. "Yeah, of course," I nod, my heart hammering harder. And then the front door slams.

"Hey, fam," Theo shouts from the foyer as he comes strolling into the kitchen. "Hope I'm not late."

He hugs my mom and waves to the other mothers.

"Theo!" Lucy runs over to him, both of their laughter filling the air as she jumps into his arms. Growing up, Lucy and Theo were inseparable and their friendship didn't stop after we all became adults. He swings her around, setting her down as he kisses the top of her head and they go their separate ways.

He strolls over to the table. "Coach," he says, nodding at Uncle Caleb before addressing everyone else. "Happy birthday, Mr. Carson."

"Thanks, Theodore."

My eyebrows tug together. "You didn't tell me you'd be here."

Theo shrugs with indifference as he pulls out an empty chair. "You didn't ask."

I had been trying to put this birthday celebration out of my mind so I didn't end up overthinking it like I normally do.

"Where are Nash and Riley?"

Nash is Theo's stepfather who played with my dad and the rest of the guys. He met Theo's mom when she was pregnant and is the only father Theo's ever known.

"My dad's at the game with Ryland and Chase, and my mom was having a POTS flareup, so she stayed home."

Ryland is Theo's younger brother. He's the same age as Bella and they're both sophomores in college.

"Alright, everyone, come help yourself to food. We'll eat first and have cake afterwards."

My dad rises from his seat, the same time everyone else does, but he walks directly to my mother. A smile tugs on his lips and he wraps his arm around her waist, pulling her close as he quietly says something to her.

She laughs softly, he plants a kiss on her forehead, and they break apart. My father's always been the hardest on me, but if there's one thing I can't say anything bad about, it's the way he's always treated my mother.

Andi Ford is the light of his life.

I wonder if he ever thinks about those five years that I was alive and he had no idea I existed.

"Come on, Matty." Theo throws his arm around the tops of my shoulders. "After that practice Coach put us through, you have to be starving."

My stomach grumbles as if in response to his statement, and Theo laughs. We file around the island with everyone else, dishing food out onto their plates buffet-style. The house is loud, filled with laughter and flowing conversation, just as it always is whenever our families are together. The seats fill up at the table and around the island in the kitchen. I opt to stand by the counter, taking it all in as my chest warms.

With all the kids grown, some in college and some not living right here in Hillford, it's not always easy for everyone to show up. We try our best to make it work if we can. There are two non-negotiables every year that everyone has to attend.

Christmas Eve and our annual summer getaway at the beach house.

Our parents all went in on a house together and it's open for all of us to use whenever we'd like, except for that one week in the summer. That's when we all show up and spend the entire week as one big, blended family.

There's a twinge of guilt as my mind drifts to Jade. Her family is all on a different continent. Here I am, surrounded by family—blood and chosen—and she has to get on a plane to fly across the ocean just to see hers.

I can't even imagine what that must be like for her.

"Did you and Dad make up yet?" Bella says as she slides next to me. I look over at the table as Theo drags Lucy's chair right next to his.

Pursing my lips, I look at my sister from the corner of my eye. "No."

"You know, he only has your best interest in mind, right? He wasn't trying to be a dick. You both blew it out of proportion."

I suck in a deep breath. "He said he wants to talk, but I don't feel like I should apologize first."

"Because you don't think you're wrong?"

It's not just me. We're both wrong with how we handled things.

"Because he started it."

Bella huffs. "That's so childish."

"Well, isn't he being childish too if he can't be the bigger person and apologize?"

"Remember what Uncle Caleb used to always say to us when we were kids?"

I bite the inside of my cheek, not wanting to answer her. I know what she's going to say before she even speaks the words.

"Don't wait until it's too late," she echoes the words from inside my head. "Stop waiting for him to be the bigger person and do it yourself."

My face contorts as my eyes slice to hers. "That's a little extreme. Dad's not dying."

"Neither was Amelia, and look what happened to her. Do you think Uncle Cale expected her to just be gone like that?"

My stomach twists into a knot. Neither of us ever met Uncle Caleb's first wife, Amelia. She was killed in a car accident when a drunk driver hit her head on.

Bella shrugs and pushes away from the counter. "Nothing is guaranteed except for the present moment."

I tilt my head to the side, letting her words creep into

the crevices of my brain, knowing she's right. "When did you get so smart, little Belle?"

She smiles. "I've always been smart. You on the other hand…" She clicks her tongue. "Your frontal lobe is unfortunately fully developed, but maybe there's still a chance you can learn new things."

My eyebrows pinch together. "I don't know whether to be impressed or offended."

Her smile reaches her eyes. "Both are acceptable, though impressed is preferred."

"Goddamn, you're a Ford," I chuckle, throwing my arm over the tops of her shoulders. Her sweetness cloaks the arrogance that simmers beneath. There's no denying she's my little sister.

Bella leans her head against my chest. "Promise you'll at least think about apologizing?"

I sigh. "I promise."

As much as I don't want to admit it, I know she's right.

———

After everyone starts to clear out, my mother and sisters are in the living room when my father asks me to meet him out back. My footsteps are heavy as I walk out onto the back patio and find him sitting in a chair, looking over the pool in the backyard.

I don't say anything as I take a seat next to him.

"I owe you an apology," he starts, his voice soft as he rubs at his chin. He slowly shifts in his seat, turning to look at me. "I'm sorry for being so hard on you." He sighs, raking his hand through his salt and peppered hair. "It's just hard sometimes, you know? We weren't taught how to parent and trying to be your parent when you're an adult is equally just as hard."

My breath quickens and I lift my brows in surprise as I look back at him. What the hell? He's apologizing to me first? I swallow hard, shaking my head. Carson Ford is a proud man and a good man. Although, the two of us butt heads from time to time.

And apologies aren't freely handed out.

"It's not your fault, Dad," I say, shaking my head again. "I'm sorry too. I shouldn't have acted the way I did about it. I don't always deal with criticism well and that's something I need to work on."

He purses his lips. "It wasn't meant to be a criticism. You're an adult and can make your own decisions. I forget that sometimes. In my mind, you're still just my little guy and I can't help but feel like I need to guide you in the right direction."

"It's just been a rough season," I admit with a shrug. "I know you were disappointed, but I wasn't fucking off. I was struggling mentally."

He stares at me for a moment before nodding. "Rough seasons happen. I'm sorry for not listening to you and passing judgment where it wasn't due. I was never disappointed. The last thing I want to see is you or your sisters throwing your futures away."

"I haven't, Dad," I assure him. "My future is still very much intact. My career is fine. I'm just still figuring some things out."

Like how to not overthink things and how to get out of my damn head.

"Sometimes I get in my own way," I add.

"I get that," he nods again, his expression soft and

warm. "I just want you to know I'm sorry and I hope we can move forward from this."

I swallow hard as the weight lifts from my chest. We'd been needing to have this conversation. Things haven't felt right since we got into the stupid fight. "I'd like that."

"I'm sorry for not apologizing sooner," he says after a moment, letting out a deep sigh of regret.

"It's okay," I chuckle, a smile breaking out across my face. "I'm sorry I didn't either. Believe it or not, sometimes my ego doesn't want me to admit when I'm wrong."

A soft laugh comes from the backdoor as it's pushed open. "Hmm. That sounds familiar, doesn't it, Carson?" My mother walks over to him, planting her hands on the tops of his shoulders. "You are your father's son," she says to me, a smile pulling across her lips.

"Let's try not to do this again?" My dad says, looking back at me. He shrugs his shoulders. "I'll let you do your thing, from now on. I'm just here to be supportive, without critiquing."

"That sounds great." I nod at him, contentment washing over me. "I'll also, you know, keep my shit together if I don't like something you said."

"Thank God you two finally got over your little fight!" Elena claps her hands from where she's standing in the doorway. Bella stands next to her, her head tipping back as laughter falls from her lips.

"Okay, the three of you can go back inside now," my father says as he reaches for Mom's waist and pulls her over to him. "I need to talk to your mom for a minute."

"Or two," she giggles as she drops down onto his lap.

"You guys are gross," Elena scoffs, spinning on her heel to head inside. I'm already on my feet, walking away from the two of them.

"Get a room," Bella calls out, still standing in the doorway.

"This is our house," Dad reminds her, wrapping his arms around Mom's waist. "I can kick all three of you out whenever I want."

Bella rolls her eyes and slips back inside. I pause just inside the doorway, glancing over my shoulder at our mom and dad. Neither are looking over at us. Mom's hands are on Dad's chest and she's staring down at him with nothing but love and adoration in her gaze.

He sweeps the hair away from her face, his eyes only meant for her. He's always looked at her as if she's the only one he could truly see.

I turn away, quietly closing the door behind me as I step into the house, feeling a tug inside my chest. I've never felt a love like what they have...

And at this point, I'm not so sure I ever will.

CHAPTER THIRTEEN
JADE

"He was close... too close. Yet, I didn't want him to move." - Clara Foss, Painted Inferno

The elevator dings as it reaches the first floor. My stomach knots and I push my curled hair over my shoulders, adjusting my purse when the doors finally open.

This isn't a date.

That's been my mantra all day. While I fixed my hair and my makeup. While I stood in front of my closet and tried on seventeen different outfits. There's no reason for me to feel this nervous about getting dinner.

I grab the top hem of my black high-waisted jeans, hiking them up a little higher, and straighten the buckle of my designer belt. Since it's not a date, I opted for a pair of black jeans, a cream-colored tight-fitting sweater, and a pair of heeled boots.

It's nothing too fancy, yet not too casual. Matteo didn't tell me where we're going tonight, so this is what he's getting.

When I reach the front door to my apartment building, I see Matteo just beyond the sidewalk. He's leaning back against the side of his sleek, black SUV, arms crossed over his chest and his legs crossed at the ankles.

Jesus Christ, looking as good as he does should be a crime.

Our gazes meet through the glass. My breath catches as Matteo's eyes hold mine. His gaze rakes down the length of my body as I slowly push open the door, swallowing hard.

He's wearing a pair of jeans, a dark shirt beneath his normal bomber jacket, and a pair of white sneakers. His hair's tousled in loose waves, brushed away from his face. I step through the doorway, welcoming the brisk air as it chases away the heat that encapsulates my body.

February has a tendency of being just as brutal as January, although we've been lucky lately with warm air coming from the coast.

However warm that air might be, it's not the cause of the fire spreading through my veins.

It's Matteo Ford and the way those steel gray eyes drink me in.

"Hey," he says softly as I stop in front of him. He pushes away from the side of the SUV, his body towering above mine.

I smile. "Hey yourself."

He shifts to the left, bending at the waist as he pulls open the car door. Those damn eyes meet mine once more, a ghost of a smile dancing on his lips.

"After you, Sunny."

"Thank you." I bob my head, half curtseying before climbing into the SUV. The dark red interior is lush and elegant. It smells like him and leather. Matteo waits until

I'm seated before shutting the door and walking around to the other side. "Where are we going?" I ask as he gets in behind the steering wheel.

He puts the car in drive, the engine purring quietly as he pulls away from the curb. "To get dinner." He looks at me from the corner of his eye. "You have a track record of forgetting to eat, so it's only right for me to make sure you do."

"I thought we were celebrating?"

"Two birds, one stone." The corner of his mouth twitches. His voice lowers. "I'm an efficient man, Jade."

I inhale sharply, my stomach fluttering as his quiet chuckle fills the air around us. Why do I keep ending up in close quarters with this man? It's impossible to escape him when we're in such close proximity to one another.

His scent, his sound. He's everywhere.

He's temporary.

"Did you do anything to celebrate yet?"

His question catches me off guard, but effectively pulls me out of my own thoughts.

"No," I admit, shaking my head. "I haven't been doing much other than writing."

"Is it hard?"

"It depends on the day. I have a tendency of over-thinking things, so sometimes it takes me all day to write a single chapter." I sigh. "I really do enjoy it, but some days, it's so taxing."

"I'm sure it's hard to stay in a creative state if you get interrupted or have to take a break when you're not ready to."

I nod and chance a look at him. "It really is. Most people don't understand it."

"I won't pretend like I do," he says with a soft laugh,

turning the car down another street. "It just seems like it would be."

"Well, your assessment isn't wrong." I glance out the window, my eyebrows tugging closer together. We're still in Hillford, only a ten-minute drive from my apartment building, but I've never ventured over this way before. "Where are we going?"

"You'll see in a second," he says with a wink. "We're almost there."

We drive to the end of the street, and he takes a left, pulling up in front of a massive brick building on the right side of the street. My brow furrows and I look at Matteo as he puts the car in park but leaves the engine running.

"We're here," he says, unbuckling his seatbelt. "Valet will park the car."

"Where the hell are we?"

Matteo chuckles again but doesn't comment as he climbs out of the SUV. I stare at him as he strides around the front of the car, confidence radiating off him. A man I didn't notice before greets him on the sidewalk. They shake hands, exchanging a few brief words before Matteo walks over to my side.

He opens the door, tilting his head as he catches my gaze. "Your seatbelt."

"What?" I look at it. My head is such a mess right now. I huff out a laugh, heat creeping up my neck as I undo the seatbelt and climb out.

Matteo smiles, offering me his elbow to lead me to the front of the building. There isn't a single window. No lights except the one above the metal door that looks like it's a hole in a brick wall.

My stomach does a somersault and my heart flutters as

I quickly look at him and then back to the door. Matteo pulls it open just as his car moves away from the curb.

This feels like the beginning of a horror movie.

"Okay, full stop." My feet freeze in place, and I give a little tug on his elbow to get him to stop. I look at him, my heart pounding with either excitement or the possibility of letting him walk me to my death. "I've seen this movie before."

"Are you always so dramatic?" He asks, cocking his head to the side. He's holding the door open, enough for me to see it's dimly lit inside. I can't make anything else out.

"When I'm brought to a place that looks like it's straight out of a scary movie, hell yes."

He raises both eyebrows, looking at the building and then back at me. "Okay, I see your point. It's a restaurant that's reservation only. It's not open to the public."

That's what they all say in situations like this.

Matteo lets out a sigh, pulling the door open farther. "Just trust me?"

I don't move at first. My eyes scan his face, searching for any hint of malevolence. He stares back at me with the same relaxed face I've grown accustomed to studying.

"Fine, but you're going in first."

His responding laughter circles around me, like a warm cloak. He shakes his head at me, rolling his eyes before he steps inside first. He holds the door for me, and I hesitantly follow him.

We step into a small foyer area with dark marble floors. The walls are a deep, forest green with elegant landscape paintings wrapped in gold frames. Across from where we're standing is a mahogany desk with a beautiful blonde woman standing on the other side of it, holding a tablet.

"Welcome to the Ivory Table." She smiles brightly. "Are you Mr. Ford?"

He nods as he walks ahead of me. "I have a reservation for two at eight o'clock."

"Right this way," the hostess says as she leads us through the door behind her.

It opens into a room that matches the appearance of the foyer. It's rich and moody in color and décor. The perimeter of the room is lined with private booths and the center has a dozen round tables perfectly arranged.

The dim lighting in the room comes from the light fixtures above. Except they aren't electric lights. They're all candles.

Matteo steps to the side, motioning for me to slide into the round booth first. I do, scooting across the seat as he slides in after me. He leaves about three feet between us with his body angled toward me.

"Is still water fine?"

"Yes," Matteo says as he takes two menu boards from her, handing one to me. "That's all I'll be drinking tonight."

I want to ask him why he isn't ordering a mixed drink, but I stop myself. It's rude and frankly, none of my business. Drinking doesn't have to be a requirement for dinner.

Although, some alcohol would definitely take the edge off right now.

"And you, miss?"

"Water is fine for me too."

She nods, pausing before rattling off the specials. I look down at the menu board, scanning the options as she disappears for a minute. We order our food when she returns with the water. I opt for a salad and the fish entrée and Matteo surprises me when he orders the same.

I take a sip of my water, and am suddenly overwhelmed with the urge to fill the silence that stretches between us.

"So, do you bring all of your dates here?"

Shit. My face pales. *Why did I ask that? Candy would never ask something like that.*

Matteo arches a brow. "Are we on a date, Sunny?"

"No," I say in a rush, shaking my head. "That's not what I meant. I —"

What the hell did I mean?

"I've never brought anyone here before. I've only been here once before, with my mother."

"Oh."

"Yeah," he says, wrapping his long fingers around his glass of water. I can't tear my eyes away as he lifts it to his lips. I'm mesmerized at the way he tips his head back, exposing the strong column of his neck as the liquid flows into his mouth and his throat works as he swallows.

Sucking in a breath, I rip my gaze from him, and look around the room, marveling at the intricate designs carved into the crown molding. "This place is amazing. I had no idea it was even here."

"Isn't it? It's hard as hell to get a reservation. They book at least a month in advance."

I tilt my head to the side. "How did you manage to get one?"

"It's a secret," he says before cracking a smile. "I'm kidding. My parents know the owner. I asked them to let me know if there was a cancellation for tonight and someone ended up cancelling their reservation last night."

"Well, aren't you lucky?"

"I am." His eyes seem to darken. "I'm here with you, aren't I?"

His words steal the air from my lungs, and I find myself struggling to form any kind of response. I blink, trying to get a grip on myself.

Man, he's good.

He can't affect me, not like that. He's just supposed to be helping me. This is everything I've been needing for inspiration.

I'm saved by our server as she appears with our salads as if I silently summoned her. "Can I get either of you anything else?" she asks, looking back and forth between Matteo and me.

He locks eyes with me, not even sparing her a glance "No, I think we're good."

I stare back at him, swallowing hard. "Yeah, we're good."

She nods with a smile and disappears from the table once again. Matteo picks up his fork, and barely glances at his plate as he pierces an apple and a piece of lettuce. His perfect lips part as he pushes the food past his straight teeth.

I allow myself the moment to take him in. Perfectly straight nose—surprising for a hockey player. Striking features. Sharp jawline. His eyes are a steely shade of gray in the dim light, but I've noticed the way they shimmer with flecks of blue when the candle light hits them just right.

"You're staring, Jade."

I shake my head to break my intense focus and bring my attention back to the present. Heat spreads through me. "Should I not?"

"I'd prefer it if you did, actually." His tone is a little flirtatious with mischief dancing across his lips. "Perhaps it can help you with inspiration."

I snort, the sound cutting through the tension. "You're insufferable," I say, rolling my eyes.

"I know," he shrugs, his laughter mixing with mine. "I think you might like it, though."

"Please," I scoff, shaking my head at him. As if that's something I'd ever actually admit out loud. "You wish."

Matteo smiles as if he's harboring his own secret and spears another forkful of salad. I let out another laugh, mimicking his actions as I distract myself with my own food knowing damn well, he might be right.

I think I might like it too.

The rest of dinner goes without a hitch. True to his nature, he remains flirty, but our conversation flows with ease as we dip from one conversation to the next.

Matteo falls in step with me as he walks me up to the front of my apartment building at the end of the night. He's quiet and pensive, just as he was the entire ride here.

"Thank you for tonight," I say quietly, turning to him as we stop by the door. "I had a really nice time."

"Yeah?" Matteo turns to face me. "So did I." I'm captured by his gaze. "I like spending time with you."

My breath catches in my throat. The magnetic pull to him tugs on me, inching me closer. "I like spending time with you too."

I need to stop, but it appears that I have no control over my own body. He takes a step closer and I tilt my head back to look up at him.

His eyes slowly search my face as if he's desperate for an answer to a question he never asked. His lips open and close, throat bobbing as he swallows hard.

"Sunny…"

He leaves the rest of his thought unsaid. His fingers brush a warm path along the side of my face, pushing the hair away from my temple. His touch drifts, trailing around my ear as he tucks the loose strands.

My tongue darts out, slipping between my lips to wet them. A ragged breath escapes me and my heart pounds erratically against my ribcage.

The muscle in his jaw tightens, his nostrils widening as his gaze flickers to my mouth. His own lips part, his warm breath fanning across my face.

We're inches apart. His fingers drift along the side of my jaw, curling beneath my chin as he lifts it higher. "You know how you said you have a tendency of overthinking things?"

I swallow the lump in my throat, my eyes slowly searching the fire burning in his. "Yeah?"

"So do I." He rolls his lips between his teeth, wetting them with his tongue before releasing them. "I don't want to overthink this."

His face lowers closer to mine, close enough that I can feel his warm breath on my lips. My heart pounds harder, my eyelids fluttering shut. Waiting. Hoping. Anticipating.

My heart stops beating. Time is frozen and so are we. After a second, he releases a ragged breath, lifting his head to press his lips to my forehead.

"Goodnight, Jade."

My heart resumes, kicking into overdrive.

The rejection stings and I pull back, my eyes flashing to him. His eyes are hooded, an ember smoldering in his irises as he stares back at me. The intensity seeps into my core and I'm so damn confused.

My feet are finally working under my command again and I turn away from him, not looking in his direction as I reach for the door. Embarrassment burns my cheeks. I thought he was going to kiss me and I can't believe that for a moment, I wanted him to.

That's not what this is or will ever be. I can't help but wonder if I misread this entire situation.

"Goodnight, Matteo," I say, letting myself into the building, leaving him outside.

I don't look back and I don't stop moving until I'm on the elevator, pressing the button for my floor. I lean against the wall, the doors sliding shut as I drag my hand down my face.

Matteo Ford almost kissed me.

And I almost let him.

CHAPTER FOURTEEN
MATTEO

"She was close... yet I wanted her closer." - Julian Hart, Painted Inferno

The cold radiates from the ice below, seeping through my socks, cooling my skin. The surface is slick beneath my blades and I suck in a breath, my lungs burning from the sheer force of my inhale. I barely notice the stinging in my nostrils.

All I really see is the puck.

I pivot hard on my right skate, the outside edge biting the ice as I drive forward, checking the other team's winger into the boards. Both of our sticks clash together, crashing into the boards. The glass shakes and I hear the faint buzzing sound of the crowd.

The cheering and the hooting and hollering—in moments like this, they all blend together. The only thing I can hear is the sound of my blood swooshing through my ears, along with my teammates and opponents yelling on the ice.

It all happens so quickly. I push forward, away from

the boards, leaving the winger falling onto the ice as I skate away. There's an opening in their defenders.

"Cross! I'm open! I'm open!"

I tap my stick twice on the ice. He passes the puck, sliding it across the slick surface. It moves directly to my blade, like there's a magnetic force pulling it to the exact place I need it.

One of their defenders applies pressure, skating toward me. I fake to the left, quickly whip around the right side of him and flick my wrist, sending a powerful shot toward the net.

The puck lifts into the air, rocketing just past the goalie as he lunges to the side. He reaches out to catch it, but he's just not fast enough

The light flashes and the buzzer sounds. Goal.

I pump my fist in the air, glancing up at the Jumbotron. There's still three minutes left in the third, and for the first time since the first period, we're up by one.

We need to keep it that way or score more goals.

My line-mates swarm me, shouting and slapping my back, but I keep the interaction brief. I share their excitement for a second and head to the bench, tapping everyone's gloved hands with my own.

My heart's pounding, the crowd's roaring, and I barely register the pain in my ribs from a brutal hit I took earlier. There's a chance I broke a rib, but during the game, if you can still skate and safely play, none of that matters.

I head back to my spot for the faceoff, waiting while Theo checks on me and my teammates before getting into position. The winger next to me starts talking shit but I block out his voice.

I need the puck. I need possession and we need to keep it from them. That's all that matters.

———

"You good, Matty?"

I lift my gaze from my skates, glancing at Shaw. "Huh?"

"Are you good, man? You played one hell of a game, but you've been quiet all night."

"Yeah," I nod as I slide my feet from my skates. "I'm good. Just tired."

Theo looks at me at the same time I look at him. His eyebrows tug together subtly but he goes back to taking off his gear. He knows it's a lie. Thankfully, he doesn't call me out in front of everyone else.

It's been a week since I took Jade out to celebrate. Everything went great that night until I dropped her off.

Everything except for the fact that I almost fucking kissed her.

She hasn't alluded to anything in our texts all week, but she's been keeping a safe distance from me since.

"Alright." Shaw sighs, bobbing his head. He's known me since our rookie season. We came into the league together, played for one other team each, and then both ended up in Hillford a few years later. "If something is going on and you want to talk, I'm all ears."

Both of Cameron Shaw's moms are therapists. He's the therapy king around here.

"Thanks, Shaw. There's nothing going on, but I appreciate the concern," I explain as I slip off the rest of my gear.

"Are you still talking to that author?" Cross chimes in as he turns around from his stall. He's our captain and plays defense on my line. He was traded to the Hillford Ice Hawks the season after me.

I tilt my head to the side. "I am."

"Have you read any of her books? Are they any good?"

"No, I haven't." I shake my head, confusion washing over me before realization dawns on me. "No way."

Cross frowns. "Come on, we said we were going to start a book club, so why not read one of hers first?"

"*We* didn't say anything," I remind him. For Cross' birthday in the fall, his grandma gifted him a book, telling him he needed to keep his brain stimulated. He tried to con us all into reading it with him, which clearly didn't work.

"Okay, boys, I'm serious about book club now." He looks around the room. "Who wants in?"

Theo stifles a laugh. "I'll do it if Shaw's doing it."

"I'm in." Shaw shrugs his shoulders. "I like to read."

I stare at the two of them in disbelief. No way is this actually happening right now. "Isn't this weird, to read one of her books?"

"Why would it be weird?" Cross counters, pushing his dark blond hair away from his face. "She's an author, she writes to provide an escape and entertainment for other people."

"Does she write under her real name?" Theo asks as he pulls out his phone.

"I don't know," I admit with a shrug. "I never thought to ask."

Shaw cocks an eyebrow. "Did you even plan on reading any of her books?"

"Well yeah. I was waiting until she finished the one she's working on."

Shaw clicks his tongue at me, shaking his head. "That's not very supportive of you."

"Okay, Dr. Shaw. Would you suggest I read one of her books?"

"Absolutely."

"We can all read it together," Cross says with excitement in his tone.

Theo lets out a laugh. "I don't know the last time I read a book."

I huff. "Probably don't know how to, illiterate asshole."

"Love you too," he coos, blowing me a kiss before turning to the rest of the guys. "If Matty doesn't want to join the book club, I'll figure it out and we can all read it to show our solidarity and support."

I narrow my eyes on him. "You're on their side?"

"Come on, it will be fun." He smiles, his green eyes shining back at me.

My chest deflates as I give in. "Fine. Let me check with Jade first. I don't want to make her uncomfortable at all."

"Brilliant," Cross smiles, bobbing his head. "I'll start a group chat in the meantime."

"We already have one," Theo reminds him. "I don't think we need another."

"Sure we do," Cross says as he collects his belongings from his cubby. "That way we can keep things separate. Book stuff in one, real life in the other."

Cam contemplates his words, nodding his head along with it. "That makes sense."

Theo laughs as Cross heads in the direction of the washroom and Cam starts putting his gear away. I look over at Theo, shaking my head. "What the hell?" I chuckle. "For the record, I was going to read her book. I just didn't think it would need to be a group thing."

"It's always a group thing." Theo laughs as he hangs up his helmet.

My phone vibrates, pulling my attention away from Theo. My stomach does a somersault, half expecting it to be Jade. My chest tightens when I see another name instead.

Dad.

DAD

Good game tonight, bud.

MATTEO

Thanks, Dad.

DAD

Love you.

MATTEO

Love you too.

I close out of the conversation, tucking my phone away as I grab my things and head toward the washroom. I catch my uncle's gaze as he passes me in the hall and he gives me a knowing look, dipping his chin.

I shower, dry off, and get dressed in what feels like record time. The rest of the guys are still lingering when I grab my keys, phone, and wallet and head out to the garage.

Just as I'm climbing into the car, my phone vibrates again. This time, when my stomach does a somersault, it's for a good reason. There's a message from Jade.

SUNNY

Don't alert the press or anything, but I watched your game tonight.

A slow smile tugs on my lips.

MATTEO

How'd I do?

SUNNY

It was impressive and entertaining.

I'd watch again.

MATTEO

Let me know before next time so I can make sure I pull out my best moves.

SUNNY

Show-off.

MATTEO

Only for you.

Maybe sometime you can come watch it in person.

SUNNY

Would you want that?

MATTEO

You in the stands while I'm on the ice? Fuck yeah.

SUNNY

Lol. Maybe if this deadline doesn't send me on a grippy sock vacation.

MATTEO

I hope not. I need you for the rest of the season still.

SUNNY

Well in that case, I'll postpone my trip to the psych unit until after your season's over.

MATTEO

If we make it to the play-offs, that just extends it, you know?

SUNNY

Are you looking for an extension on our deal, Ford?

MATTEO

What if I am?

SUNNY

You're crazy.

It's late. I'm going to try and get some sleep.

I've stopped myself from asking her when I get to see her again every time I've talked to her this past week. I think that moment outside of her door caused a shift between us. It caught me off guard just as much as I think it did her. I don't want to fuck this up. I can't afford to lose her, not now, not when everything is going right.

MATTEO

I leave tomorrow for another week of away games.

Can I see you when I get back?

SUNNY

Yeah. I'd like that.

My heart stumbles over itself. I ignore it, swallowing hard as her next message comes through.

SUNNY

Goodnight, Ford.

MATTEO

Sweet dreams, Sunny.

I lock my screen and set my phone down on the center console. Both hands find the steering wheel, my fingers wrapping around it as I stare straight ahead.

What the hell am I doing? I don't need to see her for this to keep working.

I blow out a breath, my stomach sinking at the realization.

I *want* to see her so this keeps working.

Fuck.

FROM THE TEXT THREAD
OF MATTY & JADE

JADE

Can I bother you for a second?

MATTEO

You're never a bother.

What's going on?

JADE

I'm stuck on a part in this book and need help.

MATTEO

I'd love to help.

JADE

I can't decide which way to go.

So, they're both artists who are rivals but have to work together on this collaborative exhibition. However, at the end, one artist will be selected to have their own art show.

They're at each other's throats.

133

MATTEO

I like this. Tell me more.

JADE

Well, no lol. You'll have to wait until it's done.

MATTEO

JADE

I don't know if they should kiss or not.

MATTEO

I vote yes. Always yes.

JADE

I didn't even tell you what's happening in the scene.

MATTEO

Does it really matter what's happening?

JADE

Yes. The setup has to be calculated.

MATTEO

What if it doesn't though?

What if it's one of those moments where the tension is just so thick, it's consuming them? The only way to get past it is to go through it. What if something snaps inside and he just kisses her?

JADE

I don't want it to feel like it's rushed or out of place.

MATTEO

How far into the book are you?

JADE

Half way.

MATTEO

Has there been build-up?

JADE

Oh, yeah. The tension is thick enough you could cut it with a knife.

MATTEO

Do they both want it to happen?

JADE

They're both in denial, but definitely have those thoughts.

MATTEO

I say fuck it. Do it.

JADE

Yeah?

MATTEO

If they both want it and they're holding back, let them have that moment. Time's suspended. They both stare back at one another. The air is electric.

JADE

He closes the distance between the two of them.

MATTEO

Her head tilts back, her lips parting as a soft breath escapes her.

JADE

She says his name softly—questioning—wanting.

MATTEO

He lifts his hand to cup the side of her
face. He asks her if this is what she wants,
because it's all he can think about.

JADE

She tells him she feels the same way, but
they shouldn't.

MATTEO

And he kisses her instead.

JADE

Holy shit.

MATTEO

Yeah, lol. Didn't think I had it in me,
did you?

JADE

I'm genuinely shocked.

MATTEO

You gonna bring me on as your co-writer?

JADE

You're good, but not that good.

Stick to hockey.

MATTEO

Ouch. You wound me, Sunny.

JADE

Someone has to keep you humble.

MATTEO

I'm not sure I'd want it to be anyone other
than you, at this point.

JADE

Only until the end of the season, right?

MATTEO

I don't know... Maybe I extend our pact
into next season too.

JADE

You think you can be my inspiration for
more than one book?

MATTEO

You have no idea what I can do.

Although, I wouldn't be against showing
you...

JADE

In your dreams, Ford.

CHAPTER FIFTEEN
JADE

"When the sun kissed the horizon, he kissed me." - Clara Foss,

Painted Inferno

"Nothing looks out of the ordinary," Dr. Bradshaw says as he moves the computer monitor to face me, showing me the results from my echocardiogram and EKG. "Is it just the palpitations that have gotten worse?"

I slowly nod my head. "My heart feels like it's racing sometimes and I can feel it skipping beats."

Dr. Bradshaw turns his attention back to the screen, clicking around with his mouse. "It's been almost a year since your last Holter monitor, so let's get you scheduled to have that put on. We'd want to check the electrical activity of your heart soon anyways.

He continues, "So let's do the seven days, like the last time, that way we get a bigger picture of everything." He turns to face me. "Have you thought anymore about taking medication? Having a prescription on hand, just to take when needed, is always an option."

"Do you think it's needed?"

"Hmm," he murmurs, adjusting his glasses. "Let's see what the holter monitor says first. If it is truly bothersome, we can try it regardless."

I nod in agreement. Just then, my phone vibrates in my purse. "That works."

"Okay, perfect. Stop by the front desk and they'll get you on the schedule for the monitor and a follow up appointment after we have the results."

"Thanks, Dr. Bradshaw," I say, rising to my feet as he extends his hand to shake mine. He leads the way out into the hall, saying goodbye before he heads into another room.

I pull out my phone, seeing a message from Ellie as I make my way to the front desk.

ELLIE

Dinner and drinks tonight?

I should head home and get back to work, but fuck it. I've been busting my ass with this book and quite frankly, I think I deserve a night off.

JADE

Tell me when and where and I'll be there.

ELLIE

Let's meet at Harry's Pub. Eight o'clock?

JADE

See you then!

I stop at the front desk and schedule an appointment for next week to get the monitor put on. It's a simple thing that I've done many times before. That's how they discovered the extra heartbeats and arrhythmia when I was a teenager.

It was determined to be nothing serious, although I have an annual cardiology appointment so they can keep an eye on things to make sure it doesn't turn into something serious.

The sun shines brightly, warming my body through my puffy jacket as I head to my car in the parking lot. It's already late in the afternoon, so I do have a little bit of time to kill before I'm supposed to meet Ellie.

I stop by the coffee shop on my way home, grabbing a pastry and a small drink to hold me over until later tonight. I know Ellie, and we're definitely doing girl dinner if we're meeting at Harry's Pub.

They do have the best Caesar salads, truffle fries, and dirty martinis in all of Hillford.

Well, that's debatable now that I've had a salad from The Ivory Table. They might have Harry's beat for the best one in town.

My mind flickers to that night with Matteo as I pull into the garage at my apartment building. The way Matteo's fingertips lingered, the way they felt skating across my skin. If he would have kissed me, I wouldn't have stopped him.

I would have kissed him back.

We never said anything about changing the rules of our arrangement. Is it so wrong of me to imagine what it might feel like to have his mouth against mine? To have his hands roaming over my bare skin?

I haven't been with someone in so long. I live alone. It's only natural to feel lonely from time to time... right?

My phone vibrates again as I let myself into my apartment. My stomach flutters, but I don't let myself look to see who it is until I'm in my bedroom.

MATTEO

Sunny, I think I have a problem.

JADE

What's that?

MATTEO

I can't seem to stop thinking about you.

A smile lifts my lips as I drop down onto my bed.

JADE

Why's that a problem?

MATTEO

Because Coach would be pissed if I hopped on a flight to come see you right now.

JADE

You know what my best friend Nicole always says?

MATTEO

What's that?

JADE

If he wanted to, he would.

I'm playing with fire and I can't stop myself. I shouldn't be taunting or tempting him, but he said it himself—his coach would be pissed.

JADE

I'm just kidding, I know you can't do that.

MATTEO

Are you saying you'd want me to, if I
could?

JADE

It's not an option, so it doesn't really
matter what I want.

I'm supposed to grab dinner with Ellie
anyways.

The responses are flowing from my mind like an electrical current. I'm totally channeling Candy Stone energy right now. These are the exact things she would say.

MATTEO

I have to get on the ice. I'll be home late
tonight. Send me your coffee order from
Daily Drip and I'll bring it over in the
morning.

JADE

You don't have to do that.

MATTEO

I want to. Give me your order. That's an
order.

JADE

Bossy.

MATTEO

You haven't seen anything yet.

Stay out of trouble tonight, Sunny.

JADE

Always 😏 I'm a good girl.

MATTEO

I bet you are...

JADE

Go take a cold shower, Ford.

He doesn't respond, since he most likely had to go. A stupid grin lifts my lips anyways and I shake my head to myself, trying to ignore the heat that blooms in the pit of my stomach.

Maybe I need to follow my own damn advice…

———

"Oh my gosh, Jade, don't turn around," Ellie whispers, her eyes wide as they dart past me and then back to my face.

My brow furrows and without even trying it, I start to turn my head to look over my shoulder. "What?"

Ellie's hand darts out and grabs my shoulder, turning me back to face her. "I just said don't turn around."

Her voice is barely audible due to the music playing in the bar, although I can hear her with how close she leans toward me. "I think I see Aiden standing over near the pool tables."

My stomach falls, my eyes widening to match hers. "Aiden, Aiden?"

She bobs her head. "Yeah. Your Aiden."

"He's not mine," I remind her, narrowing my eyes. "We broke up four years ago and have barely spoken since." I grab my martini from the bar, gripping the stem and bringing it to my lips with haste. The liquor burns my throat as I down the rest of my drink. "What the hell is he doing here?"

Ellie's eyes shift over to the corner, squinting as she stares back in the corner. "No idea. Looks like he's here with two other guys."

I snort. "That's surprising there's no women with him."

"You said Matty's out of town, so he can't be here for a game."

I wrack my brain for a reason and come up empty handed. "No. It's weird that he's here."

"Maybe he's here for you."

"Oh my gosh, no," I laugh, shaking my head. "I would never get back with him."

Ellie arches a perfectly sculpted brow. "Hmm." A smirk pulls on her lips. "I can't imagine why that is."

I stare at her. "Maybe because he cheated on me, God knows how many times?"

"That's definitely a reason why not to." She tilts her head to the side, resting her arm on the back of her seat. "I'm sure it has nothing to do with Matteo Ford though, right?"

Ellie's smile falters just as I'm about to respond, and her eyes shift to the side again. "Shit, he's coming this way."

Panic wells inside me. "What do I do? I don't want to see him?"

"Too late," Ellie mumbles as she purses her lips and looks past me. "He saw me and I think he saw you, too."

Fuck me.

I turn in my seat to face the bar, pushing my empty glass toward the edge of the counter. If I can get the bartender's attention, I can pay my tab and be on my merry way.

There's movement to my right. The seat next to me that was empty? Yeah, it's occupied now.

"Well, if it isn't Jade Wilson."

My spine stiffens. I draw my shoulders back and look to my right. "Oh, hey, Aiden." The last time I spoke to

Aiden was a few years ago, six months after we broke up. He called me drunk, begging for me to take him back.

He called me the next day to apologize, claiming he didn't mean it. I guess at this point, we'll never know if he did or not.

"How are you?" he asks. Ellie blows out a breath as I turn to face my ex-boyfriend. His hazel eyes rake over my body. "You look good."

"I'm great, actually." I smile. I have no animosity toward him now. It was years ago. It's water under the bridge. We were both young and people make mistakes.

With that being said, I would still never consider dating him again.

"How are you? What brings you to Hillford?"

Aiden takes a sip of his beer, nodding his head as he swallows. "I'm good. I'm here for a cousin's wedding this weekend. We have a few days off from games, so it worked out."

"That's great," I say, my brow furrowing. "I don't remember you having any family here in Hillford."

Aiden laughs quietly. "Well, we haven't spoken in a while, J. He moved here last year with his fiancée." He pauses, tilting his head to the side as his gaze roams across my face. "A lot can change in a few years."

"Yeah, it can," I agree, nodding.

Ellie bumps her arm against mine, gaining my atten-tion. "I'm going to go to the bathroom. If the bartender comes over, I'm ready to go if you are." She glares at Aiden on the other side of me.

"He's harmless, El. I'm not as stupid as I was before."

"Okay. I'll be right back."

Aiden clicks his tongue as I turn back around, looking for the bartender. "I see Ellie still hates me."

"Well, I'm pretty sure all my friends do." I give him the fiercest side eye that I'd imagine Candy Stone would throw at someone. "You did fuck me over."

His body sags, an exasperated sigh leaving him, just as I catch the bartender's attention. "My friend and I would both like to close out our tabs," I say to her after she comes over.

"Of course. I'll take care of it now." She looks at Aiden as he dips his head and rakes his fingers through his hair. "Everything okay?" she asks me.

"Yeah, yeah. We're good."

She looks at Aiden once more, back at me and nods before heading back across the bar.

"Jade…" His voice trails off for a second. I turn to look at him. "I'm sorry. I was a fucking idiot. Those girls never meant anything and I shouldn't have cheated on you. I was young and didn't know what I wanted, but I really did love you. I swear I did."

Jesus, this is like the same speech he gave a few years ago. He must be looking for a quick fuck while he's in town. He knows I live in Hillford. Hell, he has my number and I never hear from him.

"You know, after we first broke up, I was a mess. I was so upset. I couldn't figure out what I did wrong or why you didn't want me. Why the hell I wasn't good enough for you, but they were."

Aiden opens his mouth to speak and I lift my hand to silence him. The bartender comes back and eyes us both as she sets down my card and Ellie's, along with the receipts for us to sign.

I grab the pen, sign my name on the paper and tuck my card in my wallet. "I don't think I ever really loved you."

Aiden's eyes go wide. "What?"

"I was in love with the idea of you. With the version of you I created inside my mind." I shake my head at him, not giving him any room to get any other words in. I know Aiden. He's going to want to defend himself. "The person you are and the person I convinced myself that you were are not the same one."

"I don't buy it," he argues, taking another sip of his beer. He's irritated now. "You loved me. I know you did."

"I loved the picture I painted of you inside my head."

Ellie reappears at my side. "Are you ready to go?"

"Yep." I hand her the pen to sign her receipt as I get up from my seat. I look back at Aiden. "Bye, Aiden."

"Jade, wait," he says, turning on his barstool. "Come on. You don't have to be like that."

"There's no reason for me to stay and talk with you. There's no reason for us to talk again." I stare at him, my face void of any emotion. "There is nothing between us. We're not friends. We never will be. I'd like to keep you in my past, where you belong."

Aiden's pissed now. He stares at me, his face contorting in anger. Instead of waiting for him to say anything, I spin on my heel, striding toward the exit with Ellie in tow.

I will not waste my time entertaining or engaging with that asshole anymore.

"Are you okay?" Ellie asks me as we step onto the sidewalk in front of the bar. "He's such an asshole."

I am okay. I've been okay for years. Seeing him doesn't bother me like I once thought it would. If anything, he ruined my dinner. There's no sadness, no anger. I'm just mildly annoyed now. "Yeah, I'm good."

"I'm proud of you, Jade. You handled that like a bad bitch." A smirk tugs on her lips. "You were totally Candy Stone in there."

"Come on," I laugh, linking my arm through hers. "Let's go before he ends up coming outside looking for us."

She laughs, falling in step with me. "He'd be making a grave mistake. I didn't wear the proper shoes to kick his ass," she says, lifting her leg to show her heel. "Fuck, I hate men sometimes. If Matty ever acts like that turd did, I'll step on his throat with these."

A string of laughter falls from me. "It's not like that with him and me. We're just friends."

Ellie chuckles, shaking her head. "You know that, like, never works out, right?"

"This is different," I argue, adjusting my purse on my shoulder. "It will. He doesn't do relationships and I don't do athletes."

Ellie snorts. "You could. He's definitely fuckable."

My chest tightens, my stomach knotting with jealousy. "Friends with benefits is the furthest I'd go."

I know better than to get romantically involved with someone like Matteo Ford... physically, however, is a different story.

Ellie's laughter dies and she squeezes my arm. "Just be careful," Ellie says softly.

I give her a small smile. "I will."

I know she's just being a good friend and I appreciate her concern. There's nothing for either of us to worry about. I'm too guarded to make a mistake like I did in the past.

I know better than to give my heart to someone like him.

And Matteo Ford's heart isn't up for grabs.

CHAPTER SIXTEEN
MATTEO

"She said it was a mistake, but it wasn't. It was inevitable." - Julian Hart, Painted Inferno

I shift my weight on my feet, tipping my head back to look up at Jade's apartment building. I didn't pay attention to which direction her apartment looked out over the last time I was here. I'll be sure to make note of it this time when I'm inside... if she ever comes down and lets me in.

We just flew back to Hillford late last night, after our last game on the road in Tennessee. It was only a two and a half hour flight, so we didn't get home too late, although I opted to wait until the morning to try to see Jade.

My heart stutters as I see her strolling through the lobby, heading in my direction. Her hair's pulled up into a messy bun on top of her head and she's wearing an over-sized T-shirt that stops along the middle of her thighs and a pair of tight, black shorts. They hug her like a second skin, pulling my focus down her bare legs, which springs back up to meet her gaze as she unlocks the door and pushes it open.

"Hey," she says, her voice a bit breathless. Her eyes are lined with dark bags, the exhaustion obvious on her face. "Sorry. I was finishing up a call with my editor." She reaches for the drink carrier I'm holding. "Let me get that."

I lift a brow, letting her take the two coffees as I hold onto the brown paper bag with breakfast sandwiches I picked up on the way. "How did it go?"

She steps to the side, motioning for me to come inside. I step past her, the faint smell of vanilla and berries assaulting me as I move into the foyer.

"It went well." She makes sure the doors are locked before leading the way to the elevator. "I sent her the first half of the book last week and she loves it."

"I'm not surprised," I admit, smiling at her as we step inside the elevator and the doors slide shut. She reaches out, pressing the button for her floor. "Speaking of books… I actually have a question for you."

Jade turns around to face me, cocking her head to the side. "Yeah?" She covers a yawn. "Sorry," she mumbles, shaking her head.

"Some of the guys want to start a book club. Cross' trying to get back into reading and I told them about you being an author."

The air feels warmer than it was two seconds ago. My depth perception distorts, and I swear, she's close enough I could reach out and touch her.

Jade's eyes slowly scan my face, her expression unreadable as the corners of her mouth twitch. "You told them about me?"

Should I not be talking about her?

"I—well..." Shit. Heat creeps up my neck, my stomach fluttering. No sense in lying about it now. I showed my damn hand without even realizing it. "Yeah."

The elevator dings as it reaches her floor. She arches a perfectly sculpted brow, her freckles standing out beneath the fluorescent lighting above. Fuck, she's beautiful.

"Come on, Playboy."

Playboy?

A rush of dopamine courses through me at lightning speed. I can't fight the stupid grin that tugs on my lips as I follow her out into the hall. I shouldn't enjoy being called that, but it's different with her. It's playful—and fuck, I like it.

She has a nickname for me.

She leads me into her apartment, and I follow her lead, kicking my shoes off at the front door. She heads into the kitchen, motioning for me to sit as she slides onto one of the barstools. "Are you guys going to read one of my books for your book club?"

I set the bag on the counter, pulling out both of our sandwiches wrapped in aluminum foil. My breathing hitches, my stomach flipping. "Would it bother you if we did?"

She laughs quietly, unwrapping her food. "No. As long as they never bring it up to me."

"That's fair." I smile, lowering myself onto the seat next to hers.

"Thanks for bringing over breakfast."

"Of course," I say. "Someone has to make sure you're eating." I unwrap my own food. "How was your night? Did you and Ellie end up getting dinner?"

She takes a bite of her sandwich and moans. Fucking moans. "Sorry," she laughs softly. "Clearly, I'm hungrier than I realized." She takes a sip of her iced coffee. "Yeah, we did. It was alright. Some douchebags were at the bar, so we didn't stay out late."

My spine stiffens. "What happened?"

"Oh, nothing really," she says dismissively, waving her hand as she swallows another bite of food. "It wasn't a big deal. Aiden was there and came over."

My heart pounds harder against my ribcage. Fucking prick. "What did he want?"

"To apologize, I think." She shakes her head, rolling her eyes. "It was just easier to leave. I didn't really want to see him for any longer than I had too."

Seriously, what the hell did he do to her in the past?

I hate the thought of someone being that much of a problem for her. That someone hurt her so badly that she can't even stand to be in the same place as them. I should have been there with her.

I don't doubt Jade's ability to stand up for herself, but it's just the primal gut reaction I'm having. The need to protect her, to make sure she's safe. That's what friends are supposed to do, right?

I'll be seeing Aiden Scott again this season… and now I have his fucking number.

"Matteo?"

Her voice pulls me from my thoughts. I turn to look at her. Her eyes slowly search mine, the space between her eyebrows creasing. "Are you okay?"

"Yeah." I swallow hard, bobbing my head. "Are you?"

A slow smile pulls on her lips, a pink tint spreading across her cheeks. "Yeah, I am."

I hate everything about her douchebag ex. He wasn't my favorite person before I met Jade, but now there isn't a single thing about him I like. She hates the sport I love because of him.

Whatever happened between them has left her jaded. I know Aiden Scott. He loves to be the center of attention and someone like Jade... her presence alone demands everyone's attention. She shines brighter than anyone else around her.

She outshines everyone in this world.

The words fall from my lips without thinking.

"Do you want to come to one of my games sometime?"

Her eyes widen slightly. "What?"

"I know you hate hockey, but I want to try and change that for you." A smile tugs on my lips. "I'd love to know you're there in the stands."

She lifts her brows, a smirk dancing across her face. "So, it's about you. You just want to know someone is there to show off in front of."

"Yeah," I lie, nodding. "It's all about me."

It's not, though. It's not that simple and I don't even fully understand it. I don't want to show off to her; I just want her there.

I want her to not hate the one thing I love.

"I get two free tickets for every home game. You can bring a friend if you want."

"Really?" Her face lights up. "I'm not a huge fan of hockey, but I think I could stomach it for a night."

A soft laugh vibrates in my chest. "You think so?"

Her eyes shimmer beneath the light as she stares back at me. "For you? Yeah."

My heart stumbles inside my chest. Jade gets up from her seat and cleans up all the trash. She turns back to me, walking to stand on the opposite side of the island.

"I'm sure Ellie will come."

I lift my drink, slowly taking a sip as I trace the freckles across the bridge of her nose. "She single?"

Her eyes narrow, as if she's assessing me. "Yeah… why?"

Fuck, there it is. The rigidity in her spine, the darkness consuming those blue eyes. Her gaze is locked on mine, as if she's contemplating whether or not she should pounce. Is she jealous?

I'm under her skin—right where I want to be.

"Just curious," I say with a simple shrug. "I don't know much about her."

"Not much to know," she counters, her voice tense. The muscle in her jaw tightens. "She's not your type."

I love her like this. Claws out, ready to attack. "What's my type?"

"Not her," she quips.

"Right." I shake my head, chuckling. "So, what do you say? You gonna come?"

Her eyes narrow, assessing and calculating. "I'll come, but only if you promise me something."

"Anything."

"Show off to me and not to her."

My brow furrows. "To who? Your friend?" I shake my head, chuckling. "Oh, Sunny. Don't you know? You're the only one whose attention I want."

A smile pulls on her lips, slow and satisfied. The hues of blue shift in her eyes as she seems to relax again. "Good."

My phone vibrates and I pull it out. It's a message from our assistant coach, Nathan Frost.

COACH FROST

Training session times have changed today. Be there in an hour.

"Shit," I mutter, sucking in a deep breath.

"Everything okay?"

I look up at Jade, shoving my phone back into my pocket. "I have to head over to the arena. They changed our training session times today."

"That's really helpful," she laughs quietly as I rise to my feet. "I was already struggling thinking about having to kick you out so I can get some work done."

Jade steps around the counter and I inch closer, my feet stopping just in front of hers. She tips her head back so she can look up into my eyes.

"We don't have a game tonight." I can't help myself as I reach out to tuck some hair behind her ears. She's driving me fucking insane. She's every thought. Every wish. "What if I come back over later? For a creative meeting, of course."

She inhales sharply, her pupils dilating. "Yeah, of course," she rasps. "I think that would be really helpful. There's a part I've been stuck on lately, anyways."

"Maybe I can help you figure it out."

She nods, rolling her lips between her teeth before releasing them. "I think maybe you can."

Goddamn—I want to know what her lips feel like.

"I should go, Sunny."

I don't want to go, but if I don't leave now, there's a chance I'll miss my entire training session.

"Right," she half whispers, her throat shifting as she swallows. "I'll walk you out."

I follow her through her apartment, my eyes trailing

along the length of her body. Her hips shift as she walks, showing off the outline of her ass through her oversized shirt. My dick twitches.

She stops at the door, pulling it open as I slip my feet into my shoes. I walk past her, my arm brushing against hers as I step out into the hall.

I turn to face her as she stands just on the other side of the threshold. I lift my arms, grabbing the frame above the door. Cool air dances along my skin as the bottom hem of my shirt lifts. "Which of your books should I start with?"

Her eyes dart down to my waist where there's an inch of skin showing part of the V I've worked hard for that disappears beneath my waistband.

Her slender throat bobs as she swallows, her eyes flickering back to mine, heavy with want. "For Cross' book club?"

"No," I rasp, shaking my head as I lean toward her. "For me, Sunny." She tips her head back, her lips parting. If I drop my hands, if I close the small distance between us, I can finish what I started two weeks ago. "So, I can know what you like."

A soft pink hue spreads across her cheeks and I revel in the fact that I'm the one who put that color in her face. I love seeing the effect I have on her.

Her pupils dilate. "Give me one minute."

She spins on her heel, disappearing back into her apartment for less than a minute. She comes back to the door, holding out a book to me. My hands drop away from the top of the door and I take it from her. My eyes flash to hers.

"This is the one you're looking for." Her voice is low, sultry, even.

The sound vibrates through my body and I don't even

bother to conceal my hardening cock as I take a step away. "Let me know what time the creative meeting is then."

"Come over around eight." Her eyes shift to my mouth, lingering for a moment before moving back to my eyes. "Have fun."

I think I'd have more fun here with her.

"Later, Sunny."

Her smile reaches her eyes and her voice carries after me as I finally force myself to walk away, knowing I'll be back later tonight.

"Later, Playboy."

CHAPTER SEVENTEEN
JADE

"It was a mistake, yet it wasn't. It was exactly what I wanted." - *Clara Foss, Painted Inferno*

MATTEO

I'm here.

My stomach rolls with anticipation as I nervously tuck my hair behind my ears. I'm already on the elevator, heading down to the lobby, although I'm not going to tell him that.

I don't know why I told him eight o'clock earlier. It's after dinner, yet before bed. It felt like a middle ground at the time and now I'm overthinking it.

JADE

Be down in a minute.

If I was inviting him over for sex, it definitely would have been later than eight at night.

My hair falls in long waves down the center of my back and I collect it, pulling it over my left shoulder as I walk across the foyer. Matteo stands just outside the door, looking as good as he always does. He smiles when he sees me and I push open the door, holding it for him.

His hair is a bit damp and the faint woodsy smell drifts past me as he walks inside. "Hey, Sunny."

"Hey," I say softly, pausing to swallow over the nervousness that wells inside of me. "How did your training sessions go?"

"Good, good," he says, falling into step with me as we head back over to the elevator. "How about you? Did you get a lot of writing done?"

"I did," I nod as the doors slide open and we slip inside. Matteo moves to the panel on the wall to press the button for my floor.

He turns around to face me. His gaze drops down to my feet, taking in my body before finding his way back to my eyes. The oxygen in the elevator car ceases to exist. My lungs constrict and he takes a step forward, closing a foot of distance between us.

"Did you work through whatever issue you were stuck on?"

I tilt my head to the side. "If I did, do you think I'd still be wanting a creative meeting?"

A ghost of a smile dances across his lips, mischief passing over his hooded gaze. "Yes."

Heat spreads through me. "Bold assumption."

"So, you didn't then?" He takes another step closer. There's less than a foot separating us now. My back rests against the wall.

"No, I did," I admit, my voice low, tipping my head back to look up at him.

Matteo closes the remaining distance, caging me in as he plants his hands on the wall on either side of me. His tongue darts out, immediately capturing my attention. I swear I stop breathing.

My cardiologist is going to wonder what the hell happened when he looks at the way my heart's beating.

"So, why am I here then, sunny?"

My eyes flash back to his. "Because I want you here."

He groans, low and guttural. His nostrils flare, pupils dilating as his face dips down to mine, his lips a breath away from mine. "What the fuck is it about elevators?"

The bell dings and the car dips as it stops on my floor. Matteo's still caging me in as the doors slide open. A throat clears behind him. Matteo blinks. Irritation flashes in his eyes and he blows out a breath of frustration as he pushes off the wall.

"Sorry to interrupt," Harry, my neighbor, says. He meets my eyes. "Oh, hey Jade." He looks over his shoulder at Matteo, who's waiting for me in the hall. "Everything okay?"

"Hey, Harry," I say in a rush, heat spreading across my cheeks. "Everything's great. This is my friend, Matteo." I shuffle out of the elevator as Harry gets on. "Have a good night!"

"Was that your neighbor?" Matteo asks, his voice low as I walk past him.

"Yeah," I say, sliding my key back into the lock on my door. "He's lived next to me for a few years now." We're not necessarily close or even friends, but we're friendly enough to look out for one another.

Matteo steps closer behind me. He's not touching me, but the heat from his body slams into mine. His breath is warm as he brings his lips to my ear. "Are you fucking him?"

My breath catches in my throat and I'm momentarily

caught off guard. *Is he jealous?* I push open the door, uncertainty and intrigue wrapping around my spine. Matteo walks into my apartment, shutting and locking the door behind him.

"What did you say?"

We both turn to face one another. He kicks off his shoes, slowly removing that stupid bomber jacket he's always wearing.

It shouldn't look that good on him.

"You heard me," he growls, stalking closer. He stops when his toes reach mine. "Are you and your neighbor fucking?"

"That's none of your business." The sentence does not come out as clipped as I imagined it would in my head.

"No?" His fingers slip beneath my jaw, tilting my head back. "It's not my business?" A shiver trails down my spine as he slides his fingertips along my jawline, slowly trailing down the side of my throat.

"Your body tells me otherwise, Sunny." His eyes darken, the muscle in his jaw tightening. "Do I need to worry about him?"

"No," I breathe with a subtle shake of my head. "It's never been like that with him. We're not even really friends, just acquaintances."

"That's good," he draws, his eyes flicking down to my lips.

"Why does it matter?"

His eyes shift back to mine. "Because I don't like to share."

Oh my god.

My heart stutters inside my chest. He slides his hand around my neck, cradling the back of my head. His free hand lifts, his fingertips grazing against my skin as he brushes the hair from my face. Anticipation hangs in the air and I swear, my heart is going to break through my ribcage.

My breath catches in my throat. "What are you doing, Matteo?"

His eyes slowly search mine. "What I should have done earlier."

His face dips and my eyelids flutter shut. My heart's a mess, pounding against my ribcage. I reach for him, my hands gripping his white T-shirt. He pauses, his lips a fraction of an inch from mine, his warm minty breath fanning across my mouth.

"Do you want me to stop?" he murmurs, his lips brushing mine.

I inhale sharply. We're crossing that line we drew in the sand. And once we cross it, I don't know if there's any way we can come back from it.

"No," I exhale, tugging him closer. I don't care about what happens after this moment. All I know is I want him. I want this. "Don't stop."

He lets out a soft breath, his lips grazing mine. He pauses for a beat, my eyebrows tugging together as his mouth lingers, unmoving against mine. His fingertips dig into my skin, as if he's grasping for his slipping self-control.

And then it's gone.

He groans, the sound wrapping around my brain, sliding down my spine, and his mouth crashes into mine. His lips are hot and soft and he kisses me with an intensity that has my core melting. His mouth melts into mine, lips moving, tasting and teasing.

My hands slide around his torso and his left hand falls down to my waist, pulling me flush against his solid body.

"Goddamn, Sunny," he moans against my mouth. His tongue slides along the seam of my lips and I part them, letting him in.

The kiss deepens. His tongue dances with mine, the heat spreading along the nerves throughout my body. I'm on fire and he's the flame. His fingers tangle in my hair, his other hand grips my hip.

I slide my hands down the sides of his torso, feeling his taut muscles beneath the thin layer of cotton between us. He moans into my mouth, rolling his hips as he presses his erection against me.

My fingers twitch with the urge to reach between us and grip him. I want to feel him in my hand. I want to feel the length and girth of his hard cock.

He presses his leg between mine, using it to push me farther into the apartment. At some point, we spin around, so I'm the one guiding him. With the open concept, we make it into the living room with minimal damage to anything in my home.

We reach the couch. Matteo spins me back around, his arms snaking around my lower back as he eases me down onto the couch. He follows me, hovering above as he stares down at me.

"Fuck, you're beautiful." His voice is hoarse, thick with need and my heart skips a beat, my stomach fluttering with his words. His mouth crashes back into mine, stealing the air from my lungs as he kisses me deeply. Our tongues meet, dancing together as our lips move.

I'm so wrapped up in him, so lost in the moment. If I had a choice, I don't think I'd ever come up for air again.

Matteo Ford can never be anything more than this to me, and I know that. I knew that when we came up with our arrangement.

He's simply fulfilling his end of the agreement and I'm doing it for the plot. This is only research. It's burning inspiration.

It's just a deal.

He kisses me until my lungs are screaming for oxygen. His mouth leaves mine, both of us sucking in deep breaths as we struggle to fill our lungs with something other than each other.

"Jade." Matteo breathes my name as if it's the only word his brain can formulate. "Sunny, baby, we gotta stop."

Sunny, baby.

I don't let myself get caught up on the words that fall from his swollen lips. I stare up at him, my hands still linked together around the back of his neck. "Says who?"

"Do you want me to fuck you?"

Every single syllable vibrates through my body. He grinds his hips against mine, his hard cock pressing between my legs. I think I might fucking explode.

"Yes."

His eyes slowly search mine. His face is flush and his chest rises and falls with every shallow, ragged breath that slips from him. "Not tonight."

My stomach sinks and embarrassment heats my neck. "Why not?"

What did I do wrong?

His throat bobs. "I don't want you to regret it."

Words fail me for a second as I'm caught off guard. "Wha—"

He shakes his head. "We're caught up in the moment. You know what I want, obviously," he murmurs, his cock throbbing against me. "I need you to make the decision with a clear head."

I stare at him for a moment. My eyebrows cinch together. What the hell is he talking about? He's supposed to be a fuck boy. This kind of thing is supposed to be exactly what he likes.

"You want me to take some time and think about whether or not I actually want to sleep with you before I do it?"

"Yes," he says without hesitation, dipping his chin. "If we fuck, there's no going back to just this, Sunny. You're under my skin. You're in my fucking head. I've had a taste of you and once I get to devour you, I can't promise it won't change things between us."

My throat constricts. "Change things in what way?"

A smirk tugs on his lips. "In the way that I can't be around you without wanting to be inside you."

"What if the sex sucks?"

The smirk slowly fades from his face. His eyes burrow holes into my soul. "I'm afraid of the opposite."

"We never said we couldn't be friends with benefits, you know," I remind him, pushing my fingers through his hair along the nape of his neck. "It doesn't come with strings."

"I don't like strings," he says in a hushed voice as he drags his thumb across my bottom lip. "I don't want you to get attached because I can't give you any more than that. I told you, I don't do relationships. I don't do love."

A chuckle sounds in my throat. "I never said I wanted any of that with you, Matteo. You're not my type."

He lifts a brow. "The way your body responds to me tells me otherwise."

"I've been abstinent for the last year. My body's desperate for any kind of touch." A slow smile drifts across my lips. "Maybe Harry would be up to being more than just neighbors…"

"Don't test me, Jade." Matteo pushes his thumb past my lips, pressing it into my mouth. I close my lips around it, cradling his thumb with my tongue as I suck on it. He moans, his eyes dark as he grips my jaw with his fingers. "If you want someone to touch you, someone to make you feel good, you call me. Not your fucking neighbor. Not anyone else."

He pulls his thumb from my mouth.

"Does that mean you'll fuck me tonight?"

He holds my face, tipping my chin up as his mouth lowers to mine. "No," he groans against my lips. "This is all you get tonight."

"Not fair," I pout, not kissing him back at first.

"Life's not fair, Sunny." He nips at my lips. "Get used to it."

His tongue pushes back into my mouth, tangling with mine as he threads his fingers in my hair and drains the oxygen from my lungs. I don't need Matteo Ford to protect me from any regret. There's nothing about anything with him that I could possibly regret—even if it can never be more than this.

CHAPTER EIGHTEEN
MATTEO

It's been four days since I last saw Jade.

"When can I see you again?"

She bites back a grin, tucking her hair behind her ears. "I'll call you."

Four days since I finally kissed her.

My brows lift and I breathe out a laugh as I pull her back to me. "This is fun for you, isn't it?"

"You started it." She pushes up onto her toes, her lips finding mine in a soft kiss before she swiftly pulls away. "Two can play this game, Playboy."

Four days since I asked her if she wanted me to fuck her.

I release her, a smirk tugging on my lips. "I'll win."

"We'll see." She winks, closing the door before I get the chance to slip back into her apartment.

And I can't stop replaying that night on repeat in my mind.

"Wake the fuck up, Ford!" Cross barks from behind me as I fumble an easy pass in the neutral zone. I shake my head, my legs pushing. I am awake, that's the problem. I've realized every fuck up I've had on the ice all game. It's been four days and I haven't heard a single word from Jade.

I can't text her, not when she said she'd call me. I didn't think she'd actually call, but I didn't think it would be radio silence.

I didn't think I'd be this damn affected by it, either.

I'm a step behind when I get possession of the puck again. I lose control of it at the blue line. It does a weird bounce move, flopping over the blade of my stick and the winger on the other team grabs it and starts racing toward our defensive zone.

"Fuck!"

My blades cut into the ice as I quickly stop and push off to head after him in the opposite direction. I lose an edge and fall a few strides behind him. Cross and Volkov are both beat. The shot flies past our goalie and they score. They celebrate, we deflate. The energy feels like it did when we were on our losing streak.

The horn feels louder than normal. The sound rings inside my ears as I skate back over to the bench, filing on after Theo and Shaw.

"The fuck you doing out there tonight? Are you trying out to be a figure skater or something?"

I cut my eyes at Theo. "Fuck off."

"No, seriously," he presses, lifting his eyebrows. "You pulled a little twirl move in the zone. Judges gave it a 9.2. Impressive and artistic."

Cam shakes his head, leaning forward. "I don't know. The technical score might put it lower than that."

What the hell is this? I cut my eyes at both of them. "I lost an edge."

"Hence the 9.2 score instead of a 10," Theo muses, rolling his eyes.

"Still feels like too high of a score," Shaw chimes in.

My lips part, my rebuttal on my tongue with anger simmering when Coach cuts in.

"Ford," he barks my name. I meet his eyes and he looks less than pleased. "Get your head in the fucking game."

I give him a curt nod, feeling his disappointment mixing with my own. I prop my elbows on my knees, dropping my face down into my gloves. I can't get my head in the game because it's still in Jade Wilson's apartment.

Shaw elbows me on my other side. "You heard him. We need you."

"Yeah, I know."

Theo shrugs. "You're overthinking shit again. I thought you were past this?"

Yeah, so did I.

Jade's supposed to be a calculated, controlled distraction. Not one that's derailing my ability to perform on the ice.

———

The second shift isn't any better. I miss another pass. I hesitate. My movements are delayed. Even when I'm not thinking about her, I still can't get my brain to engage.

I try to get the puck out of the zone. They get a shot in from the point. Cross blocks it and it changes direction, just at the right angle for one of their wingers to tip it in.

Gray slams his stick against the ice. My stomach sinks

as I skate back to the bench. That's three goals that were my fault so far. I sit down on the bench, my eyes flicking up to the jumbotron.

3-1.

"You need different skates?" Theo tilts his head to the side, squinting his eyes. "Or maybe a sequin dress?"

I grab my bottle, squirting water into my mouth before I turn it and squirt water at his face. "I'll fight you, Simmons."

"Won't be much of a fight," Shaw quips, rolling his eyes. "Matty's too distracted thinking about what his costume might look like."

The muscle in my jaw twitches. "I'll fight you too, Shaw."

Theo arches a brow. "Jeez, we're your best friends. What has you ready to fight us both?"

I stare at him, irritation rolling over me. "Neither of you are helping."

I have no one to blame or be irritated with other than myself. I shouldn't be letting this bother me like this.

I don't know why I haven't heard from her yet.

"Neither are you," Shaw snorts. "You were doing so well last month. What happened?"

Theo looks at Shaw. "There's another period left. Maybe he'll turn it around."

It's wishful thinking because the third period only gets worse.

Coach is short shifting me and when I finally get the opportunity to shoot, I fuck it up. I get a rebound shot while the goalie's still in the left side of the net. Half the damn thing is open to me and what do I do?

I shoot high and wide, sending it over the net and into the glass. The crowd groans, my shoulders sag, and Coach calls me off the ice. No one bothers to say anything to me on the bench. I don't blame them. I deserve the silence after the shit game I've played.

Coach benches me for the rest of the period. I can't blame him for it. I've been nothing but a liability on the ice tonight.

In the last two minutes, Coach pulls the goalie and sends five skaters out instead. They end up in the other team's zone, applying the pressure and Theo ends up sneaking in a goal. Coach sends one of our other wingers, White, back out onto the ice, putting us back at full strength. The energy is still off, even if everyone's buzzing from our second goal, and we end up losing the game by one.

"You had half the net," Theo says quietly, pursing his lips as we're sitting in the dressing room. "You had plenty of time. You had a clear shot."

"Hell, he could have done a full routine before taking a shot," Shaw chimes in.

I close my eyes, turning away from them as I strip off my gear. "Can you both please stop?" I mutter, letting out a deep, exasperated sigh.

"What has you all out of sorts?" Theo questions me as I turn back around and sit down. "I thought Jade was distracting you in a good way, not a bad one."

"Yeah," I huff, shaking my head. "Me too."

"Shit, so it is her," he says, scooting closer as Shaw busies himself with his skates. "What happened?"

I rake my hand through my damp, sweaty hair. "I went to her house four nights ago. I haven't heard from her since."

"Oh shit." Theo's eyes widen. "Did anything happen?"

Shaw's head pops up, eyebrows lifted as he looks between us.

"We kissed, but nothing more," I admit, letting out another breath. I don't tell him I asked her if she wanted me to fuck her. He doesn't need to know that. "She said she'd call me and I haven't heard from her."

Shaw laughs loud. "Dude. You're out here shitting the bed on a whole game because you haven't heard from her?"

"I didn't try to. I just don't know if I did something wrong or why she hasn't texted me." I pause, playing the night over again in my head for the thousandth time. Is it because I stopped anything from happening between us? I thought it was the right thing to do, but what if I went and fucked up any chance with her?

Maybe she realized I'm not worth it, decided I'm not worth the trouble. Sleeping together changes things whether we want it to or not. I'm decent at pretending, but maybe she isn't.

"Just text her," Shaw says, shaking his head at me. "It's been what? Four days? That's plenty of time to say something to her without being a weirdo."

"He's right." Theo nods, bobbing his head eagerly. "If I were you, I'd just say something."

"I don't know," I say, pursing my lips. They might be right. I've been letting this occupy too much space inside my brain. The worst thing that happens is she tells me to fuck off.

And then I'm fucked without my good luck charm...

"You know what figure skaters do?" A smirk breaks out across Theo's lips as he leans closer. "They commit. You don't. You panic."

I groan, shoving his shoulder. "Theodore Simmons, I swear to—"

"Shut up," he laughs, shoving me back. "Stop dancing around and just text her already."

I let out a breath, my chest deflating as I stand up and grab my phone. "Fine, I'll do it." I open our messaging thread and my stomach flips when I see her name on the screen. "Wait, she texted me earlier."

SUNNY

You looked like shit tonight.

A smile tugs on my lips. Theo rises to his feet, grabbing for my phone.

"What'd she say?" He shifts to the side of me, laughing as he sees her message over my shoulder. "She's not wrong."

I move away from him, rolling my eyes as I type out a response.

MATTEO

I know. My head's elsewhere.

SUNNY

Where's it at?

MATTEO

Your place.

SUNNY

Come by tonight and get it.

My stomach flutters, my heart hammering harder.

MATTEO

Yeah?

I haven't heard from you in four days, Sunny.

SUNNY

Maybe I was trying to play hard to get.

MATTEO

How'd that work out?

SUNNY

Not well, since I caved and texted you.

My palms itch and–*fuck*–I want to see her. I *need* to see her.

MATTEO

I can't stop fucking thinking about you.

SUNNY

Yeah?

MATTEO

Yeah. It's becoming a problem.

It's fucking me up. It's making me fuck up.

SUNNY

So, what do we do about it?

MATTEO

I need to get you out of my system.

Just once...

SUNNY

Do you think that will fix your problem?

MATTEO

Yes.

SUNNY

Come by tonight.

Holy shit.

MATTEO

I'll be there in an hour.

My heart races and for a moment, I forget I'm in the same room with my teammates.

"Did she ever say anything about reading one of her books?" Shaw adds in.

Theo whips his head to the side. "You're the worst at reading the room."

Shaw shrugs. "He never said anything about it."

I lock my screen, clearing my throat and tucking my phone into my front pocket. "She said we can read one for Cross' book club."

"Yes!" Shaw pumps his fist. He looks at me, cocking an inquisitive eyebrow "What'd she say just now?"

I swallow hard, ignoring the warmth building in the pit of my stomach. "She told me to come by." I look back and forth between both of them. "I don't want to hear a single word out of either of you."

"Hey, if it helps you get your groove back," Theo says with a shrug.

"We need you distracted in the way only she can provide," Shaw adds with a wink

"I hate you both," I mutter, shaking my head as I head for the washroom to take the fastest shower of my entire life.

I've waited four days for Jade to reach out.

I'm not wasting another damn second.

CHAPTER NINETEEN
JADE

Matteo's quiet as he walks into the building, falling into step with me as we walk over to the elevator shaft. The tension is palpable and thick in the air around us. My heart races and I glance at him from the corner of my eye.

"Is everything okay?"

He pushes his hand through his hair as I press the button to call for the car. "No, Sunny. It's not okay."

My stomach twists with dread and falls onto the floor. "What's wrong?"

The elevator's on the top floor and stops a few floors above us.

"This," he rasps, waving between the two of us. "We have a pact. A deal. We laid down rules and I can't seem to find the fucking willpower to keep following them." He shakes his head and looks down at the floor.

I swallow hard. We drew lines in the sand, specific ones we said we wouldn't cross. When we first made this pact, I told him I wouldn't be trading sexual favors for him helping me. That's not what this is. God, this is the farthest thing from that.

"So, don't."

His eyes flick to mine. The elevator starts to descend toward the lobby. "Don't what?"

"Follow the rules." I pinch my lips between my teeth and my heart hammers harder. This is probably a mistake, but I'm done worrying about that. I'm done worrying about how I might feel in the future, when I can feel and experience so much in the moment. "Sometimes they're meant to be broken."

"Jade…" his voice is hoarse, his eyes hooded. The elevator dings as it reaches the lobby. "You said no sexual favors."

I lift a brow. "It's not. We have an agreement to help each other outside of that. This is more like an added benefit."

A smirk tugs on his lips. "I like added benefits."

The elevator doors slide open. He reaches for my hand and I slide my fingers through his, tugging on his arm as I step through the doorway. "So do I."

Matteo walks in after me, pulling on my arm as he spins me around to face him. "Fuck the rules," he murmurs, stepping into my space, until my back hits the wall. His eyes search mine, as if he's silently asking for my permission.

A ragged breath slips from my lips and I repeat the same three words back to him. "Fuck the rules."

His fingers slide through my hair as he cradles the back of my head. "Fucking elevators," he murmurs, his face dipping down to mine. "I've been waiting to do this in here."

His mouth claims mine, his lips hard, yet soft as he kisses me with a fervent need. He steals any words I could have possibly spoken in response. I kiss him back, my lips moving with his, tasting, teasing, melting. We cease to exist separately.

He groans, his hips pushing against my torso, tearing his mouth away from mine. "Are you sure this is what you want?"

"Yes," I murmur, tugging his mouth back to mine, sucking his bottom lip between my teeth. "You said you need to get me out of your system."

And I think I might need him out of mine too.

"Just once is all we need."

The elevator dings when it reaches my floor. I pull back, my eyes searching his for a brief second.. "What if it doesn't work?"

"It has to," he rasps, his nostrils widening. I love seeing him like this, unraveling for me.

The doors slide open and I give him a gentle shove, smirking as I reach for his hand and walk out into the hall. "It's cute that you think you won't be the one getting attached."

Matteo's silent as I lead him into my apartment, but as soon as the door shuts behind him, his hands find me once more.

"I'm already attached, Sunny baby," he murmurs, grabbing my hips, pulling me flush against him. "Let me pretend I still have some control over what's happening here."

His hands slide around my back, slipping down over the back pockets of my jeans, and beneath my ass. He grabs the backs of my thighs, lifting me into the air in one fluid movement. Instinctively, my hands go around the back of his neck and my legs wrap around his torso. He kicks off his shoes the same time mine fall off my feet.

"Which room is yours?"

"End of the hall, on the left," I murmur, trailing my lips along his sharp jaw covered in day-old stubble. I like it. It makes him look a bit more…undone.

Matteo moans, his hands gripping my ass as he stalks through my apartment, his strides long and purposeful. My lips move to his ear, finding the soft skin beneath it. I nip at his flesh, sliding my hands through his damp hair.

"Jade," he pants as I drag my tongue along the side of his throat. His cock presses against my ass and he quickly turns to the left.

We don't make it past the kitchen.

He sets me down on the island, shrugs off his coat and leaves it on the floor. His hands reach for the bottom hem of my shirt. "Do you want me to stop?" he asks, his voice quiet, eyes searching mine as his fingertips dance across my skin.

"No."

He grips the bottom of my shirt, sliding it up and over my head before tossing it onto the floor. His eyes immediately widen as they roam across my bare chest. My nipples instantly hardened under his burning gaze.

"No bra," he rasps, his throat bobbing as he swallows hard. His hands start at my collarbones, tracing the dips and curves of my body. He drags his fingertips around the outer swell of my full breasts, his eyes flickering to mine. "Is this okay?"

"Yes," I breathe, nodding my head. My heart gallops. "Everything you're doing is okay. If something isn't, I'll tell you."

His nostrils flare and he nods once. His palms are hot

against my skin as he slides them beneath my breasts, cupping them. His eyes are still on mine as he brushes his thumbs over my hard nipples.

I suck in a sharp inhale, my lips parting with a ragged breath. His pupils dilate before he lowers down to pull my pebbled flesh into his mouth. My head falls back, warmth spreading through my body as he draws my nipple between his teeth, sucking and tasting. Teasing and nipping.

He trails his lips across my chest, giving the same attention to my other breast as he plays with the other with his hand. I'm coming apart at the seams, melting like candle wax in his palms.

"I need you, Matteo," I moan, lifting my head as he releases my nipple. He stands upright, not stopping me as I reach for his shirt and drag it up and over his head. I toss it onto the floor and reach for the front of his pants. He grabs my hands, pulling them away from his zipper. In one fluid movement, he lowers me onto the counter, the marble cooling my skin as he sweeps my arms above my head and pins both wrists with his right hand.

"Not yet," he murmurs, his mouth finding mine. He kisses me deeply, his tongue tangling with mine before pulling away. "If I'm going to fuck you, I'm going to fuck you the right way."

Holy shit. I've never wanted someone as badly as I want him right now.

My breath catches, my pulse thundering as he trails his lips along my jaw, down my throat. He drags his hands down my body and they roam across my flesh as his mouth makes a path to the waistband of my pants.

He slips the button through the hole of my jeans, his fingers finding the zipper and slowly dragging it down.

"Do you want me to stop?"

"Never," I rasp as he slips his hands beneath the waist-band of my jeans.

"Lift your hips for me, Sunny," he murmurs as his hands move around my bottom. I lift and he drags my jeans and panties down the length of my legs, discarding them as he slips them from my feet.

He's on his knees pushing mine apart as his fingers press into the insides of my legs. "God, you're soaked," he growls, inching his fingertips closer to the apex of my thighs. "I just need one taste."

"Please," I moan, my voice desperate and unrecognizable.

"Since you asked so nicely," he murmurs, his breath hot on my flesh as he lowers his mouth to the center of my thighs. He licks me once, his groan vibrating against me as he swipes his tongue through my arousal.

He doesn't lift his head, but he looks up at me from where he's positioned between my legs. His eyes are dark with lust and need. "I need more," he pants, his voice a plea. "I need another taste."

I pull my lip between my teeth, biting down, tasting copper. It's the alternative to grabbing his head and pushing his mouth to me. "Please," I breathe, nodding. "Don't stop."

His mouth is back on me without a second thought. He's hungry. Ravenous. Feral. He eats me alive. His tongue is his weapon and I'm at his mercy. He slides his tongue inside me, driving deep strokes in and out before dragging it along flesh again.

He's teasing me, testing me to see how much I can take. His tongue flicks my clit and he growls against me as my body writhes beneath his touch. He plays with it, sucking it into his mouth, rolling his tongue over it, driving me closer and closer to the edge.

"Oh god, yes," I moan, my fingers pushing through his hair, tangling in the silky locks.

My body starts to tighten, teetering on the precipice as my orgasm creeps in closer. He skillfully moves his tongue away, slipping it back inside of me again.

Frustration rolls over me, but the heat in the pit of my stomach melts it away. "Goddammit, Matteo," I groan, gripping his hair tighter. I don't want him to stop. I've never experienced anything like this before. "I'm so close."

The other men I've been with could take a few lessons from him.

I don't want to think about anyone Matteo's practiced this on before.

He chases the thoughts away when his tongue hits my clit again. My hands are between my legs, fisting his hair as he feasts upon me. He works the bundle of nerves with his mouth and his tongue until the levees break and the heat spreads through my body.

"Oh my god, Matteo," I cry out, my face screwing up with pleasure.

My orgasm hits me with a ferocity that has my back arching, body coming undone. My fingers grip his hair, and he pins my legs down as he licks and sucks until I'm completely spent, floating in the abyss of ecstasy.

He stands upright, leaning over the counter as he cages me in. "How you feelin'?"

"So good," I murmur, a lazy orgasm induced smirk tugging on my lips. My arms stretch between us as I reach for his pants. "I'll feel even better when you're inside me."

His mouth finds mine, soft and tender as he kisses me. I taste myself on his tongue and he moans into my mouth as I undo his pants and try to slide them down. He chuckles, lifting his mouth from mine.

"Whoever taught you how to do that deserves an award."

"No one taught me." He stares down at me, biting his lips. "I don't go down on the women I sleep with."

My brow furrows and my stomach does a somersault. "Who do you go down on?"

"No one," he admits, shaking his head. His voice grows softer. "You."

I'm the only one who's had him like this.

My breath hitches, my heart crawling into my throat as his words slide under my skin and into my veins. His vulnerability has me at a loss for words. It's not what I expected him to say. I like the thought of being the only one for him. He's nothing like I expected him to be.

His eyes are still on mine as he stands upright and pushes his pants down, pulling his boxer briefs with them. I lift up, resting on the back of my elbows, my eyes sliding down the length of his torso to his cock.

I inhale sharply, my eyes widening. His cock throbs, standing at full attention. He's thick and longer than I imagined. The head glistens, the tip wet with precum... and the metal ball of a barbell sticking out. *Holy shit.*

"You're pierced."

The corners of his mouth twitch. "I am. Is that okay?"

I swallow hard, bobbing my head. I've never been with anyone who was pierced before. "Does it hurt?"

He chuckles softly, dipping his head as he spits into his hand. I'm practically panting as he wraps his hand around the shaft of his cock, slowly stroking the length of it as he steps back between my legs.

"No," he murmurs, shaking his head. "It won't hurt you, either."

"Okay," I rasp, my eyes still on his cock as he pumps it with his left hand. "I want to feel it…" I look up at him. "Without anything between us."

His nostrils flare as he sucks in a breath. "Yeah? I'm clean."

"Me too." I point to my arm where there's an implant underneath my skin. "I'm on birth control, so that's not a concern either."

He lets go of his dick, his hands finding my hips as he drags me to the edge of the counter. "I'm not going to last long, Sunny," he rasps as he presses his cock against me. The barbell brushes my clit and my body quivers. "God-damn, look at you. You're fucking beautiful."

He pushes into me with a moan, his movements slow and calculated. I'm so wet and ready, I stretch around his cock with ease, taking every inch as he sinks into me. His hands find my hips, gripping my flesh as he slowly pulls out, stopping with just the tip inside.

He slowly enters me again, his piercing leading the way, stroking my insides as he drags his cock in and out of me. It's the slowest, sweetest form of torture that has me lifting my hips off the counter, about to fall apart.

His fingers tighten, his movements becoming faster. He pumps his hips, pounding into me. Every stroke is harder than the one before. It's obvious he's starting to lose control as his breathing becomes choppy. I'm barely holding myself together.

We're both a mess of moans as he stands at the edge of the counter, his body positioned between my thighs. He slides his hand between us, planting his palm against the bottom of my stomach as he rolls his thumb over my clit. Heat spreads through my body, pleasure erupting as he fucks me harder, thumb applying a delicious amount of pressure.

I clench around him, the pressure building inside. His eyes latch onto mine and the fire burns brightly in his eyes as he thrusts into me once more, my orgasm hitting me like a tidal wave, pleasure rolling throughout my body.

His face screws up, his hips rocking into me as he loses himself inside of me, my name falling from his lips in a ragged exhale.

There's absolutely no way either of us are coming back from this…

CHAPTER TWENTY
MATTEO

Jade sits on top of me, her head tipping back, waves spilling down her back as she rides my cock. Moving my left hand from her hip, I slide it down between us, working my fingers over her clit. Jade inhales sharply before sighing with a moan as she starts moving faster.

"Fuck, Jade," I moan, my balls drawing closer to my body. A heat builds in the pit of my stomach, my own hips lifting to thrust into her as she rocks on top of me.

She shudders, her pussy clenching around my length, legs shaking as her orgasm hits her full force. She collapses against my chest. I wrap my arms around her lower back, holding her against me as I take full control and fuck her from the bottom.

I thrust into her, once, twice and then I'm losing myself deep inside her cunt, filling her with my cum for the third time tonight. First was in the kitchen, second in the hallway and finally, we made it into her bedroom.

Jade slowly lifts her head, her dazed eyes finding mine. "That was…" The words die on her lips with an ecstasy laced sigh.

A smile creeps onto my face. "Yeah…"

She lifts off my lap, rolling onto the mattress and off the bed. Her feet hit the floor and she slowly stands up, soft laughter falling from her lips. "Dear God, I don't know if I can even walk."

Pride swells inside my chest and I roll over, reaching for her. "Get back here and you won't have to walk."

She swats at my hand. "I need to go to the bathroom. I'll be right back."

She saunters out of the room, not bothering to put on any clothing. The bathroom door closes, and I roll onto my back, my head floating as I smile up at the ceiling. I can see why people get addicted to things. Jade is fucking intoxicating. I'm drunk on her… and desperate for my next hit.

Jade comes back into the bedroom with both of our clothes in her hands. I slowly sit up, my cock twitching at the sight of her standing naked in front of me again.

"Come here," I growl, holding my hands out to her.

Jade's head moves back and forth, a mischievous grin tugging on her lips. "No way. I'm not falling for that again." She tosses my clothes at me. "Time for you to go, Playboy."

I tilt my head to the side, my eyebrows lifting. "You're kicking me out?"

"I am, I need to get some sleep and I don't think that will be happening so long as you're here."

I rise to my feet, sliding on my boxer briefs and pants. It's all she threw at me. I look up at her, my chest warming as I notice the T-shirt she's pulling on. "That's mine," I say, padding across the wood floor until I reach her.

"It's mine now," she quips with a shrug and a wink. "You can have it back next time."

I smooth the material over her shoulders, my hands trailing down her arms as my gaze flickers to hers. "Is there going to be a next time?"

"Maybe not," she says slowly, challenging me with an arched brow. "Maybe tonight is all we get."

"Fuck that," I growl, sliding my hand around the back of her neck, tugging her closer. "I lied when I said one taste. One taste was never going to be enough."

Her lips part, as if she's going to counter and I silence her, claiming her mouth with my own. I swallow her words and the air from her lungs as I kiss her with an intensity that has my toes curling. She kisses me back, her tongue dancing with mine as she grabs for my waist, holding onto me as if she's afraid she'll drown.

If I go under, you're going with me, Sunny baby.

We break apart, breathless and flushed.

"You should go." She kisses me again, her nails biting into my skin.

"I could stay," I murmur against her mouth.

She shakes her head, her lips still molded to mine. "Not tonight."

She's right, I should go home. Spending the night feels an awful lot like strings and that's something neither of us want.

"Yeah, you're right," I breathe, kissing her once more before we finally break apart. It takes every ounce of self-control I have to release her. If I don't leave now, I'm going to have her naked, spread out on the bed for me again.

Goddamn. That's an image I'll never be able to erase from my mind.

And I'm not sure it's one I ever want to forget.

I force myself out of her room, heading into the kitchen for my jacket. I pick it up from the floor, ignoring the cold material sliding against my skin as I put it on. My heart crawls into my throat as I lift my head and see her walking down the hall toward me.

She's breathtaking.

Her hair's a mess with that just-thoroughly-fucked look. My T-shirt swims on her and stops just along the middle of her thighs. I want to push it up and bend her over the counter, exposing her bare ass and pussy.

"You're so fucking sexy," I rasp, my eyes raking the length of her as she walks over to me. She grabs the bottom of my jacket, sliding the zipper up to the base of my throat. Her fingers dance along my skin, toying with the white gold chain around my neck.

"Likewise."

"Do you have plans this weekend?"

She shakes her head. "No, I don't think so."

"My sisters and some of the guys are coming over. I didn't know if you—well, if you'd maybe want to come too."

My stomach flutters, heat creeping across my face and I replay the stupid sentence inside my head. Why the hell did I stumble over my words like that? I'm a grown ass adult, not a little schoolboy.

Jade lets go of my chain, running her hands down the front of my bomber jacket. My cock's already hard but I try to ignore it. Clearly, I'm not in control of anything anymore.

"Are you sure?" She rolls her lips between her teeth, her expression unreadable. "I don't want to intrude with your friends and family being there."

I cock my head to the side, my eyes scanning her face.

"You're not intruding if I invite you over. Plus, I want them all to meet you."

She's silent for a beat. Her throat bobs and her eyes widen, just slightly, as she stares up at me. "Why?"

My heart gallops inside my chest. I've never met anyone like her before. She challenges me and keeps me on my toes. Things with her, they never feel dry or boring. When I'm not with her, all I can think about is when I get to see her again.

I've become an addict and she's my drug of choice.

"I think everyone should know you."

She sucks in a shallow breath. "Matteo…"

I need her to stop. She can't say something to send reality crashing down around us. I don't do this, ever. I've never invited a woman over to meet my sisters or my friends. Hell, I never invite women to my home, I only ever go to theirs.

She's causing me to change the game. The rules and the lines—they cease to exist.

I want her in my space. I want my friends and family to know her. If I sit and think about it, if I acknowledge the significance of that, everything's going to go up in flames.

"Don't overthink it, Sunny. I'm not, so you can't either."

"Okay," she says with a little shrug, a small smile tugging on the corners of her lips. "I need your address and a time. I can bring something too."

I step closer, my hands cupping the sides of her face as I tilt her head back. "Just bring yourself. That's all I need."

Fuck me.

Before she can say anything, I bring my face to hers, silencing her with my lips. I'm making a lot of mistakes, saying a lot of things without filtering my words first.

"Goodnight, Sunny," I say, pulling away from her—forcing myself away. She follows me to the door, where I stop to slip my shoes on. "I'll text you when I'm home."

"Dream of me," she says with a wink as I pull open the door. Her eyes shimmer beneath the light, soft and blue.

"Oh, I will."

Jade blows me a kiss, shutting the door before we end up stumbling back into her bedroom, wrapped up in one another. I rake my hand through my hair as I step onto the elevator, a heavy sigh escaping me. Things between us, they'll never go back to what they were before we fucked.

Jade Wilson is everything I thought I never wanted… and everything I can't imagine not having now.

BOOK CLUB BOYS
GROUP CHAT

Cross added you to the Book Club Boys Group Chat

CROSS

Shaw found a book for us to read.

Before You Go.

I ordered copies for each of us already.
They'll be here in two days.

SIMS

What's it about?

SHAW

No idea. I liked the color of the cover.

SIMS

What happened to the Zamboner Boys chat?

SHAW

It's still there. This is the one for book club only.

SIMS

Send me the link for the book. I wanna read what it's about.

CROSS

You can look it up yourself, you know…

SHAW

No way, we're all going in blind.

SIMS

Where's Matty boy?

Mattyyyyy.

CROSS

He's ignoring us.

SHAW

Probably working on his figure skating routine.

SIMS

I'll send him some costume inspiration.

SHAW

Make sure it has sequins. Lots of them.

SIMS

What color do you think he'd look best in?

CROSS

Purple.

SHAW

Where is he actually?

SIMS

I think he went to Jade's.

CROSS

It's late... I didn't know it was like that
with them.

SIMS

I think it is now.

CROSS

Shit, I'm out of the loop.

SHAW

Matty was being a little bitch, afraid to
text her and then ended up going over
there tonight.

I hope for all our sake, he's getting laid.

CROSS

Has anyone met her yet?

MATTY

Listen up, fuckers.

SIMS

There he is!

MATTY

My sex life is none of your business. If I
hear any of you say ANYTHING that has
to do with Jade or what I'm doing with her
again, it won't be good.

SHAW

We're just kidding, Matty.

MATTY

I don't care. I'm not. It stops now.

SHAW

Sorry, I didn't mean for it to be offensive.

CROSS

I didn't technically say anything, but sorry.

SIMS

You're right. We're all sorry.

MATTY

Thank you.

And you will all meet her this weekend.

SIMS

Wait, this weekend, weekend?

CROSS

No, last weekend, dummy.

SHAW

Should we bring the books to get signed?

SIMS

You don't have to be a dick, Cross.

SHAW

The books. Do we bring them?

MATTY

No.

SIMS

No.

CROSS

Jesus, Shaw. We don't want to make it weird for her. It's a big enough deal that Matty's bringing a girl around us.

MATTY

Can you guys not be yourselves this weekend?

SHAW

You're right. We gotta play it cool.

MATTY

If you guys could be mutes, that would be preferred.

SIMS

Wishful thinking, Matty boy.

MATTY

I shouldn't have invited her.

CROSS

We'll be on our best behavior.

SHAW

Pinky swear.

SIMS

Cross my heart.

SHAW

You have one of those?

MATTY

Putting my phone on do not disturb.

CROSS

I think we're annoying him.

SIMS

Matty, wait.

SHAW

I think he's gone already.

CROSS

He's done with us.

SIMS

Dammit.

CHAPTER TWENTY-ONE
JADE

"I wanted to paint him like this, with his gaze latched onto mine. With a fire burning in the depths of his green eyes" - Clara Foss, Painted Inferno

My eyebrows tug together as I double check the directions on the screen in my car and then look back up at the house in front of me. This is not the house I would have expected Matteo to live in. I was expecting him to live in a gate community or in some swanky bachelor pad, not a place like this.

It's a gray, stone house that looks as if it could be a manor straight out of the Scottish Highlands. Instead, it's tucked in the historic part of Hillford, just outside the main part of the city.

I pull into the driveway and to the right of the house, where the detached garage sits on the other side of the cobblestone drive. There are at least half a dozen cars parked in the grass and I find an empty space beside a white Porsche.

My phone chimes and I open up the email that came

through, seeing it's a message from my cardiologist. Relief washes over me as I read over his words. My results all look normal—for my heart—and I'm supposed to keep an eye out for worsening symptoms. They're not concerned with the palpitations, so long as it doesn't bother me.

I tuck my phone into my bag and sling it over my shoulder. I grab the reusable grocery bag filled with buffalo dip and chips, and slip out of my car before turning to the house. I'm not sure which door I'm supposed to use. It looks like there's one on the back of the house, one at the front, and there's an entrance on the side, facing the driveway.

I should have asked Matteo before I came.

Stop overthinking, Jade.

Shaking away the anxious thoughts, I opt for the side door. I head up the four short steps and the door pops open. A younger woman, who can't be but a few years younger steps out, not noticing me at first.

Her head whips to the side, her dark hair shifting across her back. "Oh! I didn't see you there." She pauses, her dark gray eyes widening for a second. "Oh my gosh, you must be Jade!"

"Yes, hi," I smile, nodding my head eagerly. My heart races and my palms are clammy.

"I'm Elena, Matty's sister." She holds open the door, stepping to the side. "Come in! I'm so glad to meet you."

"It's nice to meet you too."

I step into Matteo's home and am in awe of the elegant interior. Light pours through tall windows, settling across dark polished wooden floors. The walls are subtle tones of ivory and gray with various oil paintings hanging on the walls. I take a moment to drink it all in. There's nothing superfluous in the decor. It's as if every piece and every touch is deliberate, calculated.

I glance at the chandelier hanging above before looking at Elena again.

"Come on," Elena waves me through the mudroom and into the kitchen. A massive skylight lets light spill in. "You can put your stuff in here. Everyone's in the basement playing pool and hanging out right now."

Elena shows me where to put the dip so it stays warm, and leads me down to the basement. Voices drift up the stairwell and Elena smiles, shaking her head with a soft laugh.

"Be prepared… the guys can be a bit of a handful, but the girls are the best ever."

A nervousness washes over me as we reach the bottom of the steps. I'm about to meet some of the people who are closest to Matteo. I think it's only normal for my stomach to be in knots. We turn left into the open space and there's a bar in the corner with a television hanging on the wall, a pool table, and an air hockey table.

Matteo's bent over the table, his stick in his hands, lining up a shot. His eyes flicker to mine, a slow smirk tugging on his lips as he hits the cue ball, sending it into the black eight ball he was aiming for. It sinks into the left pocket and two of the guys whine in protest.

Matteo tosses the stick onto the table, ignoring them as he stalks across the room to me. A familiar warmth slides down my spine as my gaze locks with his.

"Hey, Sunny," he breathes, his eyes shining bright as he stops in front of me. His hand shifts forward but then he stops himself from reaching out to me. My stomach does a somersault.

"Hey. Sorry I was a little late. I got caught up with some work things."

He shakes his head. "I'm just glad you were able to come."

His sister chuckles to herself, leaving the two of us as she walks over to the bar where a younger woman is sitting.

"Come on, I want to introduce you to everyone," Matteo smiles, waving at me to follow him. He doesn't walk in front of me, instead, he stays beside me as we walk over to the pool table. His presence is comforting and it chases away the nervousness.

There's no reason to feel that way.

"Everyone, this is Jade," he announces, looking at me with a grin. "Jade, this is Cameron Shaw and Warren Cross," he motions to the two men at the pool table. They're both tall and lean, around the same height as Matteo.

"Hey, Jade," they say in unison. Cross makes a face and shoves at Shaw's shoulder. Shaw ducks out of the way, bumping into Elena. He says something under his breath, his hands wrapping around her biceps as they share a look.

Matteo's brow furrows for a second and the two men walk over.

"Everyone calls me Cross," the one with dark, almost black hair and bright green eyes says as he shakes my hand.

"I go by Cam, or Shaw," the one with dirty blonde hair and blue eyes smiles, shaking my hand too.

"You met Elena," he nods to his sister. She looks over and smiles, although there's a pink tint of frustration across her face as she takes a step back from Shaw.

"That's Theo and Lucy," he looks over at the bar to the younger woman and guy sitting together. She looks a bit younger than everyone else and her soft blue eyes meet mine from across the space.

"Hi, Jade!" Lucy calls out to me as Theo bobs his head, his dark brown hair shifting, and waves.

Two women stand behind the bar. "And that's Posey and my youngest sister, Bella."

Bella and Posey both smile and wave from where they're standing.

The three Ford's all look like they're related. Bella and Elena both have beautiful long dark hair that's the same shade as Matteo's. The three of them all have similar facial features and striking gray eyes.

"Do you guys all play together?" I ask Matteo as he leads me over to the bar. I'm a little off-kilter, not knowing anyone, but I don't think Matteo would have led me into a lion's den.

He nods his head. "Do you want a drink?"

"Water's fine," I smile at him and glance at Posey who's grabbing a bottle from the fridge behind her.

"Matty, I think the air hockey table's broken," Shaw calls over to him.

"Shit, give me a second," Matteo says to me, his eyes scanning my face before he walks over to where the guys are.

Bella comes from around the bar, heading over to the pool table with her sister and Posey hands me a bottle of water.

"Thank you," I take it from her, screwing off the top before taking a sip. I tilt my head to the side, playing out the words in my head before speaking them. "Are you guys related too?"

"No way," Posey laughs, shaking her head. "Matteo and I grew up together. Same with Lucy and Theo. Our dads all played together, and our families are close."

So, she's just a friend. Jealousy strikes my chest like an iron fist. I wonder if she's a friend like I am…

I can't even hide the way my face falls.

Posey leans over the bar, closer to me. "We've always just been friends. You have nothing to worry about." Her eyes flick past me for a second.

"Oh." My eyes widen, heat creeping up my neck as I quickly shake my head. "No, I wasn't thinking that—"

A smile creeps across Posey's lips. "Girl, your face gave it all away. It's okay, your secret is safe with me."

Lucy slides over onto the bar stool next to where I'm standing. "What's the secret? I love secrets."

"Get out of here, Luce." Posey waves her hand at her dismissively. "It was a joke," Posey winks at me and relief washes over me.

"Whatever," Lucy sighs, rolling her eyes. She turns to me. "I'm so excited to meet you, Jade. You're the first girl Matteo has ever brought around anyone."

Theo walks over, gripping the back of Lucy's chair as he stops behind her. "Lucy doesn't get out much," he chuckles, looking down at her. "She's not as civilized as the rest of us."

She tips her head back, the crown of her head pressing against his abdomen as she looks at him upside down. "That's not true."

"Lucy's finishing an accelerated master's program to be an athletic trainer." Theo glances at me with his eyebrows raised. "I promise you; she does not get out much."

Lucy straightens herself, cutting her eyes at him over her shoulder. "Go away, Theodore."

Theo laughs, taking a step away. "It's nice to meet you, Jade."

"You too." I smile and nod. Theo joins Cross, Shaw, and Matteo who are congregated around the air hockey table. I look at Lucy. "Are you and Theo together?"

She lets out a laugh that sounds off key as she shakes her head. "My god, no. Theo and I have been best friends our entire lives."

Posey chuckles softly from the other side of the bar. "So, Jade. We've heard a little bit about you, but Matty's been keeping his cards close to his chest. How did you guys meet?"

"At a coffee shop," I laugh, my mind drifting back to that day. I don't want to overshare, since Matteo's decided to keep our meeting to himself. "I accidentally got his drink, and he got mine."

"Shut up, that's the cutest thing ever," Lucy swoons.

Bella and Elena come over. "What'd we miss?" Elena chimes in.

"Jade was telling us how she and Matteo met," Posey explains to the two of them as Elena sits down next to Lucy and Bella stands at the end of the bar.

"His drinks are so gross," Elena says, curling her lip up in disgust. "There's no hint of coffee left after he's done."

"They're like dessert drinks," I laugh.

Bella shrugs her shoulders. "I don't think they're bad."

"Because your sense of taste sucks, just like his."

Bella and Elena start bickering about coffee drinks. Lucy looks bored and pulls out her phone as Posey stands there, chin propped on her hand as she listens to the two of them with an animated expression.

"Sunny," Matteo calls out to me, pulling my attention from the girls. I turn around and see him standing by the pool table. "Can I borrow you?"

"Excuse me," I say to no one in particular, holding onto my water bottle as I walk over to Matteo. There's so many new faces, so many people here I don't know, it's a bit overwhelming.

He lets out a soft sigh when I reach him, a ghost of a smile dancing across his lips. "Hi."

"Hi," I breathe, relief washing over me. Something about being near him provides a layer of comfort. Familiarity. *Safety*. "Did you figure out the air hockey table?"

Matteo shakes his head. "I think it's done." He tilts his head to the side. "Sorry for abandoning you."

"No, it's okay. Everyone seems so nice." I roll my lips between my teeth, biting down before releasing them. "They said I'm the first girl you've ever brought to meet any of them."

Matteo stares at me, his throat bobbing. "Yeah," he says softly, his chin dipping. "I've never wanted them to meet anyone else before. No one else ever felt important enough for that."

My heart stumbles inside my chest. "Are you saying I'm important?"

The gray hues swirl in his eyes like cool steel, his gaze burning into mine, captivating me. The room around us dissipates. The voices and the people—they all cease to exist. "Yeah, Sunny." The corners of his mouth lift. He takes a step closer. "I think you might be."

"Yo, Matty," Shaw calls out, shattering the moment between us, thrusting us back into reality. Into the basement where all his friends and sisters are. "Can we eat since your girl is here?"

His girl.

Matteo doesn't correct him.

"Yeah," he answers, letting out a deep breath as he rakes a hand through his hair. He lets out a soft laugh, tearing his gaze from mine. "Yeah, let's go."

As if one unit, everyone heads toward the stairs and up to the kitchen where the food is, and we fall in step behind them.

Matteo stops at the bottom of the stairs and lifts a questioning brow as he motions for me to go first. "I'm sure you haven't eaten yet?"

"You know me so well." A crooked smile haunts my lips as I pass him.

And if I weren't as tuned into him as I am, I would have missed the three words he murmurs under his breath as I head up the steps.

"Not well enough."

CHAPTER TWENTY-TWO
MATTEO

"How could I be focused on competing against her when she looked at me like that? Like she wanted my hands in her hair and my lips on her neck." - Julian Hart, Painted Inferno

Jade stands in the kitchen, her back turned to me as she slides the empty dip container into the bag she brought. It's already inching closer to midnight and everyone else cleared out a few minutes ago.

"I should probably go," she says quietly, turning around to face me with her bag in hand. "Thanks for having me over. It was really nice getting to meet everyone who's close to you."

I push away from the counter, stalking across the kitchen to her. I don't want her to leave—not yet at least.

Stepping into her space, I reach for her bag, wrapping my fingers around the handle. "Stay," I rasp, searching her eyes. "I'm not ready for you to leave yet."

"It's late." Her words are a half-hearted attempt to convince herself as well as me that she should leave, but the way her body is leaning into me suggests that's not what she wants.

"I know," I murmur as she releases her grip on the handle, letting me take it from her and tossing it onto the counter behind her.

I sweep my hand along the side of her jaw and slide my hand beneath her chin, tipping her head back. "Don't go."

Her nostrils flare, her eyebrows twitching. "Don't let me," she whispers.

Without another word, without another chance to breathe, I drop my face down to hers and steal her breath with my lips. Our lips crash into each other like waves against a shore. There isn't a single beat of hesitancy in her lips as Jade kisses me back with the same intensity.

I trail my fingers along her jaw and down the side of her neck, memorizing every single inch of her skin I stroke.

Every look, every sound. Every touch and response— it's all catalogued inside my mind, stored for safe keeping. Somewhere I can keep her forever.

Her lips are soft, and taste like strawberries and champagne. It was the only drink she had tonight. I know she's sober and I like that more than anything. She's here because she wants to be, not because she's drunk. Every decision is made from a clear, sound mind.

She parts her lips as I trace the seam of them, my tongue slipping into her mouth, tangling with hers. I'm lost in her, caught in the undertow as she pulls me into the depths.

I breathe her in, devouring her with a reverent need. My heart hammers away inside my chest, the blood pumping at rapid speed through my veins. She's in them, spreading throughout my body, seeping into my bones. She's everywhere. *She's everything.*

My hands trail across her collarbones, down the sides of her torso, stopping at her waist. She lets out a soft breath as I lift her into the air, setting her down on the counter.

"You've got me all fucked up, Sunny." I murmur against her lips. She wraps her legs around me, pulling me flush against her. "I don't know what you're doing to me, but I don't want you to stop."

Jade's fingers dance across my skin, pushing the bottom hem of my shirt up my torso. Goose bumps raise up as her hands trail over every inch of my abdomen, across the dips and curves, branding my skin with her fingertips.

She pushes my shirt up farther, her hands moving up over my chest. I pull away slightly, removing my hat and tossing it onto the counter. I grab the back of my shirt to pull it up and over my head, then toss it onto the floor.

Jade stares back at me, her lips parted, breathing heavily as her gaze rakes over my body. Desire burns brightly in her blue eyes. "Strip."

The corners of my mouth twitch. Warmth spreads in the pit of my stomach and my cock throbs. "Yes, ma'am." I'll let her think she's in charge… *for now.*

I take a step away from her and her legs fall onto the counter, spread wide as she leans back on her hands. I reach for my pants, slowly undoing them as I hold her stare. I push my pants and boxer briefs down my thighs, letting them fall to the floor, pooling around my feet.

I slide off my socks, kicking my clothes out of the way, and toss my socks with them. My cock's hard as a rock, precum beading at the tip as I stand up straight, staring down at her. She rakes her teeth over her bottom lip, capturing it between them as her gaze trails down to my feet, lingering on my dick before sliding back to my face.

She slips off the counter, her feet hitting the floor as she closes the distance between us. She presses a manicured nail against the center of my chest. A moan vibrates in my chest as she drags it down my torso and along the length of my cock.

"Tell me, Playboy…" Her voice trails off and she runs her soft fingers along the underside of my erection. "How badly do you want to fuck me right now?"

Holy shit.

"Isn't it obvious?"

"No." Her eyes narrow as she stares up at me. Her hand wraps around the base of my dick. "I assume your dick gets hard for any woman who shows you attention."

Fuck. I'm caught off guard by this side of her and goddammit, I like it. She's ruthless and confident and sexy as hell.

There must be something wrong with me because I'm ready to burst just from the way she's talking to me.

"I want to fuck you more than I've ever wanted to fuck anyone before," I admit, my voice hoarse and thick with need. I reach out for her and growl as she takes a step out of my reach, abandoning my cock. "Tell me what I have to do to be able to fuck you, Sunny baby."

She tilts her head to the side. "Prove it to me."

Heat spreads through my body at her feisty words. She doesn't stop me as I step back into her space, backing her against the counter. My hand slips around the back of her head, tangling in her hair, gripping her tightly as my mouth crashes into hers.

She doesn't protest. Instead, her nails dig into my back

as she pulls me closer, her tongue tangling with mine, kissing me with a feral, uninhibited need. I grab the bottom of her sweater, breaking apart from her just long enough to pull it away from her body and remove her bra.

My hands slip beneath the waistband of her leggings, dragging them down with her panties. Jade's eyes are hooded now, burning with desire as she stands naked in my kitchen, staring back at me.

There isn't a doubt in my mind that I could take her right here if I wanted to. Something inside me stirs. I've let her have her little bit of fun being in control. Now it's my turn. I lift her into the air, sweeping her into my arms.

"What are you doing?" She sounds shocked, not angry, as she wraps herself around me.

"Taking you to my room."

No one else has ever been in my room before, let alone in my bed, but it's where I want her right now. I want to lay her down and worship her body as if I'm begging for a way into heaven.

My room is on the first floor and I carry her there, not stopping until I'm laying her down on my king-sized mattress. I don't bother shutting the door. I want her moans and cries echoing throughout my house.

Jade lies on the center of the bed, her eyes flicking to mine as I walk around the perimeter of it, dragging my fingers across her flesh. I want to memorize every tiny detail of her. "I fucking love you like this," I rasp.

I walk to the bottom of the bed, gripping her ankles as I drag her to the edge of the bed. I lower myself back down to my knees, sliding my hands up her calves, over her knees. They fall apart for me as I pin my arms against her thighs.

My face dips down between her legs, running my nose

along the outside of her cunt, breathing in the smell of her arousal. I moan, deep and guttural, my cock pulsating. Warmth builds in the pit of my stomach.

She sighs, her body sagging as I trace her pussy lips with my tongue, deliberately teasing her with the tip. She wiggles beneath my touch, bucking her hips in protest. My lips move over the place she wants me the most, softly kissing it.

"What's wrong?" I murmur, slipping my tongue over her clit and pushing it into her, tasting her arousal.

"Fuck you, Ford," she growls, slipping her hands through my hair, tugging on my scalp. "You know what you're doing."

A chuckle vibrates in my chest and she attempts to lift her hips again, but I pin her down to the mattress. She lets out a frustrated sigh that transforms into a moan as I finally give her what she wants.

I lick her cunt, circling my tongue around her clit, alternating between licking and sucking as I fuck her with my mouth. My tongue laps against her, flicking her clit, applying pressure as I roll over it, again and again.

Her hips lift and she writhes beneath me. Her body shakes, her breathing growing more ragged with every passing second. My cock strains, the pressure building inside me as I push my tongue inside her.

My balls constrict and I moan against her, imagining my cock inside of her as she fucks my face. She moans louder, pushing against my arms, needing more. My tongue moves back to her clit and I devour her, sucking it hard into my mouth, giving her exactly what she wants.

She bucks her hips, her moans filling the air, fingers tugging on my hair. "Oh, fuck," she pants, her body coming apart on the bed beneath me. Her orgasm hits her with full force, the exact time mine does. I growl against her flesh, eating her out as I lose myself, cum spurting from my cock onto the floor.

I pin her down, consuming her as she rides out the waves of euphoria. I'm right there with her, my own body overheating as ecstasy wraps around me. My movements slow to gentle licks and kisses before I pull my face away from her.

I rise to my feet, unable to tear my gaze away from her swollen, glistening cunt. My cock is already hard again as I rake my gaze along the length of her body. Her lips are parted, her chest heaving, nostrils flaring as she stares up at me through dazed and satiated eyes.

"You're fucking perfect."

A lazy grin tugs on her lips. "No one's perfect, Matteo."

"Except you." I lower myself onto the mattress and crawl up the length of her body until I'm hovering over her. "You are, for me."

She inhales sharply, her grin falling from her lips as she swallows roughly.

"It's true," I murmur, my face dipping down to hers. "No one else has ever been here before. You're the only one who's ever been in my bed."

Her eyes slowly bounce between mine, her chest rises and falls a little quicker, before she pulls my mouth down to hers. She kisses me hard, her lips moving against mine with no sense of self control. All thoughts vanish as her legs lift to wrap around me and her hands slide around the back of my neck.

My tongue pushes into her mouth, tangling with hers as I settle between her legs, moaning into her mouth as I slowly sink into her. She whimpers as I push my cock in deeper, filling her completely. I pause when I'm fully inside of her.

I could die right here, right now, the happiest man on earth.

I pull my hips back, dragging my cock out until just the tip is inside and then I sink back into her. Her hands drag down to my torso, her nails cutting into my skin as I start to fuck her, thrusting in and out, filling her over and over. She lifts her hips, tightening her legs around me as she meets me with every thrust.

My hands slide down to her hips and I pull her legs away from my body. I break away from her, shifting back onto my knees as I pull my cock out of her. Her eyebrows tug together in confusion as I climb off the bed.

I stand at the edge of the bed, my hands reaching for her hips.

"What are you—" Her words are cut off with a sharp gasp as I drag her toward me and flip her onto her stomach. "Oh," she breathes, turning her head to the side as I push her legs apart.

"Is this okay?" I ask, dragging my fingertips down her spine and over her ass, sending a shiver through her as I push my pierced cock against her cunt. "Can I fuck you like this?"

"Yes," she rasps, the word more like a plea. "Please."

Without another word, I bury myself inside her, a ragged breath escaping me as I fill her to the brim, sinking deeper inside than before. My left hand trails up her spine, pushing into her hair, wrapping it around my fist as I lean forward.

I grab her hip with my right hand, thrusting my hips. She's a mess of moans and whimpers, as am I, as I move behind her, fucking her hard. She takes every thrust, every inch, like my cock was made for her.

Her back arches, pleasure rippling through her body as the familiar heat builds in the pit of my stomach. I stroke the inside of her pussy, feeling my piercing dragging along her insides. She clenches around me, her cunt tightening every time I pull my hips back. Fuck, she feels so good.

My grip tightens on her hips, my other hand pulling her hair. Her eyelids flutter, her face screwing up as she cries out in ecstasy. I pound into her, again and again as she trembles, shattering around my length with her orgasm.

My thrusts become more frantic, and she inhales sharply, her cunt clenching around me, pushing me over the edge. A deep, guttural moan escapes me on one final thrust, and my hips still as the heat erupts inside.

I rock my hips forward, as if I could possibly get any farther in her, as I lose myself, spilling my cum deep inside her body. She breathes heavily, still shaking as I hold my cock buried in her until we're both fully satiated.

I lean forward, pressing my lips against the top of her spine before slowly pulling out of her. Jade rolls onto her side, a heavy sigh leaving her, lips curving upwards as she turns to look at me.

Something shifts in the air between us. I stare down at her, my chest constricting as I take in the sight of her, freshly fucked in my bed. I swallow hard over the lump in my throat. This is exactly where she's supposed to be.

The thought of anyone else being where she is feels like a crime punishable by death.

"Come here, Sunny," I murmur, reaching out to her. She slowly sits up, worry washing over her expression as she takes my hands and lets me pull her to my feet. "Come with me."

Her expression relaxes and she glances around. "My clothes."

"You don't need them," I say as I thread my fingers through hers. "It's just us here."

"Okay," she says quietly as I lead her into the bathroom attached to my room. Her footsteps are soft as they pad across the tile floor.

I stop at the shower, leaning in to turn on the water before turning back to her. "Stay with me tonight?"

Her eyes widen and her lips part slightly. "Are you— are you sure?"

"Yes," I say, without any hesitation. "I want you here, with me."

"But you said you don't let anyone stay the night."

I push open the shower door, pulling her into the hot water with me. "No one but you, Sunny." I swallow hard, turning our bodies so she's directly under the stream. "Never anyone but you."

She tips her head back as I collect her hair and smooth my hands over the length of it. She's silent, but her hands reach for me, wrapping around my waist as she pulls me closer to her. I grab some shampoo, squirting it into my hand before working a lather against her scalp.

She hums in approval, relaxing against me as I wash her hair and then she washes mine. A comfortable silence wraps around us as we take turns washing one another.

I pull her to me, the warmth of her body seeping into mine as we stand beneath the stream of water. She stares back at me and I get lost in her eyes, lost in the hues of blue shifting in her irises. She stares right through me, right into my soul.

She's the only person I've ever truly felt seen with. She sees past my reputation, past me being a professional athlete. Past the mask that I put on for the rest of the world.

She just sees me.

I can't help myself as I close the distance between us, pushing her back against the shower wall. My hand slides through her hair, cupping the back of her head as she tips back to look up at me.

My chest constricts, my ribcage like a vice grip around my heart. She stares at me as if she can feel it too. As if she's aware of those threatening feelings we both swore we'd never catch.

I chase the thoughts away as my mouth claims hers, our bodies melting into each other.

This, the physical connection, is all this thing can be with her... *I can't risk either of us getting hurt.*

CHAPTER TWENTY-THREE
JADE

"Julian Hart looked at me as if perhaps my flesh was as malleable as the clay beneath his palms." - Clara Foss, Painted Inferno

I can't believe I actually did it. My first draft is officially finished.

A sense of peace settles over me as I stare at my laptop. I just typed *THE END* and feel like I can finally breathe. I still have to self-edit and get it ready to send to my editor at the publishing house, but the hardest part is done.

I sit back in my seat, a deep sigh escaping me as I tilt my head back and cover my face. "Holy shit," I say to myself, laughing as I shake my head.

Pulling out my phone, I find *his* name first.

JADE

I finished.

MATTEO

Without me?

JADE

My book, Matteo.

MATTEO

Holy shit, no way.

I haven't seen Matteo since I spent the night at his house last weekend. I was afraid it would feel weird waking up in his bed, but he woke me up with the best blueberry pancakes I've ever had before he had to leave for a morning skate.

MATTEO

That means I can finally send you these.

JADE

Huh?

MATTEO

Two tickets to my game.

I've been waiting until you were finished, just so it didn't feel like an obligation or set you back in some way.

My throat constricts as I read over his message three separate times. With the way he's been with me, there's a part of me that refuses to believe his reputation wasn't just an exaggeration.

A link comes in his next message and it's two tickets to a game later this month.

MATTEO

Bring whoever you want, as long as it's not another guy.

JADE

I would never do that.

Plus, there is no one else.

MATTEO

Same for me.

Maybe we can keep it that way?

My heart comes to a full stop inside my chest. Is this his way of saying he doesn't want either of us sleeping with anyone else? Because it sure as hell feels like it.

JADE

I would like that.

MATTEO

Me too.

Theo and I are going to the bar tonight.
Want to come?

Between his game schedule and me on the last leg of my deadline, we haven't seen each other all week.

JADE

I don't want to impose on your plans.

MATTEO

Sunny, I would drop any fucking plans if
you asked me to.

Theo won't care.

JADE

Okay, yeah. That sounds good.

MATTEO

We'll be at Harry's Pub at eight.

See you then, Sunny.

———

"Jade, you might be the funniest person I've ever met," Lucy laughs, shaking her head. She leans against the high-top table, looking at Matteo beside me. "I like her, Matty."

I glance to my left, catching his eye as the corners of his mouth lift. "So do I."

"Matty has been unstoppable on the ice, thanks to you," Theo smiles, nodding. "We all need to throw you a party if we make it to—"

"Don't you dare even say the word," Matteo cuts him off, narrowing his eyes at him. "You know we don't do that."

Theo lets out a laugh. "Shit, I know, but fuck..." He stops although he looks like he wants to continue. Instead, he shakes his head, silencing himself with a slug of his beer.

When Matteo told Theo I was meeting them, Theo asked Lucy to come too. According to everyone at the table, they're just friends—best friends, really. I beg to differ with the way I keep catching him watching her.

Or, at least there's something more there for him.

"Did you ask her about next Friday?"

I tilt my head to the side in question. "What's next Friday?"

Matteo's eyes widen slightly. "It's just some stupid charity event for the organization." He shakes his head dismissively. "I don't even know if I'm going to go."

"It's mandatory," Theo laughs.

"Please, he's downplaying it," Lucy interjects, scooting to the edge of her seat as she sips her martini. "It's only the best thing they do every year. It's basically just a gala with an auction."

"That sounds really cool." I smile at Lucy, ignoring the annoying dread in my stomach that Matteo didn't tell me about it. We're not dating, we're not together. There's no reason for him to invite me to all the things he does.

Matteo's hand touches my forearm. "Wait, really?" I turn to look at him and his face lights up. "I didn't ask because I didn't want to add anything else to your plate while you were on your deadline."

And just like that, he chases the worry away.

"I really appreciate that. Sometimes I get tunnel vision when I'm writing."

"I know," he says softly, his head bobbing. "I didn't want to stress you out or pull you away from that headspace."

"Hey Luce, let's go get another round," Theo says to her, sliding off his seat.

Lucy chuckles. Her drink is still half full. "Yeah, sure." She gets up and they head over to the bar together, leaving just Matteo and me at the table.

Matteo's eyes are soft and warm as he stares back at me. "Would you want to go with me, Sunny?" He clears his throat. "Be my date for the night?"

I know I really shouldn't, we're no strings attached after all, but, "I'd love to."

"It's a black-tie affair. We're supposed to be there a little early because they like to get pictures of the team and have the players walk in together."

"I have a dress or can go get one," I say, my stomach

doing a somersault. "Do you want to just figure out what time I should meet you there?"

Matteo stares at me for a beat, his head tilting to the side as his eyes drag across my face. They settle on mine and his expression softens into something unreadable. "No," he says, a ghost of a smile dancing across his lips as he gives his head a swift shake. "No, I want you there with me. We will show up together."

The air leaves my lungs in a rush. I thought he'd just want me to meet him there, not for us to arrive together like a couple. "Oh." The word tumbles from my lips on a breath, barely audible, but I know he hears it by the way his expression shifts.

He purses his lips, conflict knitting his eyebrows. "I know this isn't something that was part of our deal, so if you don't want to come, I get it." He shrugs, putting up a wall, like he's indifferent to it all.

"I know," I say softly, nodding my understanding. "Things change, though, right?" I hope he hears the longing in my words, and it's obvious the second he does. The indifference vanishes and there's a glimmer of hope shimmering in his eyes. "I'd love to be your date for the night."

A slow and steady grin pulls on his lips. "Alright," he says, tipping his head in one quick nod. "I'll send you the details and let you know what time I'll be there to pick you up." He pauses for a second and cocks an eyebrow, a smirk twitching to come to life. "Or, you can always get ready at my house, too."

His words catch me off guard and it takes a moment for my brain to catch up. "Yeah, I can get ready there." This is foreign territory for Matteo Ford… and honestly, it is for me too. Nothing and no one in my past compares to whatever this is with him. No one even comes close.

"Okay, great." He brings his beer to his lips. "We'll figure out the specifics before Friday."

I smile back at him. "It's a plan."

"No, Sunny." He shakes his head, mischief dancing in his eyes as they burn into mine. "It's a date."

FROM THE TEXT THREAD
OF MATTY & JADE

MATTEO

Are you up?

JADE

I was just getting ready for bed.

Is everything okay?

MATTEO

Yeah, yeah.

Actually, no.

I was thinking about what your favorite
color is and realized I don't know it.

JADE

Do you want to know what it is?

MATTEO

I want to know everything about you.

JADE

You're obsessed. Admit it.

MATTEO

I'm not denying it.

JADE

It's purple. What's yours?

MATTEO

Blue.

What's your favorite food?

JADE

I love Italian.

MATTEO

Baked ziti is Italian-American, Sunny.

JADE

Okay, well let me rephrase. I love anything with pasta.

What's yours?

MATTEO

Lobster rolls.

JADE

I've never had one.

MATTEO

We'll have to change that.

Birthday?

JADE

September 20. You?

MATTEO

August 7.

JADE

Sweatpants or jeans?

MATTEO

Lol. Sweatpants.

Do you like podcasts?

JADE

Sometimes. Do you?

MATTEO

Not really, but I listen to my sister's.

JADE

Your sister has one? Which one?

MATTEO

Elena. She and my cousin Tella started it together.

They talk about women's sports and women in sports.

JADE

Is it only about women's sports?

MATTEO

For the most part. Elena's a bit of a man hater.

JADE

Sold. What's the name of it?

MATTEO

Women Running the Plays

JADE

I'll add it to my list.

MATTEO

Elena will love to hear it.

Okay, a few more questions and then I promise I'll let you get to bed.

JADE

You know, you could always come over and ask me in person instead.

MATTEO

I have an early flight, though.

JADE

Suit yourself.

MATTEO

What I meant was, I'll have to leave before you're awake.

JADE

I don't mind.

MATTEO

Be there in fifteen.

JADE

Meet you in the lobby.

MATTEO

You should just give me a key. Then you wouldn't have to come down to let me in every time.

JADE

And give you access to my place whenever you want?

MATTEO

Duh.

JADE

Hmmm...

I'll think about it.

MATTEO

See you soon, Sunny baby.

JADE

CHAPTER TWENTY-FOUR
MATTEO

"How contradicting for someone to be so maddening, yet so enthralling at the same time." - Julian Hart, Painted Inferno

Standing in front of the mirror, I adjust my tie, my eyes raking down the length of my suit before bouncing back to my face. I look like a younger version of my father, although I have my mother's hair and darker features. The dark gray eyes are undoubtedly a Ford trait.

Jade's been in the guest bathroom upstairs for the last hour. She came over yesterday evening and has been here since. I like having her here. I never noticed how quiet my house could be until after having her over the first time.

I smooth my hand over my damp hair, brushing it to the side before rolling my wrist to check the time on my watch. We need to leave in thirty minutes. I don't want to rush her along, but I also don't want to be late.

The last thing I need is for Coach to get on my ass about showing up late to a scheduled event, even if it doesn't have to do with us being on the ice.

The annual gala is a huge event for the Hillford Ice Hawks organization. There are a lot of big people who show up—sponsors and investors. The entire team is required to be in attendance. A lot of friends and family are invited, along with other people in the community who are there for the charity tax write-offs.

I grab my dress shoes from the closet, carry them out to the mudroom, and leave them by the side door. My footsteps are light as I make my way through the house, walking to the foyer and up the stairs that lead to the second floor.

I stop outside the bathroom, raising my fist to knock on the door. "I don't mean to rush you at all, but how much longer do you think you'll be? We need to get going soon."

The door pulls open just as I get the last word out and the air rushes from my lungs at the sight of Jade standing in front of me.

She's wearing a long, black silk dress that stops just at her ankles with thin straps over her shoulders. The left side has a slit in it that stops just along the middle of her thigh. It's not too tight, yet not too loose, hugging her body in the right spots to accentuate her curves.

Her hair is brushed away from her face, revealing her slender neck, a thin chain around it with a small diamond resting in the hollow at the base, and matching diamond earrings. Her cheeks are tinted pink, her lips a shade darker, and the makeup on her eyes makes the bright blue stand out even more.

Jesus Christ.

"You look amazing," I murmur, my voice barely more than a whisper. My gaze rests on hers as I take a step closer. "You're breathtaking, Jade."

She laughs quietly. "I don't normally get dressed up like this."

"Neither do I," I admit, shrugging my shoulders. I slip my hand around her lower back, feeling her skin just above the line of her dress. "Fuck," I growl. "Turn around."

She slowly spins, my hand dragging along her torso as I take in the full sight of her. Her hair is straight and sleek down the center of her bare back. The back of her dress is completely open, the fabric starting just above the top of her ass.

"Does it look okay?"

"You could wear a fucking pillowcase and everyone would be jealous of how good it looks on you." I spin her back around to face me. "Let them all see what they can never have."

Her lips part, a ragged breath escaping her. "I'm there with you, Matteo. I'm not worried about the other men."

"Neither am I." I wink as a smirk drifts across my lips. "They all know I know how to fight."

"You're ridiculous," she laughs, shaking her head.

My breath catches in my throat as she stares up at me through her long dark lashes. Warmth spreads in the center of my chest and there's a subtle tugging sensation. I swallow hard, my nostrils flaring as I draw a deep breath and stare down at her.

I couldn't look away even if I wanted to.

I'm completely captivated by her. Enchanted. Enamored.

Obsessed.

"Thought you said we needed to get going?" she rasps, her eyes flicking to my mouth and back to my gaze again.

I slide my hand along her jaw. "We'll get there when

we get there," I murmur, lowering my face, my lips seeking hers. I can't help myself when I'm around her. If there's any reason for me to touch her or kiss her, I'm going to find it. And if there isn't, I'll make one up.

"Maybe I'll just call and say we can't make it," I whisper against her lips, tugging her closer as my cock presses against her abdomen. "We could stay here instead."

"And waste this outfit?" She laughs, pushing against my chest. "Hell no."

"I want to see how it looks on my floor."

She shakes her head and steps out of my grasp. "Later." A smirk drifts across her lips. "If you're a good boy at the Gala, I'll let you take it off me tonight."

Fuck. My cock grows harder. I reach for her again and she swats at my hand, the sound of her laughter wrapping around us. "I can't make any promises," I admit with a sheepish grin.

"Why am I not surprised?" Jade giggles as she grabs her purse from the counter and tucks a tube of lipstick inside.

"I think it's safe to say you know me pretty well, Sunny."

Better than anyone else ever has…

"I would hope so," she says with a wink and pauses in front of me again. "Should I go and put my stuff out in my car?"

I tilt my head to the side, slowly shaking it. "You can do that tomorrow. Or another day. Or never," I shrug, reaching for her again. "I like you here with me."

Her eyes shimmer. "So do I." She steps into my space, lifting on her toes as she places a kiss on the corner of my mouth. She pulls away before I get the chance to push her farther into the bathroom.

"Nice try, Mr. Ford." She taps my chest and brushes past me as she walks out into the hall. I follow her down the stairs and through the house, letting her lead the way.

"Oh shoot," she mumbles, shaking her head as she stops in the kitchen. "I forgot my heels in the bathroom."

"I'll grab them." I spin on my heel, heading back through the house and upstairs to the bathroom. There's a pair of heels sitting by the bathroom counter, exactly where I expected to find them.

She turns around to face me as I reenter the kitchen, the heels dangling from my finger by their straps. "You're so sweet. Thank you," she says softly, reaching for them, except I don't give them to her.

Her eyes widen slightly as I lower one knee to the ground, setting her heels by her feet. I slip my hands around her left ankle and she hikes her dress up, lifting it out of the way as I raise her leg.

I slide her shoe on, pulling the strap around the back of her heel, before moving to her next foot. She stands a few inches taller now and my eyes wander up her body as I stay kneeling in front of her.

My hands drift up the back of her calves, fingertips skimming along the insides of her knees and up her thighs.

"Matteo," she breathes, the sound half a moan. "You're a bad influence."

I stare up at her. "I'm on my knees for you, Sunny baby," I rasp. "If there's anyone who's influenced, it's me."

Her lips part and she inhales sharply as I slip my hands between her thighs, my fingertips skating over her pussy through her underwear. She lets out a heavy breath and I pull them away, slowly rising back to my feet.

Her eyebrows cinch closer together. "Rude."

"We have to go, remember?" I say nonchalantly, pointing my thumb over my shoulder.

Her face settles into the cutest pout I've ever seen, brow furrowed and her bottom lip sticking out just a little. "What a tease."

"I'll take care of you later," I promise, holding my hand out for hers. "Come on. I have a hot date."

CHAPTER TWENTY-FIVE
JADE

My arm's linked through Matteo's as we make our way to the front of The Hillford Country Club Clubhouse where the Gala is being held. A soft melody played on what sounds like a string quartet drifts from the front door as we approach the bottom of the marble steps.

The door pushes open and a beautiful woman in a red gown with her hair swept to the side gives Matteo and me a look through her elegant gold embellished mask.

"Finally!" she calls out, grabbing the bottom of her gown and lifting it before sweeping down the staircase. "I was about to send a search party for the two of you."

When she stops in front of us, her gray eyes meet mine and I realize it's Elena, Matteo's sister.

"Sorry, kid," Matteo says, shrugging his shoulders, slipping his arm from mine to give his sister a hug. "We got a little distracted."

Elena looks me up and down, from head to toe. "Listen, I like men, but I too would be distracted by her." A smile curves on her lips as she looks at me again. "Girl, you're a fucking bombshell." She pulls me in for a hug. "Making me question my sexuality and shit."

"I'd gladly remind you of your sexuality," Cam Shaw calls from the top of the stairs. I don't know how long he's been standing there. Elena releases me and gives him the middle finger.

"Watch yourself, Shaw," Matteo warns, stepping beside me and his sister.

"A guy can dream, Ford. She's your little sister. I'd rather keep the teeth I have."

"You look rich," I say to Elena, ignoring the guys.

Elena hooks her arm through mine. "Babe, I am rich," she chuckles. "Come on. I see Matty forgot it's a masquerade. I set two of the masks aside that they have inside, just in case."

She leads me up the stairs with Matteo rushing past us. He stops beside Shaw and they both open the doors for us, letting us walk through first. To the right, just inside the foyer, is a velvet-draped table with ornate masks.

Elena crouches down, fishing out two masks from under the table. She hands me an ivory colored one, dusted in delicate crystals. For Matteo, she has a matte black mask with sharp gold detailing. He slips it on, a smirk tugging on his lips.

He looks dangerous as hell.

Matteo takes my mask, stepping behind me to tie it around the back of my head. He rests his hands on my shoulders and gently turns me around to face him, his gaze burning into mine as he lets out a shallow breath.

"Perfect," he murmurs, brushing his fingers along the side of my face.

A bright flash blinds me from my peripheral vision. It happens two more times and Matteo turns, his glare murderous as he looks at one of the photographers.

"Can I get a photo of the two of you?"

My stomach does a somersault. What will they use the photos for? Does Matteo even want there to be evidence of us at an event together?

Matteo's hand snakes around my back, gripping my hip as he pulls me flush against his side. "Is this okay?" he whispers into my ear.

"Yes," I breathe, smiling as we both look at the photographer. She takes a few photos before disappearing from the foyer. Matteo's grip loosens, but he doesn't release me.

"Come on," Elena urges. "People are waiting to speak with you." She looks over at Shaw. "Come on, Cam. No more hiding out here."

Shaw lets out a sigh and shakes his head as he starts to walk into the reception hall.

"He's not a fan of events like this," Elena explains to me as she grabs two flutes of champagne and hands one to me. "He hates the auction."

Matteo nods toward the doors and Shaw falls in step with him as the four of us head toward the door.

"Why doesn't he like the auction?" I half whisper to her.

She glances at me, arching a brow. "Of course Matty didn't say anything." She rolls her eyes, huffing. "They have an auction for an outing with each player."

"Like a date?"

Elena shrugs. "Depends on what the winner and player decide. Sometimes it's golf or some fun activity or even dinner." She leans closer. "You'd better outbid someone for Matteo tonight."

Realization washes over me. Someone else could bid and win him tonight. Jealousy rolls in my stomach. It's not like it's for a real date or anything sexual, but still.

"Sunny, come here, I want you to meet some people," Matteo says, breaking into mine and Elena's convo. She gives me a wink as Matteo slips his hand to mine and leads me over to a small group of three at a standing table near the corner. "Hey guys," he says as we reach them.

A woman with long dark hair and the two men turn to look at me. Her red lips pull into a smile, her gaze soft as she stares at me for a moment. The three of them are older and the two men could pass for twins.

And they both have gray eyes. Eyes that look exactly like Matteo's.

"This is Jade." Matteo's thumb strokes the back of my hand. "Jade, this is my mom, Andi, my father, Carson and my Uncle Caleb."

Holy shit. He brought me over to meet his parents.

My heart races. "Hi!" I smile at the three of them. Nervous doesn't begin to touch the way I feel right now. Hell, I don't even know what I'm feeling. An anxious feeling rolls through my stomach.

"Hi, Jade," Andi says, taking a step closer to pull me in for a hug. "It's so lovely to meet you." She pulls away for a moment. "I love your dress."

"Oh, thank you." Heat creeps across my cheeks and I glance at Matteo. His smile doesn't leave his face.

"Jade." His father nods and holds out his hand to shake mine. He looks like an older version of Matteo. "It's nice to meet you."

"You as well."

His uncle steps over, holding out his hand. "Thank you for coming tonight." He nods his head toward Matteo. "Thanks for keeping this one out of trouble too."

Matteo chuckles, pulling me back to his side. "The three of you do not get to interrogate her tonight."

"Does that mean we'll get to another night?" Andi asks him without missing a beat.

Carson arches a brow as he grabs his drink from the table and takes a long sip.

Matteo looks at me, his eyes scanning my face. "I hope so."

A smile tugs on my lips and I turn to them. "I'd love to be interrogated."

"Don't tempt them, Sunny," Matteo laughs, his fingers wrapping around my side. "They can be ruthless."

"Oh, please," Andi waves her hand. "We are harmless." She smiles at me. "I'd just love to know more about the woman who's stolen my boy's attention."

My heart crawls into my throat. With the way the three of them are studying me, I can't help but wonder if this is the first time something like this has happened before.

"Another night," Matteo promises them. "We'll be back," he says, whisking me away from the table. "Sorry about them," he says to me after we get out of earshot. "My mom loves to know everything about people."

"Don't apologize. They seemed very nice."

His throat bobs as he swallows. His eyes are unreadable and he shifts his weight on his feet, his voice dropping lower. "I just wanted them to meet you. I've uh—I've never brought anyone to meet them before."

The butterflies in my stomach flutter to life. "So, I was your first?"

A ghost of a smile dances across his lips. "You're a first for a lot of things, Sunny."

"So are you," I admit, right before we're interrupted by a few of his teammates.

And fuck me for wanting him to be my last.

———

Matteo's hidden in a separate room with the rest of his team, and Elena and I are lowering ourselves down into seats near the front row.

"Remember," Elena says quietly, grabbing two more flutes of champagne from the server who passes us. "It's all for a good cause."

The auctioneer's voice breaks through the speakers at the front of the room.

"Ladies and gentlemen, we'll be starting our auction with the first player of the night." He pauses as the crowd claps, before he begins again. "First up, we have one of our power forwards, Mr. Matteo Ford."

My stomach flutters as Matteo comes through a doorway to the left. He's still wearing his mask and stops beside the auctioneer.

"We'll start the bidding at $100."

His mouth begins to move, the auctioneer chattering away as he moves through a few playful raises, the price climbing up to one thousand dollars. It makes a massive jump to two thousand as a woman's voice calls out from the other side of the room.

My head turns and I see a woman sitting in a sleek gold gown, lifting her paddle with a confident smile. My head whips back to the front of the room, locking gazes with Matteo.

"That's Grace Hartwell," Elena whispers to me. "She bids on him every year and usually wins."

Every year?

"Who the hell is she?"

"Someone who's always wanted Matteo's attention and never truly got it."

Without a second thought, I lift my paddle. The number jumps again and the corners of Matteo's lips slowly lift. The woman on the other side of the room counters. I bid again.

We volley back and forth, the bid creeping over ten thousand dollars.

"Twenty thousand," I call out, lifting my paddle again. I do not have twenty thousand dollars to bid, but no way am I losing.

I outbid her by a considerable margin and murmurs ripple throughout the room. A low whistle comes from somewhere in the back.

"Yes, girl. Get your man."

"I'm going to need to borrow 20k from him," I laugh nervously.

Elena laughs. "He'll pay it. It's for charity."

The auctioneer drags it out dramatically, bouncing back and forth between the woman across the room and me. I don't bother looking at her. She doesn't deserve a second of my attention.

"Going once... going twice... sold!" the auctioneer calls out, pointing at me. "To the lady in the ivory mask!"

Applause fills the room and I rise to my feet as Matteo comes stalking my way, his eyes hooded as he stops right in front of me. His mask obstructs half his face still, but I don't miss the fire in his eyes.

"That was bold," he murmurs, his eyes raking across

my face. The auctioneer's voice fills the room again and the attention shifts away from us. He leans in so his mouth is right next to my ear and says just loud enough for me to hear, "I'm glad you won."

"There was no way I was losing," I laugh quietly, giving him a sheepish grin. "I might need to borrow some money."

He chuckles, shaking his head before letting out a heavy sigh. "It's for a good cause."

"So, what did I win with you?"

His eyes darken as he drags his teeth over his bottom lip. "I have an idea." He holds his hand out to me. "Want to find out?"

My heart pounds harder in my chest as I slip my hand into his. "Yes," I rasp.

He whisks me away from the ballroom, no one noticing us leaving as he pulls me into the foyer and down the hall. The last door on the right has a brass plate on it, but I don't catch what it says as Matteo opens the door and pulls me inside.

As he pulls the door shut, I notice the coats and realize we're inside the coat closet. The door latches and we're encapsulated in silence.

My heart races, my stomach fluttering. "Matteo, I can't see anything."

"It's okay, Sunny," he says, the door lock clicking just before the lights flicker on. "Better?" He smirks, reaching for my waist and pulling me flush against him.

With one hand on my hip, he slides the other along the side of my neck, his thumb pushing against the underside of my chin as he tilts my head back.

His breath fans across my face, his lips parting as his graze drops down to my mouth and back to my eyes. I love when he looks at me like that, like he's ready to devour me.

"Is this what I paid twenty grand for?"

He snorts, arching a brow. "You mean, what I'm paying twenty grand for."

A grin spreads across my face. "Touché, touché." I giggle as his face lowers and his mouth finds mine. He kisses me with an urgency, an intensity, with a burning heat that I can't ignore. I can't extinguish it.

I let it consume me.

My hands slide through his hair, tangling in his waves, messing up the way he had it styled without a single care of how disheveled we're going to look exiting the fucking closet.

"I need to be inside you, Sunny baby," Matteo groans against my mouth. His tongue traces my lips. "Are you gonna let me fuck you here?"

There's no hesitation. "Yes."

His mouth claims mine, his legs pushing me back until my back's against the wall. His lips bruise mine, rough and demanding as his tongue tangles with mine. He breathes me in, drawing the air from my lungs.

The inferno between us burns hot, my skin on fire as warmth builds in the pit of my stomach. His hands drag down to my hips, searing me through my dress. He wraps his hand around the back of my leg and lifts it up, holding it against his thigh as he pushes my dress up to my waist.

His right hand holds my thigh and we break apart, both of us breathless as he takes his fingers and pushes them into my mouth. "Get my fingers wet for me," he growls as I wrap my lips around them, swirling my saliva around his digits.

My lips pop as he pulls them out, moving his hand

down to the apex of my thighs. He pushes my panties to the side, his fingers drifting over my bare skin before he slides them inside me, sinking into my hot center. "You're so wet for me, Sunny baby. Fuck." A moan falls from my lips. He captures it with his mouth crashing into mine, swallowing the sounds as he starts to pump his fingers in and out of me.

His thumb finds my clit and he presses against me, rolling it in delicious, calculated circles. His tongue is in my mouth and his fingers are inside me as he fucks me with his hand, working me into a mess.

I grind against him, my knees growing weak, leg shaking as he holds me up by one thigh. I'm pinned against the wall, at his mercy. Anyone could come to the coat closet at any given moment. The locked door would be a cause for concern.

And if they find the two of us locked in here together...

"Fuck, Jade," Matteo moans against my mouth, pulling his fingers from me right as I could feel my orgasm creeping in. He releases my thigh, letting my foot fall back to the floor. He lifts his fingers, his eyes glazed and filled with desire as he slips his fingers into his mouth.

His eyelids flutter shut as he sucks my arousal from his fingertips and moans. "Turn around for me," he growls, grabbing my hips, turning me to face the wall. "I'm going to fuck you, fast and hard, before someone finds us in here."

He pushes my dress up around my waist and leans forward, his mouth brushing against my ear. "Can you be quiet for me, Sunny baby? We don't want anyone to hear us."

I plant my hands on the wall, turning my head to look at him. "I'll be quiet."

"Good girl," he rasps, grabbing my chin as he kisses me, hard and deep before releasing me. His hands drag down the length of my body, his palms rubbing against my ass. "Fuck, look at you."

He undoes his belt and his pants, pushing them down, just far enough to get his cock out. He brings his hand to his mouth and spits into it before wrapping it around his length, coating it with his saliva. The tip of his dick and the cool metal of his piercing press against my center.

A ragged breath escapes me the same time a low moan falls from his lips and he pushes inside me, not stopping until he's filling me completely. He pauses for a second, both hands running over my ass, spreading my cheeks before wrapping around my hips.

He shifts his hips, pulling back slightly before slamming into me again. His fingers dig into me, holding on tight as he starts to thrust into me, over and over, dragging his length out of me to the point that I think he might slip away completely, but then slams back into me again.

I push back against him, the side of my face pressing against the cold wall. I'm a breathless mess of moans, taking him fully with every thrust. His hips work faster, pumping into me harder, the force of his thrusts shaking me to my core.

The warm pressure builds at a rapid pace in the pit of my stomach, spilling into my veins as he continues to rock into me. "Matteo," I rasp, his name falling from my lips like a desperate plea.

"Shh, Sunny," he murmurs, his left hand abandoning my hip as he slides it around the front of me. His fingers find my clit the same time he slams into me hard, drawing a whimper from me. "Gotta be quiet, remember?"

I nod, my eyes meeting his over my shoulder. My legs

shake and my entire body trembles with anticipation as I tighten around his cock. He strokes my insides, his piercing brushing against that sweet spot deep inside.

I can't stop myself from crying out as his fingers roll over my clit once more and my orgasm hits me without any further warning. Wildfire spreads through my body as I bite down on my bottom lip, swallowing my own moans as he fucks me harder, inhibitions ceasing to exist.

"Fuuuck." He drags out the word, low and hoarse as he pounds into me, filling me with his warmth. His fingers still play with my clit, my body sagging as I'm rendered powerless against the orgasm that consumes me.

His thrusts slow as he empties himself deep inside me, rocking into me once more before he stills. We're both panting, riding the waves of euphoria as he brushes my hair away from the side of my face. He slowly pulls out of me, pulling my panties back in place and he drops my dress, letting it fall back down to my ankles.

He fixes his own pants and slowly turns me around to face him. "I love the thought of you walking around with my cum dripping out of you out there."

He pauses, his face flushed and eyes glossy as they slowly search mine, as if he's checking to make sure what he just did is okay, that I'm okay. He pushes my hair back over my shoulders, smoothing it away from my face. Something shifts in his gaze, something dangerous. His lips part as if he's going to say something, but instead, he presses them to mine.

He kisses me with such tenderness—the kind of kiss that seeps into your bones.

"Come on," he says softly, breaking apart as he drops his hand back down to mine. A ghost of a smile dances across his lips. "Or my sister's going to send that search party she threatened earlier."

A soft laugh escapes me as he unlocks the door and pulls me back into the hall, both of us walking hand in hand to the ballroom filled with people who have no idea that we just snuck away and fucked in the coat closet.

That twenty thousand dollars I now owe him?

Totally worth it.

BOOK CLUB BOYS
GROUP CHAT

CROSS

Book club check in.

What chapter is everyone on?

SIMS

Don't hate me.

SHAW

Chapter seven.

SIMS

I...uh. I haven't started yet.

CROSS

What the hell, Sims? Our first meeting is at the end of the month.

SHAW

Technically he still has time.

MATTY

I'm on chapter eighteen.

CROSS

Damn Matty. Star book club member.

SIMS

Show-off.

SHAW

You're making us look bad.

SIMS

What about you, Cross? How far are you?

CROSS

Finished.

MATTY

You don't do anything else with your time, do you?

SHAW

How the hell?

SIMS

Okay, you're the show-off.

CROSS

Matty, your girlfriend is crazy talented.

MATTY

Not my girlfriend.

SHAW

Does that mean she's fair game?

MATTY

That means I'll kill you if you even think about it.

SIMS

So, she's your girlfriend.

MATTY

No.

CROSS

It just means he's too afraid to put a label on it, but doesn't want anyone else to have her.

MATTY

She's not my goddamn girlfriend.

But she is mine.

Does that clear things up for you imbeciles?

SHAW

Loud and clear.

She's your girlfriend.

Matty has left the chat.

CHAPTER TWENTY-SIX
JADE

"IF LOOKS COULD KILL, MY DATE WOULD HAVE BEEN STONE COLD DEAD ON THE FLOOR." - CLARA FOSS, PAINTED INFERNO

"Jade, I'm going to need a weekly update on what's going on between you and Matty."

My lips tug into a frown as I stare back at my best friend, emotion welling in my throat. Ellie lets out a deep sigh, her head turning to look at Nicole with the same degree of sadness that's consuming me.

The three of us met for lunch today at our normal spot. The one café that's halfway between all our apartments. The place that has the best brunch menu and mimosas.

Next week, it wouldn't matter anymore. It will just be Ellie and me left for lunch dates.

Nicole will be in New York, starting her new life there with Ben.

"I don't know that I'll have much to update you on, but sure," I say after a moment, clearing the emotion from my throat. "It just sucks we won't be able to do this anymore."

"I'll only be a few hours away," Nicole smiles, her gaze

drifting between Ellie and me. "We'll still make time to see each other, okay?"

Sadness settles in my chest, because I know exactly how things like this go. There's always a hopefulness when someone moves away. Hope that you'll still make plans to see each other. But then, as time goes on and as you grow apart, the opportunities to get together seem to dissipate. I know from my own experiences with my family.

"You're right," Ellie says after a moment, lifting her glass in the air. "As much as it sucks, I think this is really a good thing for both you and Ben."

Nicole's smile spreads and I swear, it looks like she's glowing. There's excitement that bubbles from her. I know she'll miss us, but I also know she's equally excited for this new chapter in her life.

"I think so too." Nicole lifts her glass, holding it toward Ellie's.

I lift mine. "To New York," I say as the three of us clink our glasses. "To a new chapter, a new city, and new beginnings for you and Ben."

"To Ben becoming a corporate powerhouse and forgetting us completely," Ellie adds.

Nicole laughs softly, shaking her head as she rolls her eyes. "He wishes. I'd never let that man forget my two best friends."

As much as I'll miss my best friend, I am excited for her. It just…it isn't going to be the same without her here.

"I can't believe it's actually happening," I say, quietly, draining the rest of my mimosa. "It seemed so far away and now it's here."

Nicole's smile grows softer. "I know. It feels like we blinked and here we are."

"Time just disappears without us even realizing," Ellie muses, shaking her head as her eyes grow distant. Our server comes back to the table with three salads, setting them in front of each of us, along with fries we ordered to share.

When I said their brunch menu was amazing, I didn't mean we'd order anything but our normal meal we get when the three of us are together. Girl dinner can be had at any time of day, honestly.

"Just think," Ellie starts as she pierces some of her lettuce with her fork. "You're going to a brand new city, with new people who don't know every embarrassing thing you've done."

"I'm pretty excited about that. They'll know the version of me now, not all the cringy versions I've been in the past."

I tilt my head to the side, chewing a bite of salad and swallowing it before adding, "So, are we just baggage now?"

Nicole laughs, her eyes turning glossy for a fraction of a second before she blinks it away. "You two are my favorite baggage."

"The highest compliment," I smile, amusement dancing in my expression.

"It truly is," Ellie says, nodding.

"I'm going to miss you guys," Nicole says after a moment, her voice barely audible. "More than either of you understand."

Emotion washes over me and the corners of my eyes burn. I will not cry here in the middle of the café. "Like you said, we're only a few hours apart."

"And we'll talk every day," Ellie adds before taking a sip of her water.

Nicole slowly nods in agreement. "You guys will have to come visit too."

"Girls weekend in the big apple?" Ellie smiles, glancing at me with a mischievous grin.

I smile back at her. "We're so there."

The conversation shifts as we finish our salads, our mimosas, and argue over who gets the last fry. The server comes over to clear the table and refills our waters, not the mimosas.

Nicole leans back in her chair, giving me that look that says I'm about to be the center of attention. And I know exactly what it's going to be about.

"So," she says casually, a smirk toying with her lips. "You never did tell us about the gala."

"Oh yes," Ellie says eagerly, leaning forward in her seat as she sips her water. "You must tell us everything."

"I mean… there's no law that says I have to."

"Oh, please," Ellie rolls her eyes. "Only the first rule of best friendship says that."

"Come on," Nicole presses, raising her eyebrows. "You're the only one dating a swanky, professional athlete. Indulge in our fantasies, babe."

An exasperated sigh escapes me. "You two are so annoying."

"You love us," Nicole retorts.

"Spill," Ellie says at the same time, swirling her straw in her water, creating a cyclone shape with her ice cubes.

"The gala was great." I tuck my hair behind my ears. "It was a masquerade ball, which I didn't realize until we got there. The venue was amazing, the food and drinks were so good, and it was just a lot of fun."

Nicole raises an eyebrow. "What a generic answer."

"There was an annual charity auction where they

auctioned off a 'date' with the players, but really it's just for time spent with them doing something they both agree to."

Ellie's face lights up. "Did you partake in the auction?"

"I did." I smirk, the façade of coolness finally breaking. "I bid on Matteo and won."

"My girl," Nicole smiles with satisfaction, nodding her head. "What are you guys going to do, since you won?"

Heat creeps up my neck. "Ah, well." I pause, swallowing. "We already did something."

Ellie raises her eyebrows, eyes wide and eating up every tidbit of that night I'm giving them. "Do tell."

"It was a spur of the moment thing."

Nicole tilts her head to the side. "Yeah? The suspense is killing me."

"Um, well… we had sex in the coat closet during the auction."

Nicole spits her water out and Ellie's jaw drops. "Shut the fuck up," Ellie laughs in disbelief.

"Oh my god," Nicole says, her eyes wide. "Like in the middle of the gala?"

I smile sheepishly, my cheeks burning. "Yeah."

"That's so hot," Ellie says, fanning herself dramatically. "Did anyone try to come into the closet?"

"No," I admit, breathing a sigh of relief. "That would have been horrific."

"Could you imagine?" Nicole laughs, shaking her head. "Thank God no one saw you guys."

"I know," I chuckle, sucking in a deep breath as I push the memory of last weekend from my mind. "It wasn't exactly planned, but it was definitely worth the risk."

"I'd say so," Nicole smiles.

Ellie pulls out her phone and taps away on the screen. "Adding that to my list of things I want to do."

Nicole and I lock eyes before we burst into laughter, Ellie joining us after she adds "public sex" to a list neither of us knew she was keeping.

"How are things with him?" Ellie asks. "He's good to you, right?"

"Of course," I say without hesitation. "Too good sometimes. He's very thoughtful and kind… nothing like I imagined he would be." I laugh and shake my head. "I thought he'd just be a fuckboy, you know? But he's not. He has that persona, although I think it's just a mask. The Matteo beneath it is a great guy."

Ellie and Nicole both stare at me, slow smiles lifting their lips.

"What?" My stomach does a gymnastics routine as I lift my brows at them.

They share a glance. "You're in love," Nicole accuses.

"I—what? No," I swiftly shake my head. "No. We agreed we wouldn't catch feelings."

"Oh, babe…" Ellie gives me a sympathetic look. "I think it's too late."

My breath catches and my eyes grow wider as I stare back at both of my best friends. Ellie's right. It is too late. "Fuck," I mutter, letting out a breath as I close my eyes. "I caught feelings."

Nicole reaches for my hand and gives it a gentle squeeze. "It's okay. It happens."

"I mean, how could you not?" Ellie offers. "With everything you said about him and the way he's come through for you."

"And the two of you are sleeping together," Nicole adds.

I open my eyes and press my fingers to my temples. "Fuck," I say again, dropping my elbows to the table. I hold my head in my hands. How the hell did I let this happen? And what the heck am I supposed to do about it now? "What do I do? I can't tell him."

"Why not?"

I look at Ellie. "Because we agreed this wouldn't happen."

"Okay," Nicole cuts in. "This is what you're going to do. You're going to play it cool and feel him out. If it seems like he might have feelings too, subtly say something to him."

"Subtle never works with men," Ellie says, shaking her head. "You have to be direct. Don't beat around the bush. When the time feels right, just lay down your cards."

The thought of being that vulnerable makes my skin prickle.

"What if the time never feels right?"

Ellie sighs. "I say life is too short. If you're feeling something, say something about it. And if he's not feeling it too, which I'd doubt that's the case, then you just say goodbye and move on."

Nicole tilts her head to the side. "Just do what you feel is right, Jade."

"What if I don't know what is right?"

What if he rejects me completely? What if I've gone and ruined it all?

Nicole smiles. "You will. When you see him, when the time is right, trust me… you will."

The server comes back to us, and we order dessert that none of us need, but we do it for the sake of extending our lunch date. I'm the one who shifts the conversation to Ellie and her job. Now is not the time to spiral over the feelings I have for Matteo. The feelings I swore I wouldn't have.

Dessert comes and goes, then the server comes back with our bill and our time is up. Like all good things, the moment comes to an end. We head out to the sidewalk, the three of us lingering, tears threatening to spill as we all come together, arms wrapping around one another.

"New York isn't that far," Nicole says again and I'm not sure if she's telling Ellie and me or herself.

"We'll talk every day," Ellie chimes in, her voice thick with emotion.

"This doesn't change our friendship," I add, sniffling as Nicole pulls back from us. I wipe the tears away from my face.

Whether our friendship changes or not, everything will look a little different after next week.

Her eyes glimmer with hope and excitement as she smiles at the two of us. "Love you, besties."

"Love you too," Ellie and I say in unison, smiling back at her, knowing it's only fair for us to feel the same excitement for her.

Nicole deserves nothing but happiness. Nothing but all the good things life has to offer.

And honestly… I think we all deserve that, too.

CHAPTER TWENTY-SEVEN
MATTEO

Tonight was one hell of a game. We almost lost it in overtime but thank god Cross came through and won the damn thing for us.

We've been unstoppable lately. The entire team has stepped it up and has been playing on a completely different level than we were at the beginning of the year. We've been winning most of our games, with an occasional loss here and there.

We need all the points we can get right now if we want to have a chance at the playoffs. There's still a month left until the regular season is over. Anything can happen. Things can change within the blink of an eye.

I shake the thoughts from my head, walking down the hallway to my hotel room. There's a tightness in my chest as I slip into the empty room, heading into the bathroom to get ready for bed.

I used to love being on the road. Now, I hate it.

We're only away for a few days, and all I can think about is getting back home to Jade.

I can't help but open up my messages as I climb into bed, immediately opening the thread with her. My fingers move across the screen, typing out a message and then deleting it.

I miss you, Sunny. I wish I was in bed with you instead of alone in this hotel room.

My stomach knots. What the hell is wrong with me? This isn't good. This isn't normal. There's no reason why my thoughts should be consumed by her. When I'm not with her, I want to be. When I'm not talking to her, I want to hear her voice.

I signed up for a distraction, but not this kind. Not the kind that settles inside your bone marrow. Not the kind that tangles in your soul.

My phone vibrates. My heart stutters, my breath catching.

A sigh escapes me when I see it's my dad.

DAD

Good game tonight, bud.

You looked great out there.

I drag my hand down my face. I need someone to talk me off whatever goddamn ledge I'm on.

MATTEO

Are you busy? Can I call you?

DAD

Of course.

The phone rings once and he answers just as it's about to ring a second time.

"Matteo." His voice is gruff and something rustles in the background. "Is everything okay?"

I swallow hard, sucking in a deep breath. "I don't even know," I admit with a ragged exhale. "I need help."

"What's going on?" There's a twinge of concern in his voice. "Are you safe? Did something happen?"

"No, Dad, I'm okay. I'm safe. I'm in bed in the hotel room." I pause, closing my eyes as I press my palm against my forehead. "I think something is wrong with my mind and I don't know if I should go see a therapist or what to do."

He's silent for a second. "What's going on, bud?"

"You remember Jade from the charity gala?" I rub my eyes, pinching the bridge of my nose. "We've been spending a lot of time together."

"Okay…" His voice trails off.

"I—um—I can't stop thinking about her," I say with a heavy sigh.

My father's quiet for a moment. "This is what you want to see a therapist about?"

"I don't know," I say, shaking my head. "Is that someone who could help? This isn't normal and I don't know how to get it to stop."

"Matteo." There's a soft chuckle that sounds through the phone. "Bud… This is normal when you develop feelings for someone."

"I'm not supposed to have feelings for her," I say in a rush, raking my hand through my hair as I lean back against the headboard. "We agreed this whole thing was just supposed to be friends with benefits. I don't get involved with women like this."

"I know you don't want to have a relationship with anyone, but what I don't understand is why? What are you afraid of?"

My mind circles around the words I've never spoken to my parents. The things I've kept to myself because it's not something I could ever just casually bring up to my mother or my father.

"Fully trusting someone," I admit, my voice barely audible. "I leave before it gets serious. Before I have to put any kind of real trust in them."

"But why, Matteo?"

I swallow hard, the words falling from my lips before I can stop them. "Do you think you would have ever known about me if me and mom didn't go to Aston after Aunt B died?"

My father doesn't say anything at first, the silence stretching between us. "I would like to think I would," he admits, his voice quiet. "I don't know. I know your mother didn't keep you from me on purpose, Matteo."

He lets out a deep breath. "She sent me messages and they all went to the request folder. I never saw them. It's not completely her fault. The phone numbers she found for me and the addresses—none of them were real."

"But she knew you were in Aston, right?"

"She did," he admits again and my stomach sinks. "A quick search on the internet told her exactly who I was and where I played."

"And she didn't confront you?"

"No," he says after a moment. "Your mother and I lived two different lives at the time. You're a professional athlete, you know how these things go. The way we met and what happened, it was so casual. She assumed it was something I did frequently, and honestly, she wasn't far off. She was afraid and I couldn't fault her for that."

He clears his throat. "She made a mistake and that's okay. We're all human. It may have kept us apart for a few years, but we can't do anything to change that."

"Why didn't she try harder?" I finally ask, feeling the weight lifting from my chest as I let go of the one thing I've been holding on to for years. "Why did she keep me a secret from you?"

"Bud," he says softly, his voice tender and filled with sorrow. "You were never meant to be a secret. Things aren't always so simple or easy."

"Were you upset?"

"I was caught off guard by it all," he says. "I didn't believe her at first. But after the paternity results came back, I knew there was no way I was going another moment without being a part of your life. I could see where your mother was coming from. I won't lie to you and say it was easy, but we got past it. I forgave her, with time, and look at what we have now."

Silence wraps around me, the confliction compounding inside my chest. "You just trusted her without any reservation? Without any resentment?"

"I was hesitant at first, but I knew she was worth the risk. Your mother had a lot of guilt and regret and those feelings wouldn't change anything. Together, we took a chance and now, look at what it has given us." I can hear the smile in his voice. "We have created such a beautiful life together filled with so much love."

I've been wrong about them for so long. I've created this scenario inside my mind of how things were between them. I questioned the validity of trust because of not knowing the truth. I never once thought of my mother's feelings at that time in her life. All I could see was the deception, not the emotional turmoil beneath it all.

I never knew of her regret and guilt.

"I'm sorry you've been carrying this around for so long, Matteo. I wish you would have come to one of us sooner with these questions."

"I was afraid to bring it up," I admit, my voice soft. "I was afraid that maybe she never wanted us to find you."

"I can see how you may have felt like that, but I can assure you it was never that." He's quiet again before he says, "I didn't realize it had affected you this long after it happened."

"It doesn't, not really. It just made me question how to trust someone without any reservations," I say, the emotion thick in my voice. "I should have asked you about it sooner."

"It's okay," he says. "Trust is never an easy thing, regardless of outside forces. Taking a risk can be scary, especially because you never know what could happen."

My chest tightens. "How do you know a risk is worth taking?"

"You don't. You have to trust that feeling inside that tells you it's worth it. You'll never know for sure unless you do. The rest will fall into place, however it's meant to."

I blow out a breath. "You say it like it's so easy."

"Because it is. The mind is powerful, but ultimately, you control it. You control your thoughts and what you do with them. You trust yourself on the ice, you can do the same off it too."

"That's different," I argue.

"Is it though?" he questions. "Trust is such a funny thing. Sometimes, it must be built. Sometimes, it has to be earned. And sometimes, you have to take a chance and trust that the right person can hold your heart without breaking it."

I inhale sharply as his words sink into my mind. "How do you know they're the right person?"

"You'll just know, bud," he says softly and I can hear the smile in his voice. "I have a feeling you might know already."

My heart stumbles inside my chest.

I have a feeling I might too…

CHAPTER TWENTY-EIGHT
JADE

ELLIE

Girl, please don't hate me, but I can't make it tonight.

I'm behind on so much stuff with work and my boss is making me stay at the office late until it's all done.

I stare down at Ellie's two messages, feeling the disappointment and dread mixing together in the pit of my stomach. "You've got to be kidding me," I mutter to myself as I look up at my reflection in the mirror.

Matteo sent me tickets for the game tonight. Tickets for the two seats he has for every game. His sisters or family normally take the seats, but tonight was open and he gave them to me after I finished writing my book.

This was a planned night and Ellie was supposed to be my emotional support human.

My lungs deflate with a sigh as I type a response.

JADE

It's fine, I get it. Your job is definitely more important.

ELLIE

I owe you mimosas for life.

My gaze rakes over my reflection once more. My makeup is subtle and I'm just wearing a simple sweater and jeans. It's not too late for me to change into a pair of sweatpants. I could pretend to be sick and just tell Matteo I can't make it.

Before I get another chance to think over my possible plan, my phone lights up again. I'm half expecting another text from Ellie, but instead, it's Matteo calling me.

"Hey," I say, answering on the second ring.

"Hey, Sunny," he says, and I can hear the smile in his voice. "Is this a bad time?"

"No, no," I sigh again. "Ellie bailed. She has to stay late at the office tonight."

"Bailed?" His tone shifts and his voice is quiet, almost as if he's hesitant to ask. "You're still coming, though, right?"

I swallow. "I mean, yeah. But I feel weird showing up by myself and sitting alone."

He's silent for a second. "I'll come get you. You can ride to the arena with me."

My eyes widen slightly as I stare back at myself in the mirror. "I don't want to trouble you. You have a game in—"

"Two hours," he interjects. "I'm walking out my door now. I have plenty of time."

"Matteo," I start, shaking my head to myself. "You don't have to do that."

"I know I don't," he responds, his voice softer. "I want to. I'll be there in fifteen."

My heart kicks into overdrive as we end the call and suddenly, I'm moving like a whirlwind around my apartment. I wasn't anticipating leaving just yet, so I quickly make sure everything is in place, double checking my outfit before grabbing my purse and heading down to the lobby.

I head out onto the sidewalk in front of my building to wait for him and he shows up in record time, pulling his dark SUV along the curb. The passenger door pushes open from the inside and Matteo is leaned across the center console, a smile tugging on his lips.

"You goin' my way, beautiful?"

A giggle escapes me and my purse swings as I jog over to the car, hopping into the passenger seat. The car smells like him, woodsy and bold. He's wearing a black sweatsuit with the logo for the Hillford Hawks over his left breast.

"Hey," he says, mischief dancing in his eyes as I slide in.

I'm a little breathless. "Hi."

His eyes linger, his gaze raking the length of my body as a slow smile creeps across his lips. "You look amazing."

Heat spreads across my cheeks. "It's just jeans."

"Yeah," he muses, pulling away from the curb. "But it's you in jeans."

"Thanks for giving me a ride," I say, settling into my seat and securing my buckle.

He reaches for my hand, sliding his fingers between

mine, resting our hands against my thigh as he runs his thumb along my skin.

"I'm just glad you're coming."

A warmth settles in my chest. "Me too."

We fall into a comfortable silence, his thumb stroking mine as we head to the arena. My stomach does a somersault as he pulls into the parking lot for the players. A sudden nervousness settles over me.

This isn't weird, right? We're not together, we're just friends showing up at the game. It doesn't mean anything else.

I glance down at his hand still holding mine, resting against my thigh.

I swallow roughly. Yeah, totally doesn't mean anything.

"Are you okay, Sunny?" he asks as he pulls into a parking spot, putting the car in park and killing the engine. "You look like you've seen a ghost."

I turn to look at him, my heart hammering away in my chest. "Are you sure this is okay?"

He tilts his head to the side. "Why wouldn't it be okay?"

"I don't know. I know usually it's family and stuff who come in this way with the players and—"

"Sunny," he says softly, his hand squeezing mine. "You're overthinking it. I promise it's okay. Lucy is supposed to be coming tonight. I'm sure she'll sit with you so you're not alone."

I wince. I don't want to be an annoyance or a burden to anyone else. The last thing I want is for Lucy to feel obligated to sit with me.

"If you don't want to come in, you can just take my car and pick me up later."

I shake my head immediately, shoving away the negative thoughts. "No, I want to come in."

"Okay." He rolls his lips between his teeth. "If you want to leave at any time, you can. No questions asked."

Relief washes over me at his words. It's not that I feel uncomfortable... it's just what he said exactly. I'm overthinking things. Overthinking things because we've been sharing a bed and now, he's holding my hand, pulling up to his game.

But we aren't together. We aren't anything.

Matteo gets out of the car, walking over to my side like the gentleman he is. We bypass the players entrance, and he shakes his head at the photographers as we head over to the family entrance instead.

His hand finds the small of my back as he guides me inside and I try my hardest to ignore the flutter in my chest at the small gesture. He pulls out his phone and taps on the screen as we head down the hallway.

The entire arena buzzes with a palpable electrical energy. It's been so long since I've been to a game, I forgot how intoxicating the atmosphere is.

"Lucy is going to meet you by the elevators," he says after a second, turning down another hall. "She came with Theo and planned on sitting alone in his seats."

"Oh, perfect," I smile, glancing at him as we reach another hallway that leads to the dressing rooms to the left and the elevators to the right.

Matteo stops, turning to face me. "Lucy is coming down now." He glances over his shoulder at me. "I have to head in. You remember which seats?"

"Yes," I smile, nodding. "I have the tickets in the wallet on my phone."

Matteo lets out a breath. "Okay. Text me when you get to your seats."

"Okay," I nod. "I will."

His eyes slowly search mine before dropping down to my mouth. My heart stumbles over itself as he takes a step closer, his hand sliding along the side of my face. "For good luck," he murmurs, leaning down as his mouth brushes mine.

Anyone could see us, yet he doesn't shy away from kissing me in the middle of the hallway.

"Good luck," I breathe, my eyelids fluttering open as he pulls away.

His thumb brushes against my bottom lip and he smiles down at me. "See you after the game, Sunny."

And then he's gone.

My head and heart are in the clouds as I slowly turn around, walking over to the elevators in a daze. I lied. The atmosphere here isn't what's intoxicating.

It's him.

"Hey, Jade!"

Lucy's voice carries down the hallway and I catch sight of her, weaving around a few employees. She waves as she jogs over to me.

"Hey!"

"I'm so glad you're here tonight!" She pulls me in for a hug, as if we're old friends. I don't know Lucy well, but she's never been anything but nice to me. There's a warmth to her that just makes you feel welcomed.

"Do you want to sit in Matty's seats or Theo's?" She pushes the button to call for the elevator. "Actually, we can see which has a better view."

I laugh softly, unable to fight the smile tugging across

my lips. "That's a good idea. Are their seats not near each other?"

"No idea," she shrugs as the elevator doors slide open and we step inside. "Guess we'll find out."

Our laughter fills the space as the doors shut and we ride up to the floor we need. We compare seats, which are both in the lower bowl, but we ultimately end up sitting in Matteo's. His has a better view of the entire sheet of ice.

We have time until warmups start so we end up walking around, buying merch and some candy and fries. The concourse is packed full of people getting food and drinks and we duck into the section where we're sitting, making our way down to the seats in the third row, just along the aisle.

"So, you and Matty have been spending a lot of time together," she says casually as we settle into our seats and wait for the guys to come out.

My stomach does a somersault. "Yeah, we've been hanging out a bit."

"He really likes you, Jade," she says after a moment, her voice soft. "I've never seen him like this before."

I turn to look at her, my eyes widening slightly. "We're just friends."

She tilts her head to the side. "I'm not so sure that's what you guys are anymore."

The lights grow brighter and the music grows louder, the bass vibrating through the floor. The crowd roars, echoing around the arena, filling the space. It's my own personal reprieve from having to formulate a response to Lucy.

Matteo skates out, stopping for a drink at the bench before skating along the blue line. His head lifts, turning in our direction. His gaze flickers to mine and I don't miss the way his lips curl upwards.

Lucy glances at me from the corner of her eye, shaking her head with a knowing smile. "Friends don't look at friends like that."

Matteo holds my gaze and my stomach flutters.

No, they don't, do they?

———

The first and second period fly by and Matteo's unstoppable on the ice. They're down by one going into the third, but he scored a goal in the first and got an assist in the second.

Lucy and I rise to our feet. "Want to get a drink?"

I glance down at our now empty cups. The drink we got in the first period is long gone. "Sure!"

We head up the stairs to the main concourse and make our way over to one of the crowded bars. You wouldn't think the Ice Hawks were losing with how excited and loud the crowd is.

Lucy grabs my hand, pulling me through a small gap to find us a place to stand and order our drinks. "Next game, we're getting our food and drinks downstairs." She shakes her head. "The boys need to just get us a suite."

I laugh. "I wouldn't be against that."

"You tell Matty and I'll tell Theo. Neither of them will be able to say no."

The bartender comes over for our order and Lucy tells them two vodka cranberries, just to make it simple.

"Did you see the photo of Matteo Ford with a new woman on his arm at the charity gala?"

My spine stiffens immediately as I catch his name

coming from another woman's lips. I look past Lucy, over to a group of three women crowded together at the bar.

Lucy's fact contorts. "What the hell?"

My stomach is on the floor. I give her a small shake of my head.

"I'm not surprised," one of the other women chimes in. "He always has a new girl."

I pull my eyes away from them, staring straight ahead at the rows of liquor on the shelf. This cannot be happening right now. Don't these women have anything better to do than creep on professional athletes.

"How do you know all this?" the woman with red hair asks.

"It's all over the internet." Cackling laughter follows. "Just look up his name and you'll see images of him out with different women."

I think I'm going to be sick.

"He's such a player."

Lucy inches closer. "Don't listen to them, Jade. They don't know him."

The muscle in my jaw tightens. The bartender comes over with our drinks and I grab mine from him before he can even set it down.

"I'm sure that girl he was pictured with will be old news in a few weeks."

"So true," one of the other women says. "He only likes the chase. Once it starts to get real, he's gone."

It feels like a blow to my chest. I pinch the straw of my drink, gulping down half of it. Lucy pays the tab and slides her arm through mine, turning me away from the bar. "Come on, let's go."

I nod, letting her pull me back through the crowd, away from those women. I knew Matteo had a reputation. I'm not stupid or naïve. He's extremely attractive, super successful, and has enough confidence for his entire team.

It's impossible not to notice him. It's impossible not to be drawn to someone like that.

But hearing the things they were saying, like I'm just another name on his list of conquests. The way they spoke of me as if I'm that disposable to him... my stomach twists at the thought.

"Hey," Lucy says as we sit back into our seats and she turns to face me.

I shake my head dismissively as I tuck my emotions back into a box. "I'm fine."

She purses her lips. "They're wrong about him, you know."

"Are they?" I ask, the question slipping out before I can stop it.

Her expression softens. "They don't even know him. All they know is the bullshit they've read on the internet." She pauses, her eyes searching mine. "*You* know Matteo, the man behind the mask that no other woman has ever seen."

Do I, though?

Or is he just playing me?

My mind drifts to the way he kissed me in the hallway earlier. The way he did it without caring if anyone saw us. The way he drove me today, his hand not once leaving mine. The way he looked at me from the ice and no one else.

I swallow hard, my mind flashing back to the women at the bar. "What if they're right?" I ask her, my voice barely audible.

"They're not."

"But you don't know that," I argue, taking another long sip of my drink.

Lucy's eyebrows cinch. "Do you feel like he's playing you?"

My lips part and I pause for a beat. My heart pounds harder because the truth is, no. The way he looks at me, the way he does things for me—it all feels...real.

But sometimes things really are too good to be true.

"I don't know," I admit.

The buzzer sounds as intermission ends and the crowd grows louder as the patrons settle back into their seats, eager for the third period to start. The players come down the tunnel, filing onto the bench as the guys on the first line get on the ice.

"If he hurts you, I will personally ruin his life and his career," Lucy says, leaning close. "Don't let some women who peaked in high school make you question things between you and Matty."

I snort, a small smile lifting the corners of my lips. I look back out at the ice and immediately I find him. Matteo looks over at me as he skates to the center. It's impossible for my eyes not to find him. He's the flame and I'm the moth.

He's magnetic and I'm drawn to him.

I watch the game mindlessly, unable to pay full attention until halfway through the period, when Matteo scores again. The crowd goes wild and Lucy grabs my arm, pulling me to my feet.

Matteo skates past the bench, bumping his glove against his teammates, but he doesn't stop there. He skates along the boards in front of where we're sitting, his eyes finding mine through the glass.

He smiles, the grin stretching across his lips as he

winks at me. For a split second, I feel the familiar warmth in my chest, but it dissipates as soon as that woman's voice enters my mind.

I'm sure that girl he was pictured with will be old news in a few weeks..

He only likes the chase.

Nausea rolls in the pit of my stomach as I force a plastic smile and clap my hands together. We made a deal that's over at the end of the season. We agreed we'd use each other for our own benefits.

It was only supposed to go this far.

I was never supposed to fall for him…

CHAPTER TWENTY-NINE
MATTEO

Pulling up to a red light, I push my foot on the brake, turning my head to look at Jade. We won tonight and I can't help but wonder if I did something wrong instead. She's been damn near silent since Lucy gave me a dirty look and left us alone after the game.

We're ten minutes from her apartment and she hasn't said more than a dozen words to me.

"Sunny," I say, my voice catching in my throat. My stomach is in knots. "What's going on? Did something happen?"

The muscle in her jaw tightens. "Everything's fine."

"Bullshit," I shake my head, refusing to accept her answer. I stare at her, even when the light turns green, and she still doesn't look at me. She just stares blankly through the windshield.

I'm still staring at her, my wrist draped over the steering wheel with my body angled toward her. A horn sounds from the car behind us. "Fuck," I mutter, glancing in my rearview mirror before grabbing the wheel with both hands.

I turn it to the right, onto a street I didn't plan on going down, pulling my car into the parking lot at the park right down the road from the stadium.

"What are you doing?" Jade's eyebrows draw together and she looks fucking pissed as she turns to look at me. "Take me home, Matteo."

"No," I say, putting the car in park and killing the engine. I turn to look at her. "Not until you tell me what is wrong."

"Oh my gosh," she breathes, rolling her eyes as she shakes her head. "You're acting like such a spoiled little brat." She sets her jaw, turning to look at me. "Didn't get your way so you're throwing a temper tantrum?"

What the hell? Where is this even coming from?

"No, it's not a temper tantrum, Sunny," I huff, shaking my head at her. "This is what it looks like when someone fucking cares. When someone knows something is wrong and they want to know what it is so they can fix it."

She stares back at me, blinking. "What?"

"Everything was fine before the game and now... you're icing me out." My face contorts, my stomach rolling. "What's going on?"

Her throat bobs as she swallows hard. "I don't want to do this anymore."

My stomach falls to the fucking floor. "What do you mean?"

"This!" She waves her arms, frustration and hurt laced in her voice. "You were right when you said things would change after we slept together. They did and I don't like it."

I stare at her, a heaviness settling on my chest. "You don't like it."

She blows out a breath. "I don't like being another name on your list. People saw us in public and now I just look like a goddamn fool, falling for your shit like every other woman you get involved with."

I drag a hand down my face. "What the hell are you talking about, Sunny? You are not another name on my list."

"You just like the chase," she says, her voice monotone as if the words are rehearsed. "As soon as things start to feel real, you bail."

My breath catches. "You think I'm going to bail? You think I fucked you and that was enough for me?" My chest expands. "Sunny baby," I murmur, reaching for her. She doesn't stop me as I cup the side of her face. Instead, she leans into me, her eyes falling shut. "I don't think that was ever going to be enough."

Her eyelids flutter open and they grow wide as she stares back at me. "What?"

"I'm fucked," I shrug my shoulders. "I don't know what I'm doing. I don't know what we're doing. All I know is I don't want to keep pretending that I don't want this with you."

I can't say the words. If I speak them out loud, that makes them real. And once they're out in the open, there's no way I can take them back.

She stares back at me, gazing directly into my soul. That's where she resides now. There was me before her and this is me after. I'll never be the same, not when I know that my heart belongs to her.

"What are you saying?" she whispers, her eyes slowly searching mine.

"I broke the one rule we had." I give her an apologetic smile. Her nostrils flare. "I caught feelings."

"I—" She pauses, the words failing on her lips. "Don't say things you don't mean, Matteo."

I tilt my head, giving it a swift shake as I purse my lips. "Why do you think I don't mean it? Why would I say it to you if I didn't?"

She rolls her lips between her teeth. "There was a group of women at the bar tonight." She swallows audibly. "I overheard them talking about you."

I inhale deeply, straightening my head as I close my eyes for a second. "What were they saying?"

"How you're such a player. How you're with different women all the time." She lets out a sigh. "One of them saw us at the charity gala and said I'll be gone in a week."

Anger pricks my skin. "Who were these women?"

Jade shrugs. "Fans, I guess."

I lift my other hand to cup both sides of her face, shoving away the anger that flicks at my veins. "Jade. They were complete strangers. Delusional women. They don't know me, or you, or *us*." I pause, the muscle in my jaw tightening. "I know I have a track record that doesn't look good, but things are different with you. I swear to fucking god, it's never been like this with anyone else."

She's silent for a second. "But what if you get bored? What if you decide you want someone different? Something new and exciting."

My heart sinks at her words. "Oh, Sunny baby," I murmur, shaking my head at her. "I'll never want anyone different. Out of all the people on this planet, you're the one who's got my heart."

Tears well in her eyes and a shallow breath escapes her lips. "Matteo…"

She deserves to know the truth, even if it leaves me completely exposed.

"I'm in love with you, Sunny." I let out a soft laugh, in disbelief that I just spoke those goddamn words. "And that's something I'll never be sorry for."

Her lips part as if she's going to say something, but instead, she closes the space between us, leaning over the center console and her lips find mine.

She kisses me with tenderness that used to feel safe, but now almost feels as if she's saying goodbye. Her lips move with mine, sweet and slow, before we break apart.

"I don't trust easily," I whisper, leaning my forehead against hers as my eyes close. "My parents… they had a rough start. I was unplanned and unexpected. My mom couldn't reach my father after discovering she was pregnant. We went five years without him knowing." I pause, letting out a sigh. "I blamed my mom for a long time."

"They're together now, right?"

"Yeah," I say, my voice still quiet. "They've been together since I was five and they're still so in love. So much that I almost thought it was all a façade, like my father was constantly trying to make up for lost time." I swallow over the lump lodged in my throat. "I didn't understand it until you."

She inhales sharply, her eyes flashing to mine as she pulls away. She searches my face, as if she's searching for some hidden lie. A hidden agenda I'm not sharing with her.

Guess I'm not the only one afraid to let someone in.

My chest constricts as the silence wraps around us. I can't force her to say anything. Hell, I don't even know what I'd want her to say. I can see the hesitation in her expression. The things those women said are still in the back of her mind.

And I need to find a way to erase them.

"Do you want me to take you home?"

She shakes her head, igniting a spark of hope inside my chest. "Can I go back to your place instead?"

"Yeah?" I ask her, almost in disbelief.

A ghost of a smile dances across her lips. "Yeah."

CHAPTER THIRTY
JADE

"What is obsession, but a matter of the heart?" - Clara Foss, Painted Inferno

Matteo backs me up against the side of the car, my heels scraping on the cobblestone drive-way. His hands travel the length of my body, around the back of my neck before tangling in my hair. I reach for his waist, pulling him flush against me. "Fuck, Sunny," he growls, leaning into me as his mouth finds mine.

His lips are hot and urgent, kissing me with a desperate need. His tongue dances with mine, tasting and teasing me. His mouth moves, trailing along my jaw and down the side of my neck, licking and nipping at my skin.

"Shouldn't we go inside?" I pant, holding him firmly against me. My head tips back against the window, my eyelids fluttering shut as he runs his tongue along the side of my throat.

"No one can see us here," he murmurs against my

flesh. "My property's lined with foliage thick enough to keep any wandering eyes away."

The driveway's lined with small lights, but it's still dark here. Matteo's hands abandon my hair, sliding down the length of my torso, curling his fingers around my hips.

"Goddamn, I'm addicted to you." He pulls back, his mouth leaving the side of my neck as his gray eyes search mine. "I need you to know, this isn't the only thing I want from you."

My breath catches in my throat. I didn't think we were going to talk about our feelings again. After our conversation in the car, I'm not so sure I trust myself with my words right now.

He told me he's in love with me.

And if I'm not careful, I'm going to tell him that I'm in love with him too.

"It's not the only thing I want either," I admit, my voice barely audible. I'm still afraid—too afraid to tell him the truth.

His eyebrows rise, just a hair, and his breath catches as he stares back at me. "I want it all, Jade. The good, the bad, the in-between. The way I feel for you, it's not something I've ever felt for anyone before. I don't know what the hell I'm doing here, but all I know is I want you."

Emotion lodges in my throat. "I want you too. I just—I need some time to process." I pull my bottom lip between my teeth, my brow furrowing. "I want to believe you and trust you, I just need a minute."

A smile tugs on the corners of his lips. "I'm not going anywhere, Sunny. I promise you, I will be right here, ready whenever you are."

The words are on the tip of my tongue, because how the hell could they not be? With the way he's looking at me and the things he's promising? I think anyone would be telling him they're in love with him.

He steps away, sliding his hand down to mine. "Do you need a minute now, or can I have you for the rest of the night?"

A smile drifts across my lips. "I can process after tonight."

He pulls me away from the car, whisking me across the driveway, leading me back into the house. We kick our shoes off in the mudroom and then he's spinning me around to face him, his hands sliding back into my hair as his mouth crashes into mine.

His lips are soft and warm, his kisses gentle as he eases me backwards into the house, through the kitchen and into the living room. His hands leave my hair, raking down my body until he's breaking away from me and lifting me in the air.

"I want you in my bed," he murmurs, holding me close as he carries me to his bedroom. "Right where you belong."

My chest warms, my heart swelling at his words as I wrap my legs and arms around him. I press my head against the side of his, my eyelids falling shut as I revel in the way he feels, inhaling the smell of him.

Matteo carries me into his room, not putting me down until his legs are brushing against the side of his bed and he's laying me on the mattress. My hands are linked around the back of his neck and I pull him with me. He hovers above me, his mouth seeking mine, lips slow and tender.

His tongue sweeps across mine and he rocks back onto his shins, pulling me with him. His hands find the bottom hem of my shirt and he pushes it up, his mouth breaking apart from mine as he drags it over my head and tosses it onto the floor.

I reach for him, mimicking his movements as I remove his shirt, discarding it with mine. The comfortable silence settles around us, it's just him and me. We take each other in with heated gazes and feather-like touches as we slowly remove the rest of each other's clothing, one article at a time.

His eyes rake over my face, his expression unreadable as he lowers me back onto the bed. "Jade," he rasps, my name like a plea. His lips part, as if he's going to continue, but instead, his mouth finds mine once more.

He kisses me with a silent emotion. With a heated reverence. With a warmth that settles in my chest, encapsulates my heart. *He's in love with me.*

His fingertips are soft as he drags them over my skin, across my flesh, as if he's memorizing every inch of my body. My legs fall to the side as he settles between them. His mouth leaves mine, trailing down the length of my body until he's spreading my thighs, bringing his lips to my center.

My hands slide through his hair, tugging on the locks as he sweeps his tongue against me. My heart pounds harder, an unsteady thumping against my ribcage. He takes his time, drawing the pleasure from my core until I'm a mess of moans beneath his mouth on the bed.

"Don't stop. Don't stop. I'm so close."

The inferno in the pit of my stomach spills into my veins, consuming me in a delicious euphoria as my orgasm tears through my body. Matteo pins me to the bed, not coming up for air until he's had his fill and I have nothing left to give.

He lifts his face, pulling back as his heated gaze

collides with mine. He wipes his mouth with the back of his hand, his eyes shifting down to the apex of my thighs before sliding back to my face.

He crawls up the length of my body, my hands reaching for him, sliding along his torso and up over his chiseled shoulders. He hovers above me and I get lost in his eyes, in the shimmering, swimming steel of his irises.

"Sunny," he breathes, the tip of his cock pressing against my entrance. He sighs, his hips dropping, sinking deep inside of me. A soft moan falls from my lips and he groans, his eyelids fluttering shut. "Fuck…"

My legs lift from the bed, wrapping around his torso as he pauses for a moment, his eyelids lifting as he stares down at me. A fire burns in the depths of his irises, but there's so much more than that inside them. There's an intensity that seeps into my soul, into my marrow.

His throat bobs as he swallows hard and he lowers himself down to me, caging me in with his forearms pressed against the mattress. His lips brush against mine. "I could fuck you forever," he rasps, his mouth claiming mine.

There's no him or me anymore. It's just *us*.

He shifts his hips, pulling back before pushing into me again. His tongue tangles with mine, kissing me deeply as he fucks me so gently that my heart is melting inside my chest.

His arms move from the mattress, sliding down to my hips and in one fluid movement, he rolls onto his back, taking me with him. The change in position leaves me breathless as his cock sinks in even deeper.

"Fuck me, Sunny baby."

His hands grip my hips, fingertips digging into my flesh as I plant my hands on his chest and start to rock on top of him. His eyes drag down my torso and flicker back to my face as he watches me moving on top of him.

I bounce up and down and he moves with me, his hips lifting to thrust into me every time I sit back down on him. His left-hand slides to the front of my body. He presses his palm against my lower abdomen and finds my clit with his thumb.

He pounds into me the same time I slide down the length of his cock. His thumb rolls in circles over the most sensitive part of my body. My head tips back and I'm losing control as the warmth starts to build in the pit of my stomach again.

"That's it, Jade," he moans, his hand gripping me tighter as my face screws up, my eyelids slamming shut. "Come all over my cock."

One more sweep of his thumb, another thrust of his pierced cock, and I'm losing myself around him. I shatter into a million pieces, my body shaking with pleasure as I rock on top of him, needing every inch. He's right behind me, chasing after his own dose of ecstasy.

His hand leaves my clit and he pulls me down to his chest, his hands grabbing my ass as he pounds into me. One, two, three pumps and he's losing himself inside of me, my name falling from his lips as if this is his dying wish.

His grip loosens on my cheeks and he slides one hand over the small of my back, the other moving to stroke my hair. He holds me close against him, my legs straddling his waist with his cock still deep inside me.

"Stay with me tonight?" he whispers, his breath warm against the side of neck.

My heart and my brain are at war with each other. "If I do, it doesn't change anything. I still need time."

He kisses the pulse bounding beneath my skin. "I know," he murmurs. "I just want you here with me tonight."

My heart crawls into my throat. I know how I feel about Matteo, but I don't know if I trust him with those feelings. I don't know if I can trust him with my heart.

"Me too," I admit, my voice barely audible. I don't want to leave. I want to stay here with him, cocooned in his familiar warmth. I want to believe this is something we can have. I want to believe he is someone I can have.

I don't know what tomorrow will bring, but we have this moment, and for now—it's enough.

My heart wins the battle. "I'll stay."

CHAPTER THIRTY-ONE
MATTEO

"The art she created was unlike anything I had ever seen before. It was breathtaking—an experience in its own right—yet somehow, it didn't come close to touching the true masterpiece. Her." - Julian Hart, Painted Inferno

I stare down at the toes of my skates, biting down on the inside of my cheek as my eyes roam over the scuffs. The room hums around me with music playing at a lower volume and the guys talking about the game last night as we get ready for practice. I can't hear anything they're saying. There's a different replay happening inside my head.

"I'm in love with you."

The way those five words fell from my lips with zero hesitation is either astonishing or alarming. They weren't planned. They weren't calculated. Hell, I didn't even realize at that moment what my actual feelings were for her.

It hit me out of nowhere… and I needed her to know.

There's nothing else to it, other than that.

Theo scoots closer on the bench next to me. "Are you good?"

"Yeah, I think so."

Jade left early this morning and I can't stop thinking about last night. She didn't say it back. I couldn't have expected her to. But in a way, there's a burn of rejection.

Maybe I read things wrong. Maybe I said it too soon.

He nudges my shoulder. "You're not good. You're quiet again and you're only like that when something's going on."

"Yeah…" My voice trails off for a moment. I don't look at him. My gaze is glued to my laces, but I don't move to tie them. "Jade came over last night."

Theo chuckles. "When is she not over anymore?" He's silent for a beat when I don't respond or laugh. "Did something happen?"

"I—uh." I hesitate, deciding how honest I want to be with Theo, and my stomach flips. "I told her I'm in love with her."

Silence. That's all I get. It stretches between us and I have no choice but to lift my head and turn to look at him.

"Wait, what?" He looks confused and scratches the side of his head. "You were just saying last week how she isn't your girlfriend, but now you're in love with her?"

I blow out a breath, dragging my hand down my face. "I know, man. I fucking know."

His brow furrows. "When the hell did this happen?"

"Overnight." I shake my head. "I don't even know. I'd been ignoring my feelings for her for weeks now. It's like I just woke up. Something clicked inside my head and it's just what it is."

He stares at me in disbelief. "Hell must be freezing over." He cracks a smile. "I never thought I'd see the day that Matty Ford is in love." He looks past me. "You owe me a hundred bucks."

"No way," Cross says back to him, laughter following his words. "No way."

I look between the two of them. "You guys had a bet going?"

Cross nods, grinning. "Theo said you'd be head over heels before the end of the season."

"Cross said by the summer," Theo chimes in.

I scoff, shaking my head at them. "Was anyone else in on this?"

"No," Cross says with a sigh. "Thank God. I'm not paying anyone else because of this."

Cross turns back to his stall and Theo looks at me again. "So," he says carefully. "How did she take it?"

I drop my gaze back down to my skates, sucking my teeth before looking back at him. "She said she needs some time to process."

He winces, a frown pulling on his lips. "Shit." He blows out a breath, slowly nodding his head as he secures the velcro on his chest protector. "Do you think you scared her?"

"I think so." I suck in a deep breath, slowly exhaling it as I bend forward and tie my laces. "I don't think she was expecting it. Hell... I wasn't either."

Theo straps on his elbow pads and grabs his jersey, shrugging it on while I move onto the next piece of my gear. I'm finally dressed from the waist down, so it's at least a start.

A lot of the guys are already dressed, their chatter carrying with them as they funnel out of the locker room.

"You don't really have the best track record," Theo

starts, shrugging his shoulders as he grabs his helmet. "I can see why she'd be a little afraid of it."

"I'm not going to hurt her," I say without hesitation, shrugging my shoulders and tossing my hands out in front of me, like it's a given. "I've never felt this way about anyone else before. I just—I don't know how to get her to believe me."

Theo chews on the inside of his cheek for a second, his eyes drifting off as if he's deep in thought. "You just have to give her the time and the space. Don't disappear. Don't take off like you normally do. Just be consistent. Committed."

I swallow hard, strapping my last elbow pad. "What if she's just looking for a way out?"

"You mean if she's trying to pull an old fashioned Matty Ford move?" He chuckles and pats my shoulder. "You're panicking, bud. If she wanted a way out, she'd just walk now."

His words settle around me like a cloak of security. He's right. There's no reason why she would need the time if there was no point to it in the end. There's nothing tethering the two of us together. There's no reason for her to hang around if it's not something she truly needs to process.

Theo pulls on his helmet as one of the coaches blows his whistle in the distance. "Come on. You can spiral after we get off the ice."

I pull on my jersey, quickly standing up as I slip my helmet onto my head, my hands in my gloves, and grab my stick. Theo waits for me, even though he knows there's a chance we'll both end up having to practice without pucks if we're late.

The guys are still skating around, warming up their

legs while the coaches are standing in a circle in the center of the rink. The cold air hits my lungs as soon as our blades bite into the ice.

No one acknowledges Theo and me being two minutes later than everyone else. No one says anything and practice commences as normal. My lungs are tight and my movements are a bit stiff. It's like I can't get my legs under me, no matter how hard I try.

I'm not even thinking about Jade at this point, although I think it's just the lingering uncertainty after last night. It has me all kinds of fucked up.

We end up in a half ice scrimmage toward the end of practice and I miss a pass that I shouldn't have missed. My stick wasn't on the ice and my head was too far up my ass at this point.

"They'll make you a healthy scratch tomorrow night," Theo mutters as he skates past me. "Get your head in the game, dude."

I suck in a breath, nodding as I shake my head at myself. He's right. I can't afford to lose any playing time. I need to lock in and do what I need to do. If I'm going to stand strong and steady with Jade, I need to be able to do the same with my team.

Accountability and reliability is everything—on and off the ice.

Something inside me clicks and I put my head down and get to work. It's like a flip of a switch and I'm back in it, battling for the puck. By the time practice is over, I'm soaked in sweat, breathless, and a bit lighter.

There's something about losing myself in the game that has a way of grounding me.

"Matteo," Coach Ford calls to me as I'm grabbing my

water bottle to follow the rest of the guys back into the dressing room. "A second?"

Shit. He's going to tell me I'm benched for tomorrow's game.

"Yeah, sure Coach," I say, bobbing my head as I follow him onto the bench. Everyone else is back in the dressing room and the Zamboni drives onto the ice. "What's going on?"

"You seemed a bit distracted for the first half of practice." He pauses for a second, his expression softening. "Everything okay? You and your dad sorted out your differences, right?"

"Yeah, yeah," I say, a subtle relief washing over me. He seems more concerned rather than disappointed, so perhaps my chances of being benched are slim. "We talked about everything and we're good now."

He studies me for a beat. "Alright, well, if there's anything you want to talk about, I'm always here. So are your parents. We're all here for you, Matteo. We've all got your back."

Emotion wells in my throat. It's not often that Uncle Caleb lets his emotions show. It's not that he isn't supportive, he's just reserved. It's a vast difference from my dad, who has no issue telling you how he feels.

"Actually, can I ask you something?"

Uncle Caleb nods his head. "Yeah, of course."

"How do you know when it's the right time to tell someone you're in love with them?"

He's silent for a moment, his throat bobbing as he swallows hard. "As soon as you know that it's true in your heart. Don't say the words if you don't mean them, but if you mean them, don't keep them to yourself."

"But what if it scares the other person?"

A ghost of a smile dances across his lips. "I'd be worried if both people weren't terrified." His eyes search mine. "Love is scary and maddening and truly a beautiful thing."

"What if the other person needs time to process it?"

"Also normal," he says, this time with a chuckle. "You know how much courage it took to say it? She also needs that same courage to be able to say it back." His chest expands as he inhales deeply, his hand reaching out for my shoulder. "Time doesn't mean she doesn't feel the same way. Time is never a bad thing, Matteo. It's just not something we have a lot of."

I swallow hard as the sadness in his voice wraps around us both. He knows from experience, from losing his first wife.

"I can't speak for her since I only met her at the gala, but I saw the way she looked at you, Matteo." He smiles at me with his eyes, warm and sure. "She'll come around to it. You need to trust yourself that you made the right decision."

"How do I know I did?"

"You were honest with her," he says as he rises to his feet. "You took a chance a lot of people shy away from." He pauses, arching a brow. "Hit the showers, you stink."

A chuckle escapes me as he turns to go, heading down the tunnel toward the coaches offices. I turn back to face the ice, watching the Zamboni as it goes past. A sense of peace settles over me as I hang on to Uncle Caleb's words.

He's right. I let myself be vulnerable and took a chance a lot of people don't take.

And now I have to trust it was worth taking.

CHAPTER THIRTY-TWO
JADE

"My heart was his, long before I realized." - Clara Foss, Painted Inferno

I t's been almost one whole week since Matteo told me he's in love with me.

The morning after, I got an email from my editor with the first round of edits for my book. The relief I felt was indescribable. After fighting for my life through writer's block, producing a story my editor approved of was an amazing feeling. I'm still riding the high, back in my groove.

And it feels so good.

Thankfully, there wasn't too much I needed to rewrite, however, it was a welcomed distraction. It was a better excuse to keep my distance from him while I try to figure out what the hell I'm doing here.

We said we wouldn't catch feelings, yet here we are, both of us breaking that one rule.

I stare up at the ceiling, my eyes tracing invisible patterns against the white surface. Everything about the words he spoke have left me terrified. I want to trust him, God knows I do, but taking that leap of faith?

It left me paralyzed.

We've texted throughout the week, and he hasn't brought it up once. There's no pressure from him, no expectations. Just a steady calm, weathering the storm and waiting for me to turn my ship around to sail back to him.

I can't keep holding his past against him. People change, as do circumstances. But just as quickly as someone can change, they can always revert to their old ways.

Although, the only way he can prove he won't break my heart is if I give him a real chance to. I chew on the inside of my cheek, staring up at a small speck on the ceiling. My phone rings from where it's sitting on my nightstand.

A heavy sigh escapes me, and my head spins as I move to sit up straight. Today has been a weird day with the way I've been feeling. Sometimes, I'm acutely aware of my heart beating inside my chest. Every once in a while the dizziness happens, but today it's been coming in frequent waves.

My pulse races, the beating erratic as I take a second to catch my breath and get my bearings straight. I reach for my phone, my eyes closed against the dizzy sensation as I feel the device under my fingertips. I answer it without even looking at the screen.

"Hello?" I say breathlessly.

"Jade?" My eyes open at the sound of Ellie's voice. "Are you okay?"

"Ellie… hey." I say after a moment. I completely forgot we were supposed to meet up tonight. "Shit. I forgot about dinner. I think I'm okay, I'm just not feeling well today."

"What's going on?"

I explain to her about the way I've been feeling, giving her a brief overview of my symptoms. "I just saw my cardiologist last month," I explain, inhaling deeply. "Everything looked normal."

"Maybe you should go into the hospital, just to make sure everything's okay."

The hospital? It's the last place I want to go. Unfortunately, it's the only option since it's Saturday and the cardiology office is closed. "I don't know if it's worth going," I say slowly, chewing on my lip. Anxiety knots in my stomach.

"It's your heart, babe." She's quiet for a second. "Even if it's nothing, I think you should still get checked out."

"I don't know," I say, scooting to the edge of the bed to stand up. As I change positions, the same sensation happens, a wave of dizziness and the racing of my pulse. "Maybe you're right."

"I'll take you," she says without any hesitation. "Unless you think you need an ambulance?"

I pinch the bridge of my nose, shaking my head. "No, I'm not in that bad of shape." I blow out a breath as I collect myself again. "Are you sure you don't mind taking me?"

"Not at all. I'll be there soon." There's a rustling sound in the background. "Stay on the phone with me until I get there."

"Okay." I sigh in relief, slowly making my way out to the living room. Ellie doesn't keep talking, but I can hear her humming, so I know she's still on the phone. I've been trying to not panic with the way my body's been acting today, although there's a comfort in knowing I'm not alone right now.

It's a comfort I've been missing since putting distance between Matteo and myself.

I glance at the clock and grab the remote when I see it's a half an hour until puck drop. I was never a hockey fan before, but I never really had a reason to watch in the past. This last week, I've had the Hillford Ice Hawks playing in the background while I've been working through edits on my book.

My stomach flips when I see Matteo on the ice. I should let him know what's going on, although I don't want to worry him for nothing. I'm only going to be safe, rather than sorry.

He doesn't need the extra stress in the middle of the game.

It can wait until after I'm back home.

———

I absolutely hate hospitals.

I look away from the hockey game on the TV and stare at Ellie nodding off in the chair next to my bed. "Hey," I say, trying to get her attention. "El."

She stirs, lifting her head, blinking rapidly. "What's going on? Is everything okay?"

"Yeah, yeah," I say, nodding my head. "The nurse was just in and said they had a trauma come in, so it might be another hour or two until I get discharged."

Surprisingly, everything moved quickly in the two hours we've been here. I was accelerated through triage since it was cardiac related, and they did immediate testing. Thankfully, they determined it was nothing serious and the symptoms were stemming from something called

Postural Orthostatic Tachycardia Syndrome or POTS for short.

Apparently, it causes all the symptoms I've been feeling, not just today, but normally when I don't feel right. It mainly has to do with blood flow and transitioning from different positions, although it can occur just with standing and activity sometimes.

There's no cure, but they gave me fluids and some medicine to help me tonight. I have a follow up with my cardiologist and strict orders to increase my water and salt intake, along with medication just in case.

"It's almost ten o'clock. You can go home, and I'll just order a car whenever they let me go."

"No way." Ellie makes a face and shakes her head. "I'm not leaving you here alone."

"I promise I'll be okay."

She purses her lips. "The only way I'd leave you is if Matty were here and," she pauses, her eyes flicking to the TV. "Looks like he's a little busy."

I look at the screen, sucking in a deep breath, with my phone burning in my hand. It's the second intermission and I'm still waiting until the game is over to say anything to him. The first and second period were a lot longer than normal with a lot of penalty calls and reviews.

Matteo's been battling with one player in particular on the other team… Aiden Scott.

"Did you tell him you're here?"

"No," I look back at her, shaking my head. "The last thing I want is for him to worry or be preoccupied."

"Good point," she says, nodding her head. "Text him when the third period starts, that way he knows when the game's over."

I stare at her. "It's not anything serious. I'll tell him tomorrow or something."

"Why? Why are you so resistant to letting him in?" Her eyebrows tug together. "I know you have reservations and you're afraid he'll hurt you, but give the guy a damn chance, Jade."

Her words hit me in the chest. I've talked to her about everything, and this is the first time she's coming at me with tough love.

"Are you in love with him, Jade?"

"I—" *Shit.* "Yes."

Oh my god. My stomach flutters. I can't believe I just admitted it out loud, but now that the words are out, there's a lightness that spreads through my chest.

There's no sense in lying. Not to her. Not to myself… and not to Matteo.

"Then you need to tell him. Life is too short, stop wasting it. If anything, coming to the hospital tonight should have showed you that." She stares at me, hard. "What if it were something serious tonight? What if it were the worst case scenario? Matteo would have never known that your stubborn ass feels the same way about him."

I'm at a loss for words for a second. "It's not that simple."

"Says who?" She shakes her head. "You have a chance at something real with someone who loves you. He's not an Aiden Scott. I don't even know him that well, but it's obvious. Everyone else is invisible to that man except for you."

I swallow hard over the lump lodged in my throat. She's right. I've let my fear and stubbornness get in the way. I've been quietly holding Matteo's past against him, thinking he would end up being just like my ex.

When in reality… he's nothing like Aiden.

Aiden never looked at me the way this man does. He never did half the things Matteo does for me. He never made me feel anything close to what Matteo Ford does.

"Stop overthinking it and just jump. You're the only one holding yourself back and you don't want to lose a good thing like what you have with him."

Her words seep into my brain as I look back at the TV and see the guys lining back up on the ice. I look at her again. "You're right. I need to tell him the truth."

"Thank sweet baby Jesus," she laughs, sitting back in her chair, leaning her head back with her eyes closed. "Wake me up when it's time to go."

A smile tugs on my lips as I unlock my phone and find my message thread with Matteo. My stomach flips as my fingers start to move across the screen.

I know what I want… and it's a future with him.

CHAPTER THIRTY-THREE
MATTEO

"Switch me to the second line, Coach."

Coach Frost's eyebrows tug together. "Why the hell would we do that?"

Aiden fucking Scott, that's why.

The muscle in my jaw tics as my mind flashes back to warmups. I knew we were playing his team tonight since the game schedule came out last year.

"Hey, pretty boy," he called out to me as we both skated past the center of the arena. Normally, I'd pay no attention to him, but the next sentence had my stomach in fucking knots. "You and my ex looked good at that little charity gala."

We only ended up on the ice together once during the second period and he's lucky. He's been blowing kisses and chirping at me all goddamn game.

"Just for the start of the third," I press, sitting up straighter as I plant my hands on my thighs. "I have some shit to take care of."

Frost shakes his head. "We can't afford to do that, not when we have so much riding on the line." He purses his lips. "Handle your shit off the ice."

My heart pounds harder in my chest and I give him a curt nod, my teeth clenching to the point where it feels as if they're going to crumble beneath the pressure. He's right. Switching up lines while we're tied is a bad idea.

And Aiden's team winning might send me over the edge.

The second intermission is over and we all file back down the tunnel and onto the bench. I squirt some water into my mouth before heading over to the center of the ice for the first faceoff of the third.

Things start off as expected. We maintain possession of the puck for more time than the other team, although their goalie's a brick wall tonight. We have more shots than them and with all the saves he's making, it's just padding his stat sheet.

Volkov ends up losing an edge skating toward their net and barrels into the goalie, knocking the net out of place. Play stops and the ice crew comes out to clean the snow from the rink. Some of the guys leisurely skate around, keeping their blood moving.

And then Aiden Scott comes past.

"Hey, pretty boy," Aiden calls out as he slowly skates by on his way to the bench. He lifts his chin, a smirk pulling on his lips. "How's my ex been for you? Did she show you that little trick I taught her with her tongue?"

Nausea rolls in the pit of my stomach and I'm immediately on my feet, rage rushing through me. I can't stop myself as I lean over the boards, grabbing him by the front of his jersey, pulling him closer. "Careful, Scott. I'll turn your face inside out if you don't watch what the fuck you say about her."

"Oh, I'm so scared." He fakes a terrified look. "You must not be that important to her. When I saw her last, she didn't even mention you."

What the fuck? He's trying to get to me and it's working. He can say whatever he wants about me, but he needs to leave her name out of his fucking mouth.

Shaw grabs my arm, his grip firm as he tries to pull me away from Aiden. "Matty, not now."

"Yeah, Matty, not now," Aiden mocks.

"Shut the fuck up," I bark at him, tightening my grip on his jersey. "You don't get the privilege of speaking about her, do you fucking understand me?"

"Matteo!" Coach Ford's voice booms. "Let go of him."

I release him with a shove, even though I want to knock that stupid fucking smirk from his face. The refs don't see the exchange and Aiden skates off, rubbing at his chest as if I actually did something to him.

"What the hell was that?" My uncle's voice calls from behind me.

"Nothing," I look at him, shaking my head. "Sorry."

He stares at me for a moment, his gaze hard, the muscle in his jaw tightening and then he looks back out at the rink.

He has every right to be pissed, but so do I. And Aiden Scott has had it coming for quite some time now. I glance over at the other bench. I could easily hop the boards and be over to him in a few strides.

"Wait until he's back on the ice." Shaw says, bumping into me, as if he can see me formulating a chaotic plan inside my head. "There are too many of them over there."

The blood whooshes past my ears and I glance at Shaw.

He gives me a knowing look, bobbing his head before releasing my arm. He pats the top of my shoulder. "Just wait 'til he's back out again."

I'm on the edge of my seat, my hands resting on the top of the boards as I stare out onto the ice, watching as play commences again. We end up scoring, just before I head out for my next shift.

The rage simmers inside, a steady boil to the blood in my veins as I push harder, hitting a few of their guys just on sheer principle. I glance over at Aiden as I'm heading back to the bench for the next guy to come out. Aiden's about to hop over the boards when we lock eyes. He pushes his tongue against the side of his cheek and winks as his skates hit the ice.

Motherfucker.

Their team ices the puck and play momentarily stops. Aiden's skates hit the ice.

"FORD! COME ON!" Volkov yells for me, slapping his stick against the boards.

"Better go, pretty boy," Aiden calls over to me as he starts to skate backwards. "Tell J to give me a call after she's done with you. You'll get bored with her and I'd gladly remind her what a good fuck actually looks like." He winks at me.

That's it. That's all it takes for my self control to go directly out the fucking window. It's like he's asking for someone to put him on a stretcher and I am more than happy to deliver.

I charge at him, my blades cutting into the ice as I rush toward him. He's laughing maniacally and doesn't even bother to dodge me. Instead, he takes the hit, but he stands his ground.

My gloves are somehow already on the ice and I grab

the front of his jersey and his chest protector, holding him right where I want him.

"Aww, you gonna defend her honor?" He smiles right before I drive my fist into his face. His head whips to the side, blood flying onto the ice before he looks back at me. "You motherfucker," he snaps. His teeth are covered in blood, except one of the front teeth is now missing.

He comes at me and we're both throwing punches. Both of our helmets end up on the ice and I manage to keep him far enough away that he can't quite get a good hit on me. I hit him in the jaw and then in the side of his torso.

"Break it up!" One of the refs yells at us, but I can't stop now.

Aiden stumbles backward as I hit him in the face once more and I go down with him, landing on top of him. Just as I'm about to hit him again, I'm hauled up, ripped away from his body. "Enough!"

Aiden lies there for a second, his eyes a bit out of focus and I don't get a good look at him as I'm pushed away. Adrenaline courses through me and I can't feel my hand. I look down at it and just from the first sight, I know it's broken.

"Get him out of here," the ref barks at our bench as he pushes me over to them. Theo pulls open the door and I stumble onto the bench. I don't know where the hell my gloves, helmet, or stick are.

Coaches Ford and Frost both look at me, their eyes widening slightly as they look down at my hand. "Get him in the back. He's lucky if they don't throw him out of the game," Coach Ford orders Gabe, one of the athletic trainers.

My legs are wobbly and my heart pounds harder as I

blindly walk toward the tunnel. Gabe meets me there and falls in step with me as we head back to the dressing room. Dr. Herr, one of the team doctors, meets us at the end of the hall with an ice pack.

"What the hell happened, Matty?"

I shake my head, tasting the tinge of metal on my tongue. "Motherfucker kept running his mouth."

Dr. Herr clicks his tongue. "Guess he deserved it then."

"Oh, he did," I say, my breathing erratic as I sit down in my stall. "Shit," I mumble, the throbbing starting as I look down at my hand.

"Yeah," Dr. Herr agrees, his face wincing. "That's definitely broken."

Gabe shakes his head. "Let me help you get your gear off and we'll get someone to take you to the emergency room."

"What about the game? The period isn't over yet."

Dr. Herr lifts his brows. "There's no way you're playing with that hand… and that is if you didn't get ejected."

"Shit…"

Gabe helps me get undressed and into my street clothes while Dr. Herr calls the emergency room, letting the orthopedic doctor on call know we're coming in.

"Do you have all your stuff, Matty?" Gabe says as he grabs his keys. "I talked to the coaching staff and they said for me to go ahead and take you."

"Yeah, it's right here," I say, setting the ice pack down as I rise to my feet to fetch my keys from the top of my cubby. I tuck them into my pocket, making a mental note that I'll need to come get my car somehow. I grab my phone and the screen lights up with an unread message.

I open it, ignoring my throbbing hand when I see Jade's name.

JADE

Hey. I wanted you to see this when you get off the ice, instead of during the game because I don't want you to worry.

My stomach drops and my surroundings fade away, my eyes widening as I quickly move my gaze to her next message.

JADE

I'm in the emergency room because of some heart stuff. I'm okay and waiting to be discharged now.

I was wondering if I could see you soon. We need to talk.

I don't bother grabbing the ice pack as I stride toward Gabe with my phone in my good hand. Fuck my other hand. None of that matters right now. I just need to get to her. I need to see her with my own two eyes to know she's truly okay.

MATTEO

I'm coming, Sunny.

"You look like you're going to faint. Are you okay?"

I swallow roughly, my heart hammering against my ribcage, my stomach gnawing with fear.

"I need to get to the hospital. Now."

CHAPTER THIRTY-FOUR
JADE

"EVERYWHERE I TURNED, HE WAS THERE. TEARING OPEN MY CHEST AND BURROWING INSIDE MY RIBCAGE." - CLARA FOSS, PAINTED INFERNO

A frown pulls the corners of my lips downward as I pick up my phone and see the battery died. I didn't even notice it was that low. I want to text Matteo after I just tuned back into the game and saw he got a game misconduct for fighting.

I didn't even see the fight happen.

A soft knock on the door pulls my attention and I set my phone on the bed, lifting my gaze to the nurse who ducks in. It's the first face I've seen in a while, other than Ellie's.

Which she's quietly snoring from the chair, her head tipped back and her mouth wide open.

"Hi, Jade," the nurse says quietly, glancing at Ellie and then back at me. "We're still waiting on the doctor to sign off on the discharge instructions and then we'll get you out of here."

"Do you know how much longer?"

She lets out a sigh. "I don't, I'm sorry." She purses her lips, rolling her wrist to check her watch. "Do you need anything?"

There's commotion out in the hallway, although I'm not sure what's going on out there. "Sir, your room is back here!" A voice echoes in the distance.

"No, I'm okay," I smile at her, shaking my head. "What's going on?"

"Probably someone who's drunk," she says, glancing over her shoulder as footsteps get louder. "Just press your call button if you need anything," she reminds me as she pulls the door open.

"I'm looking for my girlfriend, Jade Wilson. I need to see her immediately."

My stomach flips as I immediately recognize his voice. I sit up straighter in my bed. "Matteo?"

His girlfriend?

Footsteps get louder and the nurse pauses in the doorway right as I see Matteo through the opening. "Do you know where I can find her?" He peers through the gap in between the nurse and the doorjamb. "Oh, Sunny," he sighs a breath of relief, the inner corners of his eyebrows furrowing.

"Matty! You need to get to your bay to get your hand looked at."

"Excuse me, sir," the nurse starts, glancing over her shoulder at me first. Matteo's eyes are locked on mine.

My heart beats harder. "It's okay, he can come in."

She steps out of the way and Matteo strides toward me, immediately closing the distance as he walks over to the side of the bed. He leans forward, his right hand cupping the side of my face only.

His lip is busted open and there's another small cut and bruise above his eyebrow. What the hell?

"Sunny, baby, are you okay?" His eyes quickly scan my face. "I'm sorry I didn't get here sooner."

I tip my chin down, a smile tugging on my lips as I shake my head. "I'm okay. And it's okay. I didn't want you to worry over nothing."

"It's not nothing," he rasps, his brow furrowing. "It's never nothing with you."

"Matty, what the hell?" A man's voice calls from the doorway. "You need to get back to your bay so the doctor can check you out."

My face contorts with worry and I stare up at him. "What's going on?"

"I'm fine. I'm here for you. My shit can come later."

"Jesus," the guy wearing an Ice Hawks sweatshirt sighs from the doorway. "Can you tell him he needs to go back?" he asks the nurse.

Matteo cuts his eyes at him over his shoulder. "I'm not going anywhere until she is. No one is touching my hand until Jade is okay."

"Matteo," I say softly, reaching for his face to pull him back to look at me. "I'm okay. It's nothing serious and I'm waiting to get discharged." My eyes search his. "I'll tell you all about it when we get home."

He pulls away from me, searching my eyes. "Home?" His voice is barely audible. "Are you coming home with me then?"

I roll my lips between my teeth, nodding. "Wherever you are is where I want to be." I stroke his cheek with my thumb as his eyes shimmer back at me.

"I'm going to go find the vending machines or something," Ellie chimes in out of nowhere.

"I'll come with you," the guy who came with Matteo says before the two of them head out of the room. The nurse walks back in with an ice pack and hands it to Matteo before she leaves us alone.

I lift my eyebrows at Matteo as he sits down on the bed and covers his left hand with the ice pack. "What do the doctors need to check out?"

He blows out a breath, ducking his eyes as he shakes his head. "My hand." He looks back up at me. "I got in a fight."

"I saw you got a game misconduct for a fight, but I was checking out some other channels and missed it." He lifts the pack of ice, revealing a swollen, bruised hand on his lap. "Oh my goodness."

"Yeah, it's broken…" His voice trails off and he shrugs his shoulders with indifference and covers his hand again. "It was worth it."

My brow furrows. "Why the hell did you get in a fight?"

I know it was with Aiden because when I flipped back to the channel, he was sitting in the penalty box due to fighting.

His eyes grow distant for a moment and he purses his lips, shaking away whatever that was. "It doesn't matter anymore. You're okay and that's all that matters."

"You stupid, crazy man," I laugh quietly, reaching for him again.

He looks at me and that stupid grin I've fallen in love with pulls across his lips. "Crazy about you, Sunny. Only ever you."

My breath catches in my throat. "I—uh—I wanted to talk to you about some stuff."

He shakes his head. "It's okay, Sunny. It can wait until later."

"No, it can't," I say in a rush, my eyes searching his as I scoot closer to him. I reach up to his face, cupping either side with my hands. The words tumble from my lips without another moment of hesitation. "I'm in love with you, Matteo. I should have told you sooner, but I was afraid."

"Sunny," he rasps, lifting his right hand to brush the hair from my face. He tucks it around my ear. "I know," he murmurs, his tongue darting out to wet his lips. "You scare the shit out of me, but I know you're worth the risk."

"I shouldn't have let what those women said get to me. I should have listened to you… should have trusted you." I slowly search his eyes. "We all have pasts, but that's where it should stay. In the past. It doesn't define you and it doesn't make you who you are."

"I would have never even looked at any of those women if I knew one day I would find you," he says. "However, I don't regret anything that's happened in my life because ultimately, it led me to you."

Warmth spreads through my chest and my heart constricts. "You called me your girlfriend."

Mischief dances in his eyes as he smirks. "I'm manifesting, baby."

My stomach flutters. "Can we maybe make that a thing?"

His brow furrows. "Manifesting?"

"No," I giggle, shaking my head. "Me being your girlfriend."

His eyes widen slightly, and he tilts his head to the side. "Seriously?"

"Yes, seriously," I assure him, my voice soft. "I'm ready to risk it all with you, Matteo."

His expression warms and he stares back at me, his gaze unwavering, resting on mine with nothing but tender adoration. "Yeah?"

"Yeah," I say, the intensity of his eyes filling me to the brim with something I've never truly felt with anyone before. *Love.* I pull his face closer to mine, his mouth but a breath away. "I am."

And then his lips find mine… just as they always have a habit of doing.

CHAPTER THIRTY-FIVE
MATTEO

Soft light spills into the room from the morning sun. I slowly lift my eyelids, lying still as I breathe deep, filling my lungs with oxygen and the scent of her. It's quiet and calm and I feel the warmth of her against my right side.

My left-hand throbs as my body begins to wake up and I raise my arm, inspecting the splint wrapped around my hand and half of my forearm. Instinctively, I flex my fingers and a sharp, hot pain shoots up my arm.

"Shit," I mutter under my breath, wincing from the sensation. The splint is bulky and awkward, weighing my arm down. I broke my wrist when I was a kid, but it's been years since I've had anything like this happen.

Thankfully the X-rays showed it was a clean break. They splinted it in the emergency room and scheduled an appointment for me to see ortho next week. They wouldn't cast it because of the swelling, so hopefully ortho will be able to cast it next week.

I don't know how long I'll be out with a broken hand, although if the internet proves to be right, I'm looking at a minimum of six weeks for healing.

Coach is going to kill me. I'm lucky we still won the game even after the shit I pulled.

The warmth beside me shifts and she exhales, groaning softly. I pull my gaze away from the window on the left side of my room to look at Jade nestled against my side. The blankets are pulled up to her chin, just the way she likes it.

Her arm tightens a bit around my ribs, her fingers curling against my skin. She lets out another deep breath, stirring in her sleep. Her hair is strewn across the pillowcase and I take a mental picture of her like this.

I've seen her in my bed plenty of times now, but never like this. Never waking up next to me as my girlfriend.

Holy shit.

She looks peaceful, like this is exactly where she belongs… because it is.

In a way, it almost feels surreal how the last twenty-four hours went down. The quiet settles around us and I listen to the sound of her breathing while she's still asleep, letting my mind run through last night.

When Gabe pulled up in front of the hospital, I was already out the door before he put it in park. It's a wonder I didn't fall face first onto the blacktop and end up breaking another bone.

They were already expecting me and had a bay waiting, but I only had one thing on my mind. Jade. I needed to see her. I needed to make sure she was okay—and thank God she was.

I don't know what I would have done if she hadn't been.

I refused to leave her room until she was discharged, and even after that, I insisted she come and wait with me until I was able to leave. She didn't argue. She explained POTS and what it means moving forward while we waited for the X-ray results.

Jade stirs again, pulling me from the remnants of last night. Her eyelashes flutter and she lifts a lid, cracking it open as she squints at me.

"Are you watching me sleep?"

A smile cracks across my lips. "What if I am?"

She smiles back, her arm tightening around me as she lets her eyelids fall shut again. "I can't stop you."

"I'll stop if you don't like it."

She shakes her head, burying her face against my chest. "No, I do."

"I was afraid I'd wake up this morning and last night would have been all a dream," I say after a moment, my chest constricting. "You're still mine, right, Sunny?"

She lifts her head, her hand drifting over my bare chest as she plants it over my heart. "I am." She turns and plants her chin against me. "I think I have been for a while."

"So, last night wasn't a dream?" I ask, even though my throbbing hand confirms it was in fact very real.

"No." Her expression is soft and warm, the love spilling from her eyes. "It wasn't a dream."

"Good," I breathe a sigh of relief as I tuck her hair behind her ear and run my hand down the length of her soft locks. "I love you, Sunny."

"I love you too, Playboy."

I tilt my head to the side, my stomach knotting. I know it's a playful name, but the meaning of it doesn't feel the same now. "Can we find something else for you to call me other than 'Playboy'?"

Her eyebrows cinch closer together. "Why? I didn't know you didn't like it."

"It's not that I don't like it… I just don't like what it stands for."

A tender smile lifts her lips. "It doesn't stand for how you're taking it." She traces invisible patterns on my chest with her fingertips. "You're flirty and fun. Mischievous and playful. It's a good thing, not a bad one."

Her words sink into my mind, chasing away the image I had tied to the term of endearment. "Well, in that case, I think I like it when you call me it."

"I'll call you whatever you want, baby."

I press my lips into a flat line. "Not that one."

"Babe?"

"Too generic."

She laughs. "What about… my love? Or darling"

"Hm. Not as bad, although it feels like something my grandma would say."

She lifts her head, slowly shaking it at me. She stops, her eyebrows lifting and her face lighting up. "Oh, what about 'Lover boy'?"

"You know what, Sunny?"

She tilts her head to the side. "What?"

"I don't care what you call me, as long as you call me yours."

The shades of blue shimmer in her eyes. "You're mine," she says with such simplicity, as if it's how it's always been.

And I can't help but wonder if it is. Since the day I saw her at the coffee shop and ended up with her bitter drink and she with mine. Since that day, she has crawled under my skin and caught my attention.

Since that day, I haven't been able to look away.

"You're mine, Sunny," I murmur, leaning forward to press my lips against her forehead.

A soft sigh escapes her and I pull her against me, her body flush with mine as I hold her with my good arm. She nestles back against me and I turn my head to bury my face in her hair.

This is exactly where I want her. Today, tomorrow, and I wouldn't be against every day after.

"What do you want for breakfast?"

She smiles against my chest, her hand trailing down the length of my torso. "Hm…I have a few things in mind."

My cock is immediately hard as she toys with the waistband of my boxer briefs. Last night, I didn't want anything sexual. I wanted her to know this is real. What we have goes beyond the line of just being physical.

I want every part of her—body, mind, and soul.

"Let me feed you first, Sunny," I murmur into her hair, my hand sliding down to the bottom hem of my T-shirt she's wearing that's riding up her side. "We need to make sure you stay hydrated and fed and that you're getting enough salt and electrolytes, all that jazz."

She turns her head to look at me, arching a brow. "Are you a doctor now, Matteo?"

"We could play doctor," I smirk.

"That's what I'm trying to get at, you idiot." She pulls her bottom lip between her teeth. "Wait, your hand." She purses her lips, shaking her head. "I'm sorry, I didn't even think about it and I don't want to—"

"Sunny." I cut her off, pulling her onto my body with

my good arm. I hold my left off to the side as her legs part and she straddles me.

Her hair falls forward, framing her face. "Yeah?" she rasps as she settles on my lap.

"Stop worrying about me," I smile, lifting my good hand to the side of her face. "I'm good. Better now," I chuckle, lifting my hips to grind my cock against her.

She chuckles. "You're crazy."

"I already told you," I say, dragging her face down to mine. "Only ever about you."

"I could get used to that," she smiles, the light from the climbing sun out the window catching on her blue eyes. I trace the constellations of freckles across her nose before losing myself in her gaze.

"Good, because that's never changing," I promise, my voice thick with emotion as my lips find her, just like they always do.

For the first time in a long time, the future doesn't feel uncertain.

It feels as though it's already started, and it's started with her.

EPILOGUE
MATTEO

A smile tugs on my lips as I read the script written across a chalkboard sign outside of theater seven.

The event is already underway as I slip inside. Her laughter echoes throughout the room, the sound tugging on the strings attached to my heart. My chest warms and I find an empty seat at the back of the room.

She doesn't know I'm here. Hell, she didn't even know I was coming. She still thinks I'm in St. Louis, getting ready to fly to Detroit. What she doesn't know is that I took a flight separate from the team to Chicago first.

This is the second to last stop on her book tour and so

far, I've had to miss every stop. This was the only one I could make and the only way I was able to make it.

After her book was finished with the final round of edits, she finally let me read it and I'm forever in awe of the story she crafted. It's a story about two rival artists who end up having to collaborate on a project together for an exhibition. It's an angst-filled story with the tender tug of war between two hearts who can't seem to stay apart, even while the two main characters fight against it the entire time.

It's perfect, just like her.

I stare up at the stage with the bright lights shining down upon Jade. She's sitting in an armchair on the left and her conversation partner is sitting in the one to her right. She'd been so nervous about all of this and seeing her up there right now—it looks as if her anxiety never existed.

A smile tugs on my lips and pride swells inside my chest. I always knew she could do it. I pull my gaze from her, glancing around the historical theater with almost every single seat filled. She was so afraid no one would show.

Doesn't she get it yet?

I may be the one who has her heart, but I'm not the only one who loves her. She has so many readers who love every single thing she writes. She deserves it. She deserves to be seen and to be heard and to be celebrated.

To be loved.

Her voice carries through the room, pulling my attention back to her. I didn't catch the question her conversation partner asked. Jade's face relaxes, her eyes crinkling at the corners as she smiles.

"My boyfriend was a huge help with the inspiration

behind the whole story. I was struggling with writer's block when we ran into each other. We ended up striking a deal where he said he would help me." A smirk tugs on her lips. "I'd say it worked, wouldn't you?"

Laughter ripples through the crowd and I can't help but chuckle to myself. I was supposed to help her with research or bouncing off ideas, but I really had nothing to do with the story at all. It was inside Jade the entire time, she just needed to believe in herself.

Their conversation wraps up and they shift gears into a Q&A to end things. There's no shortage of questions, and I listen as they pick Jade's brain or express their love for the characters and the story.

"Alright, friends!" The emcee's voice sounds through the microphone. "We have time for one more question and then we're going to conclude tonight's event with a signing." She smiles brightly, looking around the room at all the hands that shoot up.

Clutching her book in my hand, I rise to my feet and step into the aisle, lifting my arm above my head. "I have a question for Miss Wilson."

Jade pushes her head forward, her eyes squinting, eyebrows furrowing as she looks in my direction. The Emcee tilts her head to the side. "Oh.. okay."

Jade's expression softens, her eyebrows lifting in surprise as I walk closer to the stage and step into the light where she can see who it is. An audible gasp escapes her as her gaze collides with mine.

"Matteo?!" She climbs to her feet, lifting her hands to cover her mouth.

"Hi, Sunny."

I walk up onto the stage, murmurs spreading through the crowd like wildfire.

She throws herself into my arms and I willingly accept, wrapping my arms around her body. "What are you doing here? Aren't you supposed to be on a plane to Detroit?"

"Yeah, I'm just taking the long way there instead," I chuckle, breathing in the familiar, comforting smell of vanilla and berries. "I would have come to every one of your stops if I could have."

She pulls away, her hands cupping the sides of my face. "I never expected you to come to any, but I'm glad you're here." She lifts up on her toes, her lips soft and warm as they land on mine. The crowd lets out a collective awe.

Her lips curl into a smile against mine and she lets out a soft chuckle as she pulls away from me. A pink tint creeps across her cheeks and she stares up at me with those shimmering eyes. "I love you," she murmurs.

"I love you." Her arms are still around the back of my neck. I glance at the emcee. "You said there was time for one more question, right?"

She grins, nodding with excitement. "There is."

I look back at Jade, my eyes slowly searching hers. "Sunny, baby. I love you so much." I reach up to grab her wrists, pulling them away from the back of my neck. "I think I've loved you since you stared at me like I was a wild animal when I drank my drink after you had at the coffee shop."

She laughs, a sweetest melody to my soul, and threads her fingers through mine. "I mean, you were a stranger drinking from a drink I drank out of."

"Say that five times fast," I joke. My smile grows deeper and warmth spreads through my chest as I stare back at the woman my heart belongs to. "I don't know what I did to deserve you, but somewhere along the road, I must have done something right. You are the kindest, most amazing person I've ever met. You constantly keep me on my toes and you're not afraid to call me out on my shit."

She smirks. "Well, someone has to keep that ego in check," she winks.

"There's no one else who could." I release her hands, pulling the black velvet box from my pocket. Her eyes drop down to my hands and back to me as I slowly begin to lower down onto one knee. "I have a question I've been wanting to ask you for quite some time now."

"Matteo," she breathes, her eyes wide, searching mine as I pop open the box, revealing the diamond ring inside. "Oh my god."

"You're the only one I could ever imagine spending my life with." She stares back at me with tears shimmering. "Will you marry me, Sunny?"

"Yes." The word falls from her lips without hesitation. "Yes. Yes. A million times, yes."

I pluck the ring from the box, sliding it onto her finger before she reaches for me, hauling me back to my feet. Her hands find the sides of my face, tears streaming down her cheeks as she smiles up at me.

Everyone in the theater is on their feet, clapping and shouting.

"I love you, Matteo," Jade breathes, lifting onto her toes, her lips seeking mine. And they find them… just as they always do.

When we first met, she needed a muse and I needed a distraction. Our pact was supposed to be a simple agreement. It was all for the plot—*until it wasn't*. Somewhere between the lines she was writing and the ones I kept crossing, it stopped feeling like a transaction.

I broke our one rule without even realizing what was happening.

I wouldn't change a thing about the way we fell and how we got here. The ending I want now isn't written on a page... it's written in the stars. Her and I? We were inevitable.

And standing here with her now—*my fiancée*—I know it was never about the plot

It was only ever about her.

———

THE END

———

WHAT'S NEXT?

The Baby Bluff, the second book in The Bar Down Series, is coming Summer 2026!

Make sure you're subscribed to Cali's newsletter to get all the updates on upcoming books!

ABOUT THE AUTHOR

Cali Melle is a USA Today Bestselling Author of steamy, swoon-worthy romance novels that will have you feeling like you're the one falling in love.

If she isn't lost in the fictional world she's creating, she's most likely adding a new book boyfriend to her own roster or sitting in the stands at the ice rink, watching her kids play hockey.

ALSO BY CALI MELLE

ASTON ARCHERS SERIES

Make Your Move

Make Your Play

Make Your Save

Make Your Change

Make Your Shot

ORCHID CITY SERIES

Meet Me in the Penalty Box

The Tides Between Us

Written In Ice

Dirty Pucking Play

The Lie of Us

WYNCOTE WOLVES SERIES

Cross Checked Hearts

Deflected Hearts

Playing Offsides

The Faceoff

The Goalie Who Stole Christmas

Splintered Ice

Coast to Coast

Off-Ice Collision

STANDALONES

The Christmas Exchange

The Christmas Rebound

Tell Me How You Hate Me

The Art of Breathing

<u>BAR DOWN SERIES</u>

The Plot Pact

<u>SUGAR HILL HOLLOW</u>

Love Tapped

<u>THE WILD BROTHERS</u>

Love Me Wild

www.ingramcontent.com/pod-product-compliance
Lightning Source LLC
Chambersburg PA
CBHW020905060726
47591CB00004B/1091